EVIL BENEATH THE SKIN

EVIL BENEATH THE SKIN

Venezia Miller

EVIL BENEATH THE SKIN

Copyright © 2021 by Venezia Miller.

All rights reserved. No part of this book may be used or reproduced in any manner whatsoever without written permission except in the case of brief quotations embodied in critical articles or reviews.

This book is a work of fiction. Names, characters, businesses, organizations, places, events, and incidents either are the product of the author's imagination or are used fictitiously. Any resemblance to actual persons, living or dead, events, or locales is entirely coincidental.

For information contact: Venezia.Miller@gmail.com
ISBN: 9798527628586

Book and Cover design by V. Miller, Images taken from www.pixabay.com

First Edition: September 2021

CHAPTER

1

THAT MORNING IN APRIL, the lake revealed a secret few knew existed. It was a whisper in the background, just a ripple on the still water, but it would soon create a tidal wave.

Bengta peeked through the window and saw the budding flowers. Spring had come late. Against a perfectly blue sky, the swallows flew by, and in the distance, the row of towering trees swayed gently with the wind. Early weeds sprang up among the already tall grass, and tiny insects were dancing like a veil over the plowed fields. In a matter of weeks, the snow-covered garden had turned into this green wilderness.

Bengta looked at it with detachment, numb from the pain and exhausted from the constant worry.

Two months, two long excruciating months of despair and hope. Weeks of knocking on every door, putting up posters with her daughter's face, and asking strangers if they had seen the young woman. The police hadn't helped them. They had only confronted Bengta with her daughter's old exploits. She had done this before. She had run away from home seven years ago. There was nothing to worry about.

Yet, this was different. Her daughter was no longer a reckless teenager, but a confident woman who had made plans for the future. Bengta couldn't convince them, neither the police in Uppsala, nor in Gävle.

A dark, alienating quiet had fallen over Gävle. The town was still licking the wounds left by the Sandviken killer. That case had reduced the disappearance of Bengta's twenty-two-year-old daughter to a footnote, dissolved in the massive media coverage the serial killer had claimed.

As hard as she tried to deny it, Bengta felt the tragedy lurking in the background, and her family was going to be at the center of it.

* * *

The road was straight and uphill, with short rolling hills cutting through the wooded landscape. The vegetation grew denser as the path moved toward the visible horizon, and between the shrubs and trees, you could see the rooftops of the distant houses that lined the shores of the lake.

"What do you think?"

The deep voice awakened Ingrid from her reverie.

"I don't think we've been introduced," the dark-haired man said.

"Indeed, we haven't."

With his light blue eyes, athletic figure, and impressive height, towering more than a hundred and ninety centimeters above the ground, he was a remarkable presence. He had a youthful face that made it difficult to guess his age, but he was no more than forty.

"Inspector Timo Paikkala."

"Oh, yes, the new inspector! From Stockholm."

He smiled and said, "Correct."

"Paikkala? Finnish?"

"Half. My father is. My mother is Russian, and I was born in Sweden."

"Well, we have something in common. My mother is Finnish too. Oh... I forgot to introduce myself. I am..."

"Dr. Ingrid Olsson, the forensic pathologist."

"Also correct," she said.

He took a step closer to the edge. "Back to business. What do you think?"

She hesitated and looked at the body. It had taken the forensic team an hour to retrieve the corpse from the water and remove the vegetation that seemed desperate to hold onto its most peculiar and horrific find. A young woman dressed in jeans, T-shirt and hoodie, her face covered in dirt and leaves.

"Dr. Olsson? Accident? Murder?"

"I... I don't know."

A beautiful young woman. So serene, as if death had taken her without leaving its mark. Ingrid resisted the urge to let her gloved hand run along the cheek and forehead to straighten her hair, as a loving mother would. She wasn't her mother; she was just an outsider collecting the evidence. For her, emotions were a burden, not a blessing.

"I can't say anything about the cause of death," she said. "I have to examine her."

Ingrid moved to the other side, took the thermometer from the forensics kit, and put it in the woman's right ear.

"The body temperature is high," she said.

"Meaning?"

"If I take into account the impact of the cold water, I'd say she died less than twelve hours ago."

"Any identification?"

"None," she said.

"Who found her?"

"A father and his son. They live in the house over there."

"I want to talk to them," Timo said.

"They are in shock, and I believe Berger already took their statements."

"Uh... Berger?" Timo said.

Of course, he was new here. He didn't know them, and they didn't know him. The news had come two weeks earlier. Anders Larsen, the former superintendent, had announced his retirement in the wake of the Sandviken case, one of Sweden's most prolific serial killers.

The National Police Commissioner hadn't wasted time and had appointed a temporary replacement the next day. Though, everyone knew Anders was collateral damage. He had paid with his job for the indiscretion of his chief inspector, Isa Lindström, Ingrid's best friend.

"Inspector Berger Karlsson. Bearded guy, lots of dark curly hair?"

"Oh, right... of course."

It was funny and almost endearing to see how he acknowledged his ignorance. Five days into the assignment everyone had tiptoed around him. She hadn't heard the rumors and slander about the new intruder yet, but the opinions about Timo Paikkala would come.

She stood up and sighed.

"What's wrong?"

"Nothing," she said. "It seems such a waste."

"Why?"

"So young, in the prime of her life, and now... dead."

"Dr. Olsson, you know better. Don't let this get to you."

He was right, but his comment jolted her. It was condescending, and he suddenly made her nervous.

Berger joined them. "We found footprints in the bushes, and a lot of gloves, wrappers... actually people leave a lot of stuff behind."

"Anything useful?" Timo said.

"Not much. Maybe this... a handkerchief."

Timo took the plastic bag from Berger's hands and held it up to the sun.

"Blood?"

Berger nodded. "Looks like it."

"Have it examined for DNA."

"And we found skid marks, glass and paint chips on the road close to where we found the body," Berger said, holding up two other bags.

"From a dark-blue car. So, it was an accident? Hit-and-run?"

Ingrid cast a glance of compassion at the woman. "Maybe... the impact landed her in the water."

Timo let out a sigh. "What about the neighbors? Did they notice anything?"

"The houses are too far away," Berger said. "I doubt anyone has heard or seen anything. We don't even know when she died."

"Talk to them," Timo said, "assume nothing."

The groan that escaped Berger's lips was slow and filled with irritation.

Then Timo turned his head away from them and let his gaze wander over the landscape. The water was a flawed mirror. Broken images of the sky, the faint sun, the shore. It was peaceful, but he knew the harmony could be deceiving, that it muffled every source of noise, and every whisper of unrest.

"Who lives there?"

The house, about hundred meters from where they stood, stretched across the entire inlet of the lake. The fence surrounding the house glistened in the sun. On the waterfront, there was a large timber-covered patio and floor-to-ceiling windows overlooking the plain. With its wood paneling, the house almost blended with the surrounding nature. It breathed luxury and wealth.

"I don't know," Berger said. "Why?"

Timo raised an eyebrow and said with a stern face, "Well, I guess you'll find out."

Berger rolled his eyes, glanced at Ingrid who met his sigh with a compassionate smile, and sauntered over to the houses.

"I need to go," Timo said, quickly glancing at his watch. "And Dr. Olsson, keep me posted on the progress!"

"But...," Ingrid stammered.

"I assume you can handle it, or am I wrong?"

His blue eyes were piercing through her. When inspector Paikkala wanted respect and obedience, nothing was more effective than his infamous gaze.

"Yes, yes, of course."

"Oh, and Isabel Lindström. You know her?"

"Yes. Why?"

"Is she a good colleague?"

"Ye... yes," she said.

With his mouth quirked in an ironic smile, he turned and walked to his car on the main road, leaving a baffled Ingrid behind.

* * *

One month ago, police quarters in Stockholm.

"Inspector Paikkala?"

"Yes."

Why did he feel so nervous? A little self-doubt was fine, but not when he wanted to convince the boss to give him another job.

"You have an excellent track record. Chief inspector since 2015. Young and ambitious."

Young? He wasn't sure about that, but ambitious... likely.

"Still, you'd like to do something else, I heard?"

"Not something else. Somewhere else."

"Why?"

Good question. Why, and why now? Why not last year, or the year before, or... eight years ago when he had been a different man?

And why Gävle?

They didn't need to know all his motives, but the case of the serial killer intrigued him and that was good enough for now.

"I have my reasons," Timo said.

"Fine. But there are other candidates. Why should I choose you?"

Timo pointed to the document in the commissioner's hands. "That's why."

"You are a man of few words."

"I think actions and accomplishments are more relevant than words," inspector Paikkala said, "anyone can claim to be the best, but few can actually show it."

Was that a faint smile around the man's mouth? An excellent sign.

"The assignment is in Gävle. I assume you've heard about Gävle and Sandviken?"

There wasn't a newspaper, TV station, or social media these days that didn't report daily on the events in that region of the country. Stockholm was no longer the center of everything. It was Sandviken and its serial killer.

"What do you want me to do?"

"The Gävle police department is a hellhole," the man said with a straight face, "and I want you to clean up the mess."

The Swedish Police Authority needed a scapegoat. As always, they would sacrifice careers for the greater good, as long as it wasn't theirs.

"You think you can handle it?"

Without hesitation, Timo said, "No problem."

* * *

"You killed me!"

The man was in the corner. Like a dark menacing figure, the young man was staring at him, judging him. The same clothes, the same pale, perfect face and the bloodstain on the jacket that seemed to grow with every second. It was his own apartment, and then again it wasn't. Like previous times, he couldn't speak or move, and the other man repeated the phrase like a record stuck in a groove.

You killed me. You killed me.

Ten times. Twenty times.

The scene changed. The man stood over him and pointed a gun at his head. Where was he? This was no longer his apartment. It was the house of the infamous serial killer.

"Are you ready?"

He opened his mouth, but no words came out. He wanted to scream, "No, please, stop, don't... I'm not ready to die."

"Any last words?"

If only he could explain that love had blinded him, that it hadn't been personal.

"Of course, it was personal," the man said reading his mind, "it always was. Your words are hollow and too late, far too late."

A click. With a simple gesture, the man cocked the gun. Yes, too late. A slight pull on the trigger and everything would be over. In the distance there was a strange ringing sound. A blinding flash and then...

Magnus woke up, dripping with sweat, on the edge of the bed. His bedroom looked like a war zone. The sheet lay on the floor, and he found the blanket he had taken out of the closet in the middle of the night somewhere between the bed and the door. Another nightmare. Lately there were plenty of them, and they were increasing in frequency.

The doorbell rang, and almost immediately a second time. Someone was impatient. Though he needed a moment, the sensation of the dream still lingering in his mind. A splash of lukewarm water brought him to his senses, but he didn't like the face staring back at him in the mirror. He looked old, worn out, tired. How could he ever get Isa back if he didn't take care of himself? She liked her men well-groomed and handsome, and he was none of it right now.

"God, Magnus, it's ten," Sophie, his soon-to-be ex-wife, said when he finally opened the door, "you're still in bed... you knew we were coming."

"Good day to you too," he sneered.

Anna, his twelve-year-old daughter, stood quietly next to her mother. She had seen and heard it all before and sighed.

"Hey, Anna," he said and tried to pat her shoulder, but she quickly went inside without giving her parents another glance. She could do without these forced gestures of pretense.

"What's the matter with her?"

Sophie shrugged. "Maybe you could talk to your daughter now and then and find out."

"Like you know everything about her!" he said.

She ignored him and waved Anna's bag in front of his face.

"She has homework... I appreciate it if..."

"Yeah, yeah," he said. He couldn't bear another lecture on good parenting from the coldest and most disinterested mother he'd ever met.

When he took the bag out of her hands, he smelled a whiff of alcohol. Had she been drinking?

"Magnus, before I go, we should talk about Toby."

"What is there to talk about?"

"There is no point..."

"Goodbye," he said and slammed the door in her face.

His son Toby was lying in a hospital room, buried under dozens of tubes and wires that monitored about everything that was still left to register, trying to keep him alive, while he wasn't. Braindead, the doctors said, but Magnus couldn't accept his son was dead. Miracles happened from time to time. Why couldn't it happen to Toby?

His daughter had put the bag in the small bedroom.

"Anna, maybe we can catch a movie later?"

He had taken the day off to spend it with her. It hadn't exactly been to Berger's liking. After Isa's suspension, Anders' retirement, the arrival of a new boss, and a team in chaos, everyone had hoped that chief inspector Magnus Wieland had taken more responsibility, but it had turned out differently. Magnus had a hard time concentrating on his job these days and was more absent than present.

"I have homework," she mumbled while she took the books out of the bag and stacked them on the wooden desk. Everything was so crammed together. It felt claustrophobic.

"Maybe later," he said.

"Maybe..."

Disappointed, he left the room, and she breathed a sigh of relief.

It wasn't the divorce, the fact that her brother was dead or her father's forced attempts to connect that upset her, but something else bothered her. She needed advice. But who was there to talk to? She had witnessed something she shouldn't have seen. Maybe she had misinterpreted the situation, but deep down she knew she was right. And it was wrong, very wrong.

* * *

The first thing she noticed were the blue eyes. They were difficult to describe. Darker than the Caribbean sky, lighter than the Atlantic. Black hair, blue eyes, a well-known combination that always got her into trouble. Though Isa wouldn't call him handsome, not like Alex had been. He was too muscular for her taste. But the way he filled the room with his presence was intimidating and dealt an unexpected blow to her ego. A dominant, no-nonsense man.

"Isabel Lindström," Timo said.

"People call me Isa."

"Well, Isa Lindström then."

He looked at her photo in the file and then said, "Do you know why I'm here?"

"I can guess."

"I'll take over the team temporarily... now that Anders..."

"He didn't deserve that."

He sat back and said nothing for a while, his blue eyes scanning her every move, making her feel even more uncomfortable than she already was.

He finally said, "Why?"

"He has done nothing wrong. It was my fault. I have never denied that."

"The responsibility rested with him. He was the police officer in charge, and he should have had his team under control, which he didn't. It was the right thing to do."

She was seldom at a loss for words, but this was one of those occasions and she could only stare at him with open mouth.

"But you're also right. You made a huge mistake. Lucky for you, no one has filed an official complaint... yet. But there is an internal investigation."

What was this? A lecture?

"So, what do you want?" she asked.

He pushed the file across the table toward her.

"This reads like a thriller... your file. Interesting career, but Alex Nordin was not the first mistake."

"Alex was no mistake," she said.

"A relationship with a witness... suspect even, that's no small offense. You and I know that, as police officers, we can't afford such errors."

"He was a victim, not a suspect. And what if he was the greatest love of my life?"

"What if he was the worst killer ever? I don't care. There is no room for emotions in this job. If you can't handle it, this isn't the job for you."

"There are always emotions," Isa said.

"Absolutely, but I expect you to act with professional demeanor under all circumstances."

"I'm already suspended. So, what now? Are you going to fire me?"

"No, but it is your second offense. A third one and it's the end of your career."

"And I'm sure you're going to help me?"

"I'm feeling some resistance here," he said, "but yes, I will give your job back... on a few conditions."

"And those are?"

"You'll be demoted to inspector, and I'll supervise you."

"What about Magnus?"

"I'll assign him a new partner. Probably Berger Karlsson."

"And?"

"And you will have nothing to do with the Sandviken case."

"But there are so many loose ends! Irene Nordin is still free. She killed her son! She needs to be locked up!"

He watched quietly as she grew more and more excited.

"That's exactly why you shouldn't be on the case."

"But..."

"They'll take care of that in Uppsala. I want you to focus on a new case."

"Which one?"

He annoyed her immensely. But whatever inspector Paikkala had decided about what she could and couldn't do, she was determined to continue her investigation into Alex Nordin's homicide.

Timo picked a paper from the backpack on the table and showed her the photo of the woman from the lake. "This one."

"A woman was found dead in the lake near Stromsbrö. Dr. Olsson is doing the autopsy."

"Who is she?" she said.

The woman looked so unharmed, as if nothing had happened to her.

"We don't know. Inspector Karlsson is checking the missing persons list."

"Any evidence found at the scene?"

"A handkerchief with blood on it, and paint chips and glass from a dark-blue car."

"Hit-and-run?"

"Too early to say."

"Witnesses?"

"No, inspector Karlsson spoke to the neighbors, but they didn't hear or see anything. The body was found by a father taking a walk with his seven-year-old son. They were pretty shaken up by the incident."

"What... is that?"

He straightened his back and leaned over to see what she was pointing at.

"What's wrong?"

"There's something in her mouth. I can't see what it is."

He took the photo. "You're right. It looks like... a piece of wood. Maybe from lying in the water?"

CHAPTER

2

THE LIGHT, PEEKING THROUGH the imperfectly closed curtains, drew a line on the duvet. Ilan heard the door open downstairs, and someone entering the house. How long had he been sitting there? He checked his watch. Just like he thought: almost noon.

Since he'd gotten home that night, his entire body had been shaking, and he couldn't stop it. He should have seen the girl! A heavy blow, and immediately he realized he had hit something. But he hadn't been ready for what he saw when he got out of the car. The scene was still fresh in his mind.

I've killed someone!

He still remembered the heartbeat echoing in his ears. How? Why had this happened again? This time he had been sober; he hadn't been speeding. Or maybe he had? Maybe a little.

Why had he chosen to drive along the lake? A deserted, dimly lit road. He should have gone straight home.

And who was he kidding? He had drunk too much. Two beers, or maybe five?

After he saw the body, everything started spinning, and he fell against the car. He could hardly keep himself from gagging. A déjà vu!

"Help me!"

He jumped up when she tried to lift her hand. She wasn't dead. Her arms and legs lay twisted in a bizarre manner, like a rag doll, tossed and splayed across the road, almost covering the entire right-hand track. Her head was locked in an unnatural position, with eyes staring straight ahead. In the light, they emerged like two unearthly red coals of fire.

The moans faded, as if her body were shutting down.

"Please..."

Then his brain started working at full speed. He couldn't help her. He just couldn't.

He scanned the area. Had anyone seen him? The landscape lay quiet beneath the waning moon. None of the houses were close by, only the water, the road, and the trees. In the distance, he saw the outline of a car, headlights off, silent, waiting, like a Damocles' sword about to strike. Or was he just imagining things?

Get out of there!

He crawled back in the car, his hands quivering so much he dropped the key.

Quickly! Get out of here! I can't go through that again!
No, I have to help her! She saw me. If she survives...

He found the key between the clutch pedal and brake. But as he drove off, he saw a red flash in the rays of the headlights. So fast. Another figment of his imagination? Or was it the red jacket of someone running away?

Someone saw me!

Where could he go? He drove aimlessly for most of the night, thinking. In no time the police would be at his door to arrest him. He wouldn't get away with it. Not like the last time. Why had he left her on that road?

A high-pitched voice interrupted the bitter memory of the incident. "Ilan, Ilan, are you there?"

He sighed and wiped the tears from his cheeks.

"Ilan?"

His wife Eve was standing in the doorway. He turned his red-stained face away from her.

"I didn't hear you come home last night. Are you okay? Is something wrong?" Eve said.

Was something wrong? Yes. But he couldn't tell her that. He couldn't tell her he had killed someone. Again.

"I...," he said but struggled to continue the conversation. "I don't feel well. I called in sick."

"Do you have a fever? Shall I take you to the doctor?"

She walked up to him and tried to feel his head, but he pushed her away.

"No, I don't have a fever," he said. "I just need some rest. That's all."

"Okay, okay," she said and sighed. "Trouble at work?"

He said nothing, stood up, and went to the bathroom.

"You can tell me," she tried again.

He let the tap water run over his hands. Aimlessly, like he needed some kind of cleansing.

"Ilan?"

"Eve, just leave it! I'll be fine. I just need some rest."

Why is she so insistent? That annoying habit of hers to keep drilling until she gets to the bottom of it! I don't need this right now.

"How was the party yesterday?"

"Okay, I guess," he mumbled.

* * *

Eve walked into the bathroom and saw him staring at the reflection in the mirror. He looked like crap. She touched his shoulder, but he pushed her away again.

Did Ilan know something? He hadn't asked why she was home. Like him, she wasn't supposed to be there.

It had started four months ago, triggered by a drunken kiss at a New Year's party. So exciting! She had only been married to Ilan for two years, but their journey together had started more than five years ago, with frequent breakups and lots of drama. She had stood by him when he had been on trial for involuntary manslaughter after killing a pedestrian with his car, only to find herself dumped by him two months after the acquittal. But they kept coming back to each other, and they got married on a rainy day in May.

After that, the relationship worsened. He found a solid, well-paid job at a law firm, and she was working in real estate. It was all so well-behaved, goody-goody. Everything seemed so dull and rooted in comfortable settlement. She missed the excitement.

And then there was Nicolas. Handsome, sexy Nicolas, a lawyer at her husband's office, who had dared to kiss her out of the blue. Lawyers and their egos. There were plenty. Anton, another of her husband's colleagues, was a splendid example, with his annoying jokes, always trying to be the center of the attention, with his unmistakably flirtatious glances, but when it came down to it, the man would never leave his wife.

But she liked Nicolas, and he liked her. The taste of his lips lingered for weeks, and it was the trigger to take it much further than that. The midday rendezvous was just one in a long line of secret appointments where it usually ended with sex. She had sent him a last-minute cancellation when she saw Ilan was still home that day.

"Just leave me alone!" Ilan said and left the room.

What was wrong? She hadn't seen him so upset in a long while.

He knows about me and Nicolas. But then, why hasn't he confronted me with his suspicions?

* * *

"Isa, you're back," Ingrid said.

She couldn't stop smiling. It was so good to see her friend, after weeks of lengthy phone calls, trying to help Isa express the pain and frustration about Alex's death, and the moments, full of worry, when the suspended police inspector had gone in stealth-mode, not allowing anyone to see her misery. Sometimes Ingrid felt out of place. She was the woman performing the autopsies, trying to figure out how people had died, but she had no personal experience with death, which made her question the advice she gave her closest friend.

She covered the body on the autopsy table with a white cloth and joined Isa across the room.

Isa glanced at the door. "I'm back... but with restrictions."

Timo entered with a lot more noise than he should have. Isa rolled her eyes and let out a sigh.

"Ah," Ingrid said, remembering her first encounter with inspector Paikkala that morning.

"Meet my new partner," Isa said.

Ingrid knew her friend well enough to guess that the new arrangement wasn't to her liking.

"Dr. Olsson, do you have anything new for us?" Timo asked, ignoring his partner's frustration.

"Yes, I have."

She went to the other table, parallel to the one she had been working on before the inspectors had entered and removed the white sheet. The lifeless body of the young woman confronted them with the seeming senselessness of death.

Timo's eyes trailed over it as if he wanted to absorb every detail of the woman's face. So different from Magnus. Magnus couldn't stand the sight of a dead body. Most of the time, you could find him outside, about to pass out or throw up.

"The autopsy showed trauma to the thorax and abdomen, fractures to the spine and pelvis, and to the arms and legs, consistent with an accident, but that's not what killed her."

"What?" Isa gazed at her open-mouthed.

"Then what?" Timo asked.

"Bruising on the neck, facial petechiae, swollen eyelids and bloodshot eyes. Someone..."

"... strangled her," Timo said.

For a split second, Dr. Olsson felt her face frozen in an expression of sheer astonishment. He stared at her for a moment, unable to hide the smile that played on his lips.

"Uh... yes, you're right," Ingrid said, turning her attention to the dead woman.

Isa sighed. "So it was murder."

Ingrid nodded. "Exactly. She died between eight and twelve hours ago. I had to factor in the water temperature to get a more accurate estimate."

Isa said, "So, someone ran her over, then strangled her to cover up the accident and put her in the water?"

"Maybe," Timo replied. "But let's not jump to conclusions."

"It gets more interesting," Ingrid said, and pulled down the sheet, exposing the woman's naked torso. The woman had looked so perfect, but as she stood so close, Ingrid saw the terrible details. The scratches and bruises, how the red lines on her hands and arms were evidence of the struggle she had delivered before her final faith. And the Y-incision, the inevitable scar that medical examiners leave behind during autopsy when studying the organs of the victim.

"Ligature marks on the wrists indicate she was tied up for a long period of time."

"And the scratches?" Timo asked.

"Sustained before death," Ingrid said, "on the feet as well... she had no shoes."

"She was trying to get away," he whispered.

"Yes, exactly. Like she was running through a forest. And... she was pregnant."

He held his breath.

"Good God," Isa said. "How long?"

"I estimate twelve weeks. Samples of the woman and embryo were sent to the lab. We should have the DNA results in a few days. And there is more."

"Jesus, what else?"

She took the plastic bag from one of the drawer units by the table.

"I found a twig clenched in her mouth," Ingrid said, and held the transparent bag up to the light.

"Could it be a coincidence from being in the water?" Isa said.

"No, it's too well-positioned. The twig was placed there before rigor mortis set in."

She handed it to Timo, who passed it through his hands a few times before giving it to Isa.

"What does it mean?"

Ingrid shrugged. "I really don't know what to make of it. Not sure we'll find anything, but I'll send it to the lab."

"Go ahead!" Timo said.

"Do we already know who she is?" Isa asked.

"We are still checking the missing person's reports," Timo answered.

Isa said, "Then I'll check with Berger later."

Timo turned to Ingrid. "And I'll be waiting for your report, Dr. Olsson. We can discuss it at the police station if you have time. And let me know when you know anything more about the twig."

With a quick glance at the two women, he left the room.

* * *

When she heard the echo of footsteps in the hallway fade away until there was only silence, Isa turned to her friend. "He likes you."

"I don't think he likes any of us," Ingrid said and pulled the sheet over the woman's head. "He doesn't trust us."

"Not yet," Isa replied, "but he should if he wants to survive here."

Ingrid handed the tools to the diener and went to the sink to wash her hands. The test-tube rack, now filled with the dead woman's tissue and bodily fluids, stared her in the face. After all these years, she still wasn't used to it, any more than seeing the blood on the slanted, aluminum examination table, which was now being sprayed clean by the diener. In the light of the fluorescent lamps, the blood was an even deeper red, almost otherworldly.

Then she bowed her head, almost as a sign of respect for the dead, continued to scrub her hands and said, "He seems to be good."

"Who?"

"Paikkala. Upper management regards him as thorough and smart. A real team player."

"So, you checked him out?"

Ingrid shrugged and continued to dry her hands.

"What more did you find out?" Isa said.

"Not much. Some think he's a bit intimidating and strict, but I heard mostly praise for his insight, systematic way of working, and perseverance."

"Nothing like me," Isa said.

"That wasn't exactly what I wanted to say."

"It's fine. I've often put my personal interest first. But I'll be on my best behavior from now on."

This didn't sound right. For more than a decade Ingrid had known her friend as a fighter, not someone who gave up so easily. Stubborn, smart and manipulative. There had to be a hidden agenda.

"What are you up to?"

Isa said, "You really don't want to know."

"So, you're up to something," Ingrid said calmly. "Tell me. God knows... maybe I can talk you out of it."

Isa looked at the floor for a second and then said, "I want Alex's autopsy report and the forensic file of the Norman house."

A flash of disappointment crossed Ingrid's face. "No, that's not a good idea."

"I'm not asking. You know what I need to do. She's still out there, scot-free."

"Leave it up to the Uppsala guys. If Irene is guilty, she will be held accountable, and they will charge her with murder."

"I wanted to take the file without you knowing."

That was honest, but so Isa-like. Too much Isa. And for the first time in the history of their friendship, Ingrid couldn't let her get away with it.

"Please don't stop me!" Isa turned and walked out of the room.

"No, Isa, no!" Ingrid went after her.

* * *

Meanwhile, Isa was already in the next room searching the filing cabinet. It was one of those drab rooms with dozens of gray cupboards where most of the case files from years past were kept. The older files were moved to the archive room in the basement of the police station a year ago. Even though it suited her this time, Isa wondered why everything wasn't kept on the computer drives and why paper versions were still needed.

"Where is it?" Isa said and let her fingers quickly slide over the tab edges.

To get her away from the confidential documents, Ingrid tugged at her arm, but she resisted. "Isa, please stop!"

"Here it is!"

When she took out the folder, Ingrid tried to take it from her, and during the struggle, a photograph slipped out and floated to the floor. Its view froze Isa on the spot. Alex. The close-up only showed his face. They had taken it just before the autopsy. Like the woman in the lake, he appeared to be asleep, and nothing in the photo showed what a violent death he had died.

The last weeks, things had improved. There were times she didn't think about him at all. The crying had stopped, and she felt more at ease, not afraid that the slightest thing might remind her of him, but now she was once again confronted with Alexander Nordin and the incredible impact he had on her life. The tears came out of nowhere, and she couldn't stop them.

"Issie, if the picture already upsets you, the file will destroy you. You can't read the autopsy report."

Ingrid picked up the papers and Alex's photo from the floor and put them back in the filing cabinet. "This is the forensic report. Take it, make a copy, and bring it back by Friday. The Uppsala team comes next Monday."

She held the report in front of Isa, who took it.

"Never ask me anything like that again," Ingrid's voice sounded.

Isa wiped the last tears from her face and walked to the exit, the file hidden under her coat. When Ingrid had handed her the file, she hadn't been able to look her friend in the eye. Friend? Was she still Ingrid's friend?

* * *

Bengta didn't know what she was doing here. This was stupid. There was nothing. Just that eerie, elusive feeling she needed to be there.

So much noise and so many people, as if someone had turned up the volume ten decibels, piercing her ears like the sound of chilling cries.

The police officer at the counter was watching her. She had been there before. Maybe he recognized her.

"Ma'am, can I help you?" he said from behind the counter.

She looked at him without really seeing him. Numb. Everything went in slow motion. His words didn't ripple through. The hand with which she frantically held the flyers wasn't hers.

"Sorry, I have to check this," the officer said and left his conversation partner alone at the desk. "Madame, you don't look well. Would you like to sit down?"

She shook her head. Marie. She had to tell them about Marie.

"My daughter," Bengta said. "I think you found my daughter."

"Let's go somewhere quieter, and then you can tell me all about your daughter."

* * *

When Timo entered the interview room, she was biting her nails. An annoying habit from childhood.

"Mrs.... ?"

"Mrs. Lång," she said.

"My name is Timo Paikkala. And this is inspector Berger Karlsson."

Berger took a seat opposite her.

Timo said, "You told one of my officers we found your daughter. Why do you think that?"

"Marie. I don't know... just a feeling."

Timo frowned. "A feeling?"

She shrugged.

"Okay then... what happened to Marie?" he said.

"Marie disappeared two months ago."

It was all so vague and chaotic in her head. She should have listened to Oskar, her husband. She didn't want to be the crazy lady, crying wolf when nothing was wrong. How strange and stupid she must seem to them.

"Tell us what happened."

She took a deep breath. "She just disappeared."

And then she looked at her hands. She wasn't making any sense. They would react in the same way as the Uppsala police had. She had heard it all before. Her daughter was a grown woman. Marie had disappeared before. She would show up eventually. She was probably with a boyfriend.

But she had the right to be hysterical. She was her mother.

A police officer entered the room. "Marie Lång's file."

Timo opened the document and looked straight at the photograph of the young woman. Bright blue eyes. Pale skin, dark short hair.

Then he looked at the woman in front of him and sighed.

* * *

"Take your time."

Bengta Lång stood in the chilly room of the morgue. The smell was peculiar. Although the strange, musty mixture of formaldehyde and methanol clung to every nose hair, it was different from the way she had imagined it. She was scared it was Marie and she would always remember her this way, lying on that creepy dissection table, cut up by a stranger. Alone.

The policewoman was standing next to her, waiting for her to take the first step. Timo was leaning against the wall by the door.

Maybe Oskar needed to be there. What was she thinking? She couldn't do this alone. But she couldn't turn back and leave, she had to know.

Ingrid said, "Are you sure you want to do this, Mrs. Lång?"

Of course, Bengta wasn't sure, but she nodded and approached the table.

"Whenever you are ready," Ingrid said.

There was no point in dragging it any longer, and she motioned Ingrid to remove the white sheet.

Things would never be the same. Her daughter looked so peaceful and beautiful. The scratches, the bruises, the redness. Nothing mattered. She wanted to touch her daughter, take her in her arms, but she couldn't.

"It's Marie."

"I'm so sorry for your loss, Mrs. Lång."

Dr. Olsson pulled the cover over Marie's head. Then she turned and walked to the door where Timo was waiting.

"Thank you," he said.

Ingrid nodded and then left the room, giving him another inquiring look, but he had already turned his attention to Marie's mother.

Bengta was still standing by the metal table where the dead body of her daughter lay.

It was all a blur. Why didn't she cry? Why didn't she lunge, kick, scream? Her daughter was dead, and she couldn't react.

CHAPTER

3

THEY WERE SITTING AT THE DINNER TABLE with a box of uneaten pizza slices between them. Just like in the good old days, when pulling an all-nighter, they had feasted on junk food and calorie-packed soda. Magnus had barely touched the food. He loved hearing her rattle on about everything. She needed to vent, which was essential in reducing her mood swings.

"It was wonderful to see Elvin again," Isa said, and took another bite of the lukewarm slice from which she had carefully removed the anchovies. She didn't understand why after all those years he still forgot that she didn't like it. Every time.

But Magnus never forgot. He always ordered it on purpose. There were certainties in life, no matter how insignificant they looked to an outsider, that needed to surface now and then. And this was one of them: Isa Lindström, carefully turning the pizza inside out to remove every trace of salty fish before taking a bite. And the certainty she would never ask for a separate slice without anchovies of her own.

Isa smiled and said, "What was your brother doing here, anyway?"

Elvin Wieland was Magnus' younger brother. They had met a while ago, during her student days in Uppsala. Viktor, her ex-husband, had been a good friend of his. An inspector himself, Elvin had convinced her to change careers and apply for the police academy. It wasn't until much later, when she had already been appointed inspector in Gävle, that she had met his brother Magnus and the rest was history.

"Some meeting," Magnus said and shrugged.

"He works in Jämtland?"

"Yep. Happily living there with his wife and four kids. Probably the most boring place in Sweden, if you ask me."

"As if Gävle is so exciting," she said.

"Nowadays it is."

"Yeah... you might be right."

"So, how's the new boss? I haven't met him yet."

"Annoying," she answered quickly.

"Why?"

"He reinstated me."

"I'm confused: that's an awful thing?"

"No, just the way how. I need to be an obedient girl and do whatever he says. By the way, I'm no longer your partner."

"You're not? Then who is?"

"Mister almighty himself."

He wants her, Magnus. Just for himself.

Magnus turned. Where did these words come from? Did his imagination run wild? He could swear he saw a ghostly figure staring at him from the dark corner of the living room. Now it was gone. How could this be? This wasn't a dream.

"What's wrong?" Isa said.

He looked around. Nothing seemed familiar, but it was still his room, his apartment, and the woman he loved sitting in front of him. "Did you hear something?"

"No, not really. It's probably Anna."

Miss Anna had fled to her bedroom when Isa, her father's ex-mistress, had arrived, and she hadn't left it since. The teenager still blamed Isa for tearing her family apart.

"I'm sorry about Anna," he said, "she's still trying to get her head around the divorce."

And he knew Isa wasn't particularly looking to bond with a teenage girl she knew nothing about.

"I understand," she said.

"So, he'll be your partner. What is he like... besides annoying? Young, old?"

Good looking? Sexy? Her type? Another Alex?

"Our age, I guess. But you know, I want to talk to you about something else."

"About what?"

He had to let go of the topic, but her answer wasn't satisfactory. She was too evasive. Another man, another threat. He still loved her. Why didn't she see that?

"Now I have my job back, we can continue to investigate Irene Nordin. We need to go through all the reports and find evidence that could link her to Alex's murder."

Alex. His blood started boiling. There he was again. Why couldn't he just be gone? She should be over him by now.

"Issie... don't rake that up! You just have to move on!"

"Move on? What do you mean? Alex died less than three months

35

ago, and his killer is still out there."

"Maybe we were wrong, and Mats Norman killed them all."

"You don't really believe that," she said.

He just couldn't let her poke her nose into the investigation. It was risky. She was too talented a detective to unleash on a case where he had so masterfully manipulated everything to hide his involvement.

"Okay then," he said, "I'll help you."

His hand slid across the table and gently touched the fingertips of her hand. It was a tenth of a second, so brief, but he could sense the benumbing shock going through her entire body.

"Issie... I miss you," he said and took her hand, "I would do anything to make you happy."

She lowered her eyes. This conversation was bound to come.

"I... have to go," she said softly, and walked over to the wooden peg to get her coat.

"You don't have to leave."

"We can talk tomorrow," she said, walked over to him and gave him a kiss on the forehead. He pulled her head down and kissed her on the lips. And he wanted more, much more.

"Magnus, stop!" She pulled out of his grasp. "I can't... I just can't."

She picked up the bag from the floor and disappeared, leaving him alone at the table with the excitement of the kiss still lingering in his mind.

She doesn't want you. What a loser! You killed a man, and you couldn't even make that work for you.

His nemesis sat on the other side of the table. He looked so real. But he couldn't be dreaming. No, it was official. He was losing his mind. Hallucinations, just like Toby. He wouldn't be able to distinguish reality from delusion.

He could psychoanalyze it. Was it his subconscious? Guilt? Remorse?

It was too good to be true. All traces erased. Nothing that could lead to him. Safe and happy.

The bloodstain grew as the man sat there, just like in his dream... just like in Mats Norman's house, when Alex, wounded and in pain, had begged for his life.

"Why are you here? What do you want?"

Why was he shouting? The man was dead. This wasn't real.

Stop! Go away!

He needed a drink. The bottle stood beside the kitchen sink, and he took a quick sip. He had used the get-together as a reason to open the bottle of wine, but lately he had opened quite a few. Surely the warm glow of alcohol would stop these weird delusions. But Alex was still there.

"Say something! What do you want from me?"

The young man with his handsome face and his stunning blue eyes was still looking at him.

"I hate you; I really hate you... I'm glad I killed you!"

The bottle broke into a thousand pieces when it hit the wall.

"Dad, what's going on?"

Anna. He'd forgotten she was in the next room.

"Nothing, I just... I dropped the bottle and it just... never mind. It was clumsy of me."

The man was gone now, but what was he doing? He needed to get a handle on his mental state that was going into overdrive.

"Dad?"

"I'll be okay. Go to your room!"

She closed the door. The laptop was still on the bed, but she didn't feel like chatting with her friends anymore. Until a minute ago, she could have pretended it was a misunderstanding on her part. But now she knew. And it was so much worse than she had imagined.

She dropped onto the bed, next to the laptop, and stared at the ceiling for a while. Ridiculous thoughts ran through her mind. Her emotions cycled between sheer horror and the self-reassurance she had imposed on herself already weeks ago after the incident, but she couldn't fool herself anymore. What now? What was she going to do? Maybe nothing. Or maybe she needed to help her dad? Yes, that was it. She should do that. Make everything disappear.

* * *

Ilan walked around the car a few times. The windshield was intact, but there were scratches and spots where the paint had been removed. Besides a broken headlight there was also a dent in the hood on the left side of the vehicle. It could be worse. The car had hit the woman at a slow speed. He knelt and ran his hand over the bumper. Dents again, but the damage was minimal.

What was this? There were tiny fibrous structures sticking to his fingers. They looked like... hair! The dead woman's hair! And blood. How was that possible? Did he run over her? Frantically he tried to remove them from his hand. He had to get the hood and bumper replaced altogether, and as soon as possible. Eve couldn't see the car in this state. She'd start asking questions. He still had to cock up a believable story for her.

And the tires... they could probably match them with the skid marks. A jolt of panic seized him again. This wasn't the time. He needed to be calm and think it through. Everything had to be replaced. He knew people from his illustrious past who could probably do it without asking questions.

There was a beep from the phone. He sighed and took the mobile from the wooden shelf that hung on the wall next to the car.

He froze. The display showed a picture of him in the cool white headlights of the car. There was a second picture of him kneeling next to the body on the ground. The quality was poor, but enough to recognize him and the woman. The red jacket. A witness. How did they know his phone number? Who was this? What did they want?

He opened the garage door and got in the car. He had to get out of there. Fast.

* * *

When she got home, Isa changed clothes and took a long, hot shower to relax. Magnus. What should she do about him? He was still in love with her. Maybe she should give him a chance, for old times' sake, for the two years they were lovers. Alex was dead, and Magnus was right: she should just move on. But when she came downstairs, after pouring herself a glass of wine, she couldn't resist the temptation and took the laptop from the drawer of the living room closet. If she wanted to go after Irene, she had to build a solid case with evidence that would stick in court.

The document on her laptop contained the transcript of Irene's interrogation, written by Nina Kowalczyk, her former protégé. It was another file she had obtained illegally. She had read it repeatedly, like a good nail-biting thriller. Only it had been real, and the victims had paid with their lives. After Mats Norman's arrest, Irene Nordin had been questioned about her involvement in her son's death. She had denied everything and had given her interrogators Nina and Magnus a run for their money.

Isa leaned back against the soft cushions on the couch and sighed. The document gave her nothing new. The fundamental problem was the lack of evidence. The gun belonged to the serial killer Mats Norman, and they had found no fingerprints on the weapon that was wiped clean. No witnesses who saw Irene Nordin enter the house.

What did she overlook? She had to review the events step by step, meticulously. The perfect murder didn't exist. There were always clues and witnesses. She just had to find them.

* * *

"Marie... my sweet girl," Bengta cried out. Her hand trembled as she held the photograph.

Her husband grabbed her tight. A second hug in the ten minutes Timo and Isa were there. The cottage by the harbor in Gävle, once home to a family of six, was filled with despair and grief after Bengta had seen her daughter on the metal table in the morgue.

The living room had seen its best days. The couch seemed to date from the 1970s or even before that, and it clashed in style with the other furniture in the room. The wooden table with six chairs stood majestically in the center of the room. It looked as if it hadn't been used in ages for what it was intended for, as it was covered in newspapers and books. Opposite the large window, lined with creamy brown curtains discolored by the sun, was a cabinet filled with photographs and memorabilia. Sons and daughters. Grandchildren. Marie's photograph had been there until Bengta had taken it to keep it close to her while she talked about her daughter.

"How...," Bengta said.

She paused and looked at her husband. Why was she the only one talking? Sometimes he could be such a coward! Always letting her sort it out. But then she saw his face, flushed with tears, and she realized his emotions were just too strong. The pain of losing his daughter had put him in a state where he could no longer function normally.

"How did she die?" Bengta asked.

"She was strangled," Timo said. Simple and to the point.

"Mrs. Lång, Marie disappeared two months ago. Can you tell us what happened?"

Bengta shook her head and said, "All we know is that two months ago we got a call from her roommate asking where she was. Her roommate had left for a ski holiday that weekend and when she returned on Monday, Marie was gone."

"That's in Uppsala?"

"Yes, she studied economics at the university. Second year. Strange choice. We never expected that. She was always so socially engaged. Until a few years ago, she wanted to do something in the medical sector. And she passed a few biology classes, but one day she told us she had decided to study economics and that she would be sharing an apartment with an old schoolfriend. She had it all worked out."

"Who's this roommate?"

"Teresa something."

"Teresa Ljungman," her husband said.

"The Uppsala police investigated her disappearance," Timo said.

"They have done little." Mr. Lång's fingers cramped and nearly tore the fabric of the couch.

"Why do you say that?"

"They didn't start the investigation until a week after we reported her missing. And each time we were told there was no evidence anything had happened to her, that it was her own choice and that she probably didn't want to be found."

"The file mentions she ran away from home when she was fifteen," Timo said, "can you tell us why?"

"Why is that significant?" Mr. Lång said. "You are all the same... thinking she did this to herself."

"Mr. Lång, I don't..."

The man stormed out of the room. Seconds later, they heard a door open and close again.

Bengta said: "I... I'm sorry. He can't take it. It has been wearing him down."

"I understand, Mrs. Lång, but we are on the same side. We want to find your daughter's killer. That's all we want. But for that, we need all the information you can give us. So, she ran away from home. Why?"

Bengta sighed, shuffled in her chair, and then looked at the inspectors.

"Marie had bad friends when she was in high school. She was our youngest... maybe a little spoiled, but high school was tough for her. The first year she was bullied. The situation improved after the second year, but then she got involved with a group of youngsters who... well, thought they were entitled to do anything they liked. She changed."

Mrs. Lång bowed her head and stared at the photograph in her hand. She remembered the fights, the yelling, the harsh looks thrown back and forth... the beating. She had felt so helpless. The bullied had become the bully. She couldn't think of those days without a stomach-churning feeling. Her lovely daughter had turned into a monster.

"Why did she run away?"

"We had a huge fight. It got out of hand. I hit her and... They found her a month later in a crack house with some of her friends."

"She was doing drugs?"

"No, she wasn't, but it was like she was brainwashed. We had a lot of counseling as a family and things got better. She got her life back on track. She finished school and went to university in Uppsala."

"Do you think her old friends had anything to do with her death?"

"No, I don't think so. They all mended their ways. As if it had been a phase they had to go through. And especially after..."

She shook her head.

"After?" Timo said.

"After a boy killed himself. Marie was devastated. They all were. That was actually the turning point. I'm not proud of it, but that boy's death brought my daughter back. I have to admit, when she told me she was moving in with Teresa, I was afraid she might go back to her old ways. Teresa was one of those friends. But they gave me no reason to worry."

"And what about the others?" Isa asked.

"There was another boy. I can't remember his name at the moment. It'll come back to me, but I remember that a few years ago... or was it last year? Anyway, we saw him in the center of Gävle. Marie and I were shopping. She recognized him, but he didn't recognize her, or rather, he didn't want to recognize her. He saw us, turned his head, and then walked away. Espen Frisk! That's the name. He was in the same class as Marie and Teresa. He looked like a decent young man. Well-groomed, handsome, not what I thought he would be."

"Did Marie have a boyfriend?"

She took a deep breath and said, "Yes, she did."

"But you didn't approve?"

"Jussi Vinter... no, we didn't approve," she hissed.

"Why?"

"He... it just didn't click. I still don't know what she saw in him. She could have done so much better. An engineer, a lawyer, someone with a higher education, but not a simple bartender."

"I see. And where can we find Jussi Vinter?"

"Do you think he has something to do with this?" Bengta said and looked up in surprise. Until then, she had been staring at the photograph.

"We need to talk to everyone who was close to her," Isa said, and threw Timo a glance.

With his blue eyes locked on her, showing no emotion, Timo said, "Mrs. Lång, did you know your daughter was pregnant?"

The words hit her like a bomb.

"How? What? No, I didn't..."

She had to stop. The words didn't come, only tears. Tears of shock, a sorrow so deep and painful she could hardly stop the rage it had crashed her with. The sobs lasted minutes.

"Bengta?"

Her husband had come back to see what the noise was about.

"She...," she tried to say between the sighs of breathing and crying, "was pregnant."

"How long?"

"Twelve weeks," Isa said without a sign of emotion on her face.

"Mrs. Lång, do you know who the father might be?"

"I assume Jussi," Bengta said, surprised.

"There was no one else?"

"What do you mean? That my daughter was sleeping around, like a wh..."

"No, that's not what I meant," Timo said.

* * *

Marie's bedroom was tidy and organized. In the middle a single bed with a plain blue cover and by the window a small wooden desk with a laptop, a stack of books, make-up and a hairbrush, and a few pictures. A photo of Marie and a young man, photos of her parents and siblings. Maybe Timo didn't remember what the typical room of a twenty-year-old should look like, but he missed the dirty clothes on the floor, the food stains, and the accompanying smell. Maybe that was just him, remembering his own little mess of freedom, that had often triggered his parents' frustrations.

"Very tidy," Timo said.

The mother waited in the doorway. It was just too painful. As if Marie could enter at any moment and throw herself on the bed. When Marie was in the house, everything revived. She was the youngest. Her other sons and daughter had left home years ago. She only had Marie. Fair enough, there had been difficult moments. Moments when Bengta had come in the room and gone through the closets like a crazy woman. Looking for drugs, looking for something to explain the behavior. The trust, lost along the way, was so hard to rebuild. The years after the incident where Marie had eloped, they had worked on the parent-daughter relationship with ups and downs, trying to voice the frustrations, pain and mistrust, but in recent years, everything had settled in a solid bond with mutual respect.

"Is this her boyfriend?" said Isa, holding up the picture.

Bengta nodded.

"They look happy," Timo said.

"Maybe." Bengta couldn't bring herself to give Jussi Vinter any credit.

"Where's Marie?" A young voice rang through the room. A boy appeared behind Bengta and stared at them.

Bengta said, "Jakob, go to your room, I'll be there in a minute."

Then Bengta turned to the inspectors. "Sorry, my grandson is here. My son... his wife has left him, and we take care of Jakob while he's at work."

"It's fine," Timo said and walked over to him. The boy looked at him with big blue eyes, fearless and self-conscious. How old was he? Five, maybe six.

"Did something happen to auntie Marie?"

"Why do you say that?" Timo said and knelt beside him.

"Marie was crying."

Bengta looked puzzled and tried to intervene, but Timo signaled her to stop.

"When was this?"

"She didn't want to make a snowman."

"A snowman... I see."

"Uh, probably a few months ago... I don't quite know," Bengta stammered.

"And did she say anything?" Isa asked.

Jakob turned to Isa and froze. Wide-eyed and with open mouth, almost gasping for air, he stared at her and then yelled, "You're beautiful."

Isa smiled. The boy's innocence was refreshing. But it suddenly reminded her she had never been a mother to her two children, who were living with their father in London. She didn't know them and never went with them through those life-changing moments when they had taken the next leap into building character and self-awareness. She had experienced none of it. She was a mother without being one. That morning she had retrieved the mail from the letterbox and had found a letter from her former husband Viktor. He was about to get married again. The children knew her well and loved her so much that it would only seem natural if they could call his new wife "mom".

And they didn't know Isa, anyway. She was a name on a paper. She had never contacted them, never even tried, so it should come as no surprise when he asked her to give up her right as a parent so his fiancé could adopt them. But it came as a surprise. In her mind, she still had time, time to decide whether to reconnect with them. The letter, still on the kitchen counter, had left her more perplexed than she had expected, in so many ways. Viktor had moved on. Her children had moved on. She was no longer part of anyone's world, except for this boy, whose utterance had put a smile on the grandmother's face.

"Nana, she's like an angel... look," Jakob said.

Isa walked over to him and knelt next to Timo. The boy stepped back and hid behind his grandmother.

"Jakob, I'm here to help Marie. Will you help me?"

Jakob looked around. "Marie? Marie isn't here."

"Jakob, the inspectors...," Bengta said.

The boy grabbed the toys, turned, and went to his room.

"Sorry about Jakob. He's..."

"He's just a little boy, but a very observant child," Timo said, straightening up.

"I'll talk to him later," Bengta said.

"Were they close, Marie and Jakob?"

"Yes. When Jakob was born, and his mother left a few months after the birth, it was a wake-up call for Marie. Jakob was here most of the time. Although Marie was still in high school, she took care of him and became very fond of him. The last two years, they saw each other less often, but the bond was still there."

"So he probably would know if something was going on with Marie?"

Bengta frowned. "He's only five."

"Children observe and know more than we think," Timo said and restarted his scan of the room.

Isa gave him a quick glance. Irritating man! Not what he said, but the way he said it. Pedantic. Was that the word she was looking for? Maybe not, but it came close.

"Did Marie keep a diary?" Isa said as her boss opened a few drawers from the desk and then went to the larger closet standing next to the bed.

"I don't think so. She was too rational for that."

"But she went into therapy when she was fifteen."

"How... yes, she did. We all did. Look, the therapy has helped us a lot. It gave her tools to manage her anger and frustrations, but instead of writing it down, she learned to talk about it. To me, her father..."

"Jussi?"

Bengta shrugged.

"Was Jussi her first boyfriend?"

"No, there were others, but it was her first long-term relationship."

Isa opened the wardrobe. A brown jacket and two black trousers were strung up on the hanging rod, next to a series of dark-colored evening dresses. Versace. Armani. Isa looked at the mother, still standing in the doorway.

"Expensive taste! Where did Marie get the money to buy designer clothes?"

"What are you talking about? She was a simple student. She had a job now and then, but she wouldn't spend her money on expensive clothes!"

Isa opened the doors wider for the mother to see.

"I don't understand," Bengta stammered, "they weren't there before."

* * *

They had been driving along the winding roads of Gävle for nearly ten minutes. Timo had agreed to take Isa home, a few kilometers from the city center.

He broke the silence by saying, "You don't trust me."

Slowly she turned her head and looked at him. She wasn't in the mood to have this conversation. It was enough he had forced her to go with him to the interview.

"Do I need to?"

He turned the wheel and drove to the intersection.

"We don't need to be friends, but trust and mutual respect are the minimum requirements to make this work, I'd say."

"Trust and mutual respect," she said, "and why should I trust you?"

He kept his eyes fixed on the road as he said, "Is there a problem?"

"How can I trust you when you come in, reshuffle the teams, give me my job back, but at the same time threaten to take it away if I don't meet all the boundary conditions and requirements?"

"Okay, this is what we'll do," he started, "you ask me a question. I'll answer, and then you'll answer one of mine."

"Whatever."

He stopped the car in a small parking lot next to the road. The loose stones bounced against the frame of the car as the vehicle reduced speed. There, in the middle of nowhere, on a desolate road between the center and the countryside, few trees on the side of the road, no cars in front or behind, he wanted to level with her.

"Ask me anything," he said, keeping his hands on the wheel, eyes fixed on the road ahead, as if he were about to hit the gas pedal at any moment and drive off.

"It really isn't necessary," she said.

"Ask me!"

What exactly was this? Was it a trap? What did he need from her? But it didn't matter. If she would lose her job anyway, she might as well play along.

"Okay, then... why are you really here?"

He sighed, let go of the steering wheel and turned his head away from her. "I'm here to find a scapegoat."

"Other than Anders?"

"Yes. People are shocked... scared. Heads need to roll."

His reflection in the window revealed how serious he was. There was no ill-placed superiority or gloating.

"Why are you telling me this?"

Had she misread him? Was he genuinely concerned?

"A scapegoat is nice to have. It makes you feel safe, makes you feel comfortable and gives you the idea you've done everything to correct a wrong situation... until one day reality slaps you in the face and shows you it had been a false sense of security."

Outside, a car passed by. It was the first in the ten minutes they had been sitting there, next to the long, boring road that seemed to go nowhere.

"That is an interesting statement," she said, "very personal."

Timo smiled faintly. Whatever the memories were, they were painful.

"Maybe someday I'll tell you how personal it is," he said.

"You don't want a scapegoat then? Still, they fired Anders... he didn't deserve that."

"No, as I told you before, it was the right thing to do. I don't agree with what the guys in Stockholm think, but that doesn't mean everything is fine. Things are not okay."

For the first time during the conversation, he turned his head and looked at her with those sharp blue eyes.

"What do you mean?" she said.

"You think you work as a team, but there's no team. There never was. You could have solved the Sandviken case so much faster. I truly believe that."

"Really," she said, "I disagree... how can you..."

"Yes, really! During one of the most important cases of his career, inspector Magnus Wieland disappears for weeks and only Anders knows why. You... you keep quiet about crucial discoveries in the investigation, run off with a witness to test your own theory, and sleep with him along the way! No directions were given to the team. Ms. Kowalczyk quits after less than a year and Dr. Olsson... well, I think she really wants to keep the team together, but, in reality, she only looks up to you. And you've disappointed her... this time and so many times before. You let her down, and you should make amends."

"I don't see..."

"It's my turn," he interrupted. Without taking his eyes off her, he continued, "Why Alexander Nordin?"

"What do you mean?"

"Why would you risk your career for a guy like that? You don't match. I just don't see it."

"What?"

"He seemed weak, damaged, needy..."

With increasing bewilderment, she listened to him. Weak and damaged. Yes, Alex had been all of that. And then? Alex was hers. Only hers. She couldn't and wouldn't answer him. It was just provocation.

He waited for the reaction that didn't come, and then he said, "Or was it the sex... was he that good in bed?"

"What the hell!"

"It was probably the only thing he was good at."

"Fuck you! Alex was the kindest, most sensitive man I've ever met. I admired the way he tried to do something meaningful with his life after everything he'd been through with his mom and dad, how he had crawled out of that deep hole after the abuse. You would never understand!

Never!"

And at the end of his life, Alex had tried to take back everything they had taken from him.

The entire time Timo watched her, scanning every muscle movement in her face: the frowns, how her mouth was folded in an angry, almost terrifying grimace. His expression stayed motionless, until he said, "There it is... this is what I was waiting for!"

"Go to hell," she said, opened the door and stepped out of the car. She started walking down the road at a speed that seemed to take him by surprise. Quickly he got out and followed her.

"Sorry... I'm sorry," he said.

She stopped and turned around. "What the hell was that?"

"I finally saw that passion."

She gave him a confused look. She still didn't know what he was talking about.

"I was disappointed. You are the so-called rebel of the department. But so far, I've gotten nothing but polite agreement and cautious signs of dissension. I don't need another "yes" man... or woman. I need to see something more than that. And Alex brings out those powerful emotions in you. That passion makes you one of the best detectives on the team... but you don't know how to channel it. Still, I'd rather see you like that than someone who quietly and submissively follows everything I say. Argue with me! Tell me what you think! Though, I won't always agree."

"Was this a test?"

"Yes, and no. Don't let yourself go like that!"

"Go like what?"

She trudged back to where he was standing, only a few meters in front of the car. She was still so angry. Maybe not with him, but with someone.

"Well, they... you took the only case away from me that mattered. I want Irene Nordin. That will definitely bring the passion back."

"So I'll just ignore the fact that you stole two official police files," he said. She thought the shock wouldn't have been all over her face, but it was.

Ingrid. Ingrid had told him.

"You're not exactly subtle," he said and smiled.

When she saw that smile, she couldn't keep a straight face. When she got back in the car, she said, "but I still want the case."

"Okay, let's agree on the following," he said as he switched on the ignition, "you can continue your investigation... but you're on your own; I know nothing about it!"

"Typical... you want to save your own ass!"

"No, you'll need someone to save yours if you get caught," he answered and drove off.

CHAPTER

4

THE SMELL, THE GRAYNESS OF THE WALLS, everything reminded Irene Nordin she didn't want to be here. She had come every week since it happened, every week with the same question, the one he didn't want to answer. While she waited, she twisted the wedding ring on her finger, unconscious at first, but when she felt the gold rub against the skin, she remembered how her son had this peculiar tic, turning the strap of his watch whenever he had been nervous. They had more in common than she ever imagined.

The prisoner entered. He wasn't handcuffed, but he held his hands together in a strange, cramped position near his belly. Dressed in a casual gray shirt and jeans, he didn't look like the worst serial killer Sweden had ever known. Ordinary and uninteresting. And as so often he refused to look at her.

She usually did all the talking. "So here we are again."

He watched his hands on the table, emotionless, like a child waiting to be reprimanded.

"Let's get it over with," he said.

She rolled her eyes and said, "Look, I don't want to do this anymore. It brings me nothing."

He looked up, and only then she noticed the blue and red stains around his left eye.

"What happened to you?"

"Let's say people don't like child murderers and rapists... funny, most of them have committed worse crimes," he said, his lips folded in a bizarre grin.

The way he laughed it off turned her pity into repulsion in a matter of seconds. What could be worse than raping and killing teenage girls?

"Maybe you deserve it," she answered.

There was a glimpse of disappointment in his eyes, brief and almost unnoticeable, before he said, "Ah, yes, you're no longer on my side."

"Mats, I never was," Irene said.

He suddenly leaned forward and stared deep into her eyes. The sudden movement provoked a reaction from the guard in the corner, but Irene signaled him it was fine.

"You're such a hypocrite," he said with an unbelievable control in his voice, not a muscle in his face that twitched or was out of place. "You want to know what happened to Alexander? I know why! Not because you loved him... you brutalized and traumatized him in every way. No, because they think you killed him, and you want someone to take the blame... but it won't be me."

She lifted her head and tried to escape his gaze, but he had his eyes locked on her.

"You killed him," she said, pushed the chair backward and jumped up, "and I'll make sure everyone knows!"

The anger was so real. She wanted to cry out. The abuse of all these years, buried in silence, wrapped in tears and tucked away in the deepest vaults of her soul, was seeping through the cracks left by her son's death. It wasn't just the notion of self-preservation. No, it was the regret of not being able to mend the one relationship that really mattered. He had taken that away from her, forever. Alex. Why hadn't she told him she loved him in her own weird, destructive way? Love and hate had pushed him away from her while she had so desperately tried to hold on to him. She told herself he wore his father's face, and he would, just like his father, hurt women, but he had been nothing like Mats. That insight had pushed her to the limit of what her mind could handle. She could blame Isa Lindström for endangering her son, but in reality, that woman had given her son more love than she had in a lifetime. She could blame Mats for his existence, but in reality, he had treated Alex with more respect than she ever had.

"I didn't kill our son," he said.

"My son, my son alone... Alex was never your son!"

The excitement at the table alarmed the guard again, and he looked at the clock above the secured door.

Mats shouted, "Alexander, his name is Alexander! Why do you have to vulgarize it?"

"It's time," the guard's voice thundered through the room, but none of them were inclined to back down.

"I think it frightened you he looked so much like me," Mats said, "that's why you could never love him the way I do... did."

"He'll never be yours. I'll make sure the world knows what you've done."

He smiled. "While we're at it, why don't you tell the police what happened to my wife?"

Her head was in the guillotine, with her own hand on the handle, ready to pull. She couldn't destroy him without being dragged into the abyss herself. She knew it and yet she came there every time, without expectation, until today. It was the first time she had seen him lash out and refute her accusations.

"Mrs. Nordin, it's time to go," the guard said, walked to the door and pushed the button.

As they escorted Mats out of the room, he gave her a shrewd look. He had won... for now.

* * *

Anna's dad had barely said a word since she had heard his outburst that evening. Magnus wasn't angry. He was just quiet. He was always quiet after a visit to the hospital.

Anna had refused to go. It was so depressing to see her brother like that. How could her father not see it? Toby was dead and they should let him go. What was the point of all those machines running day and night if he would never wake up?

She sighed and turned her attention to the images on the television screen. How could her dad watch this stupid show? As if he had read her mind, he took the remote and switched the channel. She quickly glanced at him. There was something she had wanted to ask him for a while, ever since they had arrested the serial killer. She didn't know how to bring it up. There was probably a good explanation for what she had seen that afternoon, a few months ago. Magnus was her dad. He would never hurt her. But it was scary, and she didn't know how he would react.

"Dad, can I ask you something?" she said.

He was still staring at the TV. A familiar tune started the opening sequence of a popular detective show.

"Dad?"

"Uh... what," he stammered, awakened from a daydream.

"Can I ask you something?" Anna repeated.

"What?"

"Have you ever killed someone?"

"Why do you ask?" he finally said.

She pointed to the TV. Shots in the background. A suspect lay injured on the ground, with a policeman leaning over him.

She continued, "What is it like to kill someone?"

"I wouldn't know," he said, eyes fixed on the telly.

"You've never shot anyone?"

"No, I haven't."

Suddenly, he got up and meandered to the doorway before turning.

"And don't you have more homework to do," he growled and went to his bedroom, leaving his daughter alone.

* * *

In his room, Magnus kept staring at his reflection in the mirror. Where was the dashingly handsome and charming Magnus Wieland? A wrinkled, shabby man with gray hair, bloodshed eyes, barely standing, stared back at him. The last few days, he wasn't feeling well. He couldn't sleep; he couldn't eat. He neglected his job. Most of the time he didn't even show up. He needed help, but no one could help him without revealing his most terrifying secret.

How does it feel to kill a man, Magnus?

That voice again. He tried to ignore it but how could he when the man stood next to him and whispered in his ear. The hallucinations were coming more frequently. He was there all the time, and it became increasingly difficult to ignore the litany of accusations, incessantly cruel but true.

How did it feel when you killed me, Magnus? You can tell your daughter all about that. How did it feel when you saw me pleading for my life, when you watched the blood slowly soak my clothes and stain the floor? How did it feel when you saw the life being drained out of me? Did it make you feel powerful and victorious? Yes, what a great man you are!

He covered his ears and shouted, "Leave me alone, leave me alone!"

The stress had been building up to a point he could no longer carry it, and he fell on the bed, crying and moaning.

His daughter came rushing in and saw her dad, crawled up lying on the bed.

"What's wrong?" she asked.

"Go away!"

He cramped his hands over his ears, while the tears were rolling down his cheeks and his body was violently shaking with every sob.

"Dad?"

"Leave. Just leave!"

* * *

"Dad, I'm off." Lise Forsberg stood in the doorway of the large living room, looking at the figure sitting at the kitchen island, his eyes fully focused on the article displayed on the tablet.

"Dad?"

He looked up. "Uh, what?"

"What's wrong? You look so distracted."

"Have you seen this?"

He held up the tablet, as if he had expected her to read it from where she was standing, more than five meters away from him. She moved closer and as she walked toward him, the outline of the picture became clearer. She recognized the woman in the photograph and said, "Marie?"

"They found her," he said.

She took the tablet from his hands and read the article, while he gazed through the window. The sky was perfectly blue, but it would soon get dark. In the distance he saw the water of the lake glittering in the late sun. It looked so peaceful. No one knew what lay beneath the surface, just as no one knew what lay beneath the skin of a person. A murderer usually looked so normal, so every day. Just like the water. The lake was a place of tranquility and harmony, but beneath, in the depths of the water, a battle of life and death was going on. Hidden secrets. How many bones and bodies were there? Buried for years, decades. Never to be found.

"Dad, she was found in the lake," Lise said, "close to the house."

"I know."

"What does that mean?"

"Lise, I don't know. She's your friend."

"I wouldn't call her a friend. I just knew her. What now?"

Her father didn't react. Gerard Forsberg, self-made millionaire, entrepreneur, philanthropist, was at a loss for words. Death had never come so close. He had built an entire empire from scratch. A transport company. He had been on TV shows and the subject of articles and much debate. He had built his modern castle on the lake near Gävle where he could live a quiet life, away from the sensation, away from the eyes of the media. The last years he had devoted most of his time to art, music and charity. He had bought an art gallery in Stockholm. He was president of the sculptor's guild. He had two grown children, both studying at the university of Uppsala, but he felt alone. So alone.

"Did you see her leave?" Lise asked.

"What? What do you mean?"

"The party. Did anyone see her leave?"

"Lise, calm down! Nothing happened at the party."

"What were you and Marie arguing about?"

He turned to her, surprised by the words. She had seen more than he'd wanted.

"Nothing," he said.

"Was it about Henrik?"

He tried to dismiss it. "No, no, it was nothing."

"Dad, we need to go to the police. Tell them everything we know. They will find out eventually, and we have nothing to hide."

Silence. He kept staring at the lake.

"Dad?"

"Lise, please... I like to be alone for a while. I need to think."

"Okay," she said hesitantly and walked back to the door, but before she left, she threw him a quick glance. He was still a good-looking man. Tall, slim, with a luscious head of gray hair. Distinguished and smart. Her dad probably had many admirers, but there had been no one since mom. He looked melancholic. Not the strong man everyone used to see. And it was clear he was hiding something from her.

* * *

Why did he have to come instead of Isa? Berger had asked himself that question several times during the short drive to the center of Gävle. Sitting in a car with Timo Paikkala was like having to face a tribunal. His life had been meticulously dissected and put up for questioning, all under the umbrella of getting to know the team. He breathed a sigh of relief when they finally arrived. Five more minutes and he would have thrown himself out of the moving car. The boss was just too exhausting.

Jussi Vinter was a thin, nervous-looking man, neither handsome nor smart. He was young, but the wrinkles on his face, the raspy voice and thin, unkempt hair made him look at least ten years older. The image was hard to reconcile with the idea that he was the boyfriend of the beautiful woman they had found in the lake. He was working in a pub near the city center when Timo and Berger asked him to talk about Marie Lång. The young man was drying glasses behind the bar, which looked amazingly valuable with its mahogany panels and gold details. The rest of the room was dark, and there was a strange mist, accentuated by the dust particles swirling in the sunlight. The tables were still full of glasses with leftovers of beer and wine from the previous evening. The room seemed to reek of smoke, even though it had been more than ten years since someone had lit a cigarette there.

"What do you want to know?" Jussi said.

"You don't seem so heartbroken about her death."

"Why would I?"

"Because she was your girlfriend," Berger replied.

"No, she wasn't. Not anymore."

"When did that happen?" Timo asked.

Jussi let out a sigh of contempt and then said, "About six months ago."

"Why?"

He sighed again, shook his head and then said, "I thought we were fine and then she broke it off."

"No explanation?"

"Not at first. She ignored my calls and messages. But her roommate Teresa told me there was someone else."

"Who?"

"I don't know... Teresa claimed she didn't know either. It was all so secretive."

"When was the last time you saw Marie?"

"Six months ago, when she told me."

"And you were angry," Berger said.

"No, I was confused. I loved her."

For the first time during the conversation, Jussi's wall of indifference and carelessness broke down, and he shook his head, trying to find the words.

"Marie was twelve weeks pregnant," Berger said.

Jussi's mouth folded in a flatline, and he said, "Then it wasn't mine."

"Tell us a bit more about when you met," Timo said.

"There isn't much to say."

"Where and when did you meet?"

"We met in high school."

"During her wild years?" Berger said.

"I wouldn't call it wild," Jussi said, "it was kinda innocent."

"What was it then? Adolescent aberration?"

Jussi shrugged.

Berger continued, "How does a quiet, unremarkable girl suddenly turn into a rebel, pushing her parents away and everything that she previously believed to be true?"

"Marie wasn't all that innocent. There was a dark side to her. She could be mean, lash out."

"What was that dark side?"

"Drugs... sex."

"And you call it innocent?" Timo remarked.

"No hard drugs... some hash... occasionally. That's all."

"Who else was in your circle of friends?"

"Teresa Ljungman..."

"Her roommate?"

"Yep... Espen Frisk and... Quinten Hall."

"Do you still see them?"

"No, except for Teresa... and she hates me."

"You're not a popular man, Mr. Vinter!"

"They all think they are so much better than me, but they have forgotten that, at one moment in their lives, they were living in a dilapidated house, full of graffiti, stinking of urine and vomit, stealing to get food, dealing drugs to survive, just like me. Beggars, loafers, crackheads just like me."

"I wonder... didn't you feel betrayed, humiliated when Marie told you she wanted to move on? This must have been such a blow."

"Like I said... it was a blow... but I would never hurt her. She was the love of my life... and I lost her."

CHAPTER

5

As Ilan passed by the living room, he saw the flickering light of the changing images on the TV screen reflected in the hallway mirror. The almost deafening sound was, for Ilan, a sign his mother was in the house. They weren't the best of friends. In his mother's eyes, he was a freeloader who had killed someone, who took no responsibility, and even if his life seemed on track now, it was only a matter of time before he'd mess it up again. Of course, she took no responsibility in his upbringing. His adulterous father was to blame. He paused, stared at the gray-haired head, and then fled. He could do without another of her lengthy outbursts. Strangely, she and Eve seemed to get along well, and for the past six months, his wife had invited his mother to come over twice a week. He wasn't sure what they were doing during those hours of chitchat.

He threw the jacket on the coat rack and headed for the kitchen. Eve sat at the table, flipping through one of those women's magazines he so loathed, especially the advice on how to improve marital life, which Eve seemed to take seriously. Usually it was the husband's fault. It was strange, but lately she had kept quiet. No romantic suggestions, no advice to spice up their love life.

"Where were you?" she said without taking her eyes from the weekly.

"I had to take the car to the garage."

She looked up. He was fidgeting with the grocery list on the kitchen counter.

"What's wrong with the car?"

"Nothing. Just something with the gears. It should be fixed in a few days. I'll take the bus tomorrow."

"You didn't get a replacement car?"

"I can manage," he said, left the kitchen and walked down the hall to the stairs. The sound of the TV bounced in his ears as he passed by the open door of the living room again.

But then, through the frosted glass, he saw the silhouette of someone standing at the front door. He gasped for air.

Who was this? The police? Or the mysterious messenger?

His heart was thumping; his legs were numb. This was it. What could he do? Could he run? Or should he stay, regain his cool and welcome the stranger behind the door into his home? It almost seemed like the shadow was staring at him, and by playing that psychological game told him he would never be safe.

The shadow disappeared.

Would it be like that from now on? Always looking over his shoulder wherever he went?

"The police are asking the public for help in finding witnesses to the hit-and-run of a twenty-two-year-old woman in the early hours of Wednesday morning. Marie Lång was found..."

The words slowly permeated his mind. His mother, sitting on the couch, was watching the police report. Marie Lång. A dark-blue car. This wasn't good. Eventually they would find out it was him.

A beeping sound. He took the cell phone out of his pocket and glanced at it. A deep breath. With trembling hands, he opened the message and read it. "You see... I know where you live."

My God, it was him!

He ran to the front door and pushed it open. The kid across the street gave him an indifferent look. The empty street with terraced houses, family homes, where nothing ever happened, where most people kept to themselves, was as boring and ordinary as always.

"Hey, you... did you see anyone?" Ilan said.

The boy shrugged, took his bike and drove off.

Where did his stalker go? How could he disappear so fast? How did he know?

Another beep.

"Where is the car, Ilan? Hiding won't help."

He wrote, "Who are you? What do you want from me?"

"All in due time."

The tension in his body rose. He couldn't stand it any longer. He wanted to hide, just disappear from the world. Hide from the police, his family, and the stalker who took over his life.

"Ilan, what's wrong? You're acting strange these days."

His wife was standing behind him. He put the phone in his pocket and turned to her.

"Ilan?"

"It's okay," he whispered and ran upstairs. He needed alone-time to think about the next steps.

* * *

The dog's persistent barking had drawn her to the window. Bengta stared into the darkness. She could barely see the trees. Why was he making so much noise?

"Bengta, you should see this. I found it between Marie's papers." Oskar looked up from the document in front of him.

The entire day her husband had been reading articles about Marie. The pile of newspapers on the kitchen table was witness to his desperate attempt to find information about his daughter's death. He had read the editorials over and over. This was his way of trying to control the situation. He wasn't like Bengta. She cried most of the time, but sometimes she felt almost at peace with it. Strange how they could be so different in dealing with the pain!

Then Oskar had turned his attention to the box of papers and books his wife had collected from Marie's room.

"Bengta?"

"Oskar, there's someone in the garden," she said.

"What?"

He got up and joined his wife in the kitchen.

"Are you sure?"

A shadow, perhaps a fabrication of her mind, but when the moonlight peered through the clouds, she no longer doubted. Someone was watching the house. But in that one second when she had turned her attention to Oskar, the ghostly apparition was gone.

Oskar took her hands. "Bengta. This is difficult... for all of us. Maybe you should talk to a doctor."

She pushed him away and left without saying a word.

They had been there before. The same old story. He hadn't believed her then; he didn't believe her now. She wasn't crazy. Yes, she had those strange feelings sometimes. As if she could see things from a world beyond what most people could observe and feel, but this was different. This was real.

She trudged up the lawn to the forest. The dog was calmer now, as if the danger had passed. She was no longer afraid, just curious. Oskar was coming after her, but she ignored his cries.

And then the center of gravity shifted and pulled her down. The next moment, she lay in the wet grass, face down, flat on her stomach.

She heard her husband call her name. This time more frantic than before. She felt no pain, only astonishment. Only when she wanted to get up, she felt something at her feet preventing her from finding solid ground.

When she finally got up, she saw what it was.

A pair of sneakers. And she recognized them. Marie's shoes. They had bought them together, not long before Marie had disappeared. The person who had brought them knew what had happened to her. But why now? Why here? Why them?

* * *

Teresa Ljungman was the next witness to be visited by inspectors Lindström and Paikkala. The apartment was modern and spacious. To keep this luxury affordable, she had looked for a roommate when she had started university three years ago, but Marie had only joined a year later.

She put her long raven-black hair in a bun as she, like an accomplished hostess, invited the inspectors to sit on the couch in the living room. Teresa Ljungman, the eldest daughter of Pjotr Ljungman, entrepreneur and real estate guru, and his Filipino trophy wife, studied law. They needed to be quick because she had a lot of studying to do if she wanted to stay at the top of her year. With her centimeter-long fingernails painted light pink, she plucked a few pieces of loose-hanging fabric from the cashmere sweater and crossed her long legs. She knew how to impress men, although the handsome inspector had his emotions under control and had shown no signs of the typical ancient male urges, even if these days it came in the form of approving looks or slightly too long gazing at certain parts of her well-trained body. The woman next to him was beautiful, but old. She was no competition for her youth and sexual appeal.

When she was made aware of her teenage escapades and how her behavior at that time seemed to clash with the decency of her current situation, she replied, "An unfortunate digression."

"Well, I am intrigued," Timo said, "enlighten us."

"There is nothing to say. A few bad friends, wild teenage hormones, and the rest is thankfully a thing of the past."

"And who were these bad friends?"

"I think you already know," she said with a sarcastic grin and threw her head back. It reminded Timo of one of those movie divas who seemed to put the drama in every conversation. It reminded him of his mother.

"You disapproved of your friend's choice?"

"Disapprove is not strong enough. We regularly argued about Jussi Vinter."

"Why was that?"

"He treated her like shit. I still don't understand why…"

"That's all very commendable, but in my line of work I've learned that there are other reasons a close friend hates her best friend's boyfriend."

"Oh, what then?" she said casually.

"Sex, love. I think you're in love with him, and Marie got in the way."

"That's ridiculous! That idiot! One evening she came home… bruises all over her body and face. They got into a fight, and he hit her. You see what a saint he is!"

"Marie told you that?"

69

"Not in so many words. I begged her to go to the police, but she refused."

"Marie was pregnant," Isa said.

"Pregnant?! Really? I can't believe it!"

"Twelve weeks," Timo said. "Why is it hard to believe?"

"She had finally broken up with that loser. Her idea of marriage and kids wasn't so conventional. She said she never wanted to have children, and she was a fan of open marriages and relationships."

"She seemed to get on pretty well with her little nephew."

"But that doesn't mean she wanted kids of her own," Teresa replied.

"So, she had other lovers? Did Jussi know?"

"She had flings. Nothing serious... and no, I don't think Jussi knew."

"So he could have found out and killed her in a rage?"

"Maybe...," she said, looking down at her hands.

"She broke off the relationship. Why? If she was so open-minded, why would she end it with Jussi?"

Teresa sighed and ran her hand through the loose strands of hair.

"She had met someone else, and she had fallen in love."

"Who?"

"She didn't want to say. It was all so new, but I think he was someone important."

"Why do you think that?"

"Marie liked to go to the parties of the beau monde. She was a girl of simple folks, but she was ambitious and wanted to advance her career and herself. She wanted to get out of Gävle and see the world."

"Beau monde? The parties of the rich and famous?"

"As you well know, inspector Paikkala."

He looked at her open-mouthed.

"You are the son of Yrjo Paikkala and Valesca Ignatova, aren't you? I had the pleasure of meeting your mother a few years ago at a party organized by the Trade Partners Association."

Isa gave him a quick glance, but obviously Timo wasn't pleased. Teresa had done her homework, making this personal. What was she up to?

Timo ignored her and said, "Do you think that man was the father of her child?"

"Probably," she said and smiled.

"Tell me about Quinten Hall and Espen Frisk."

"Tragedy," she blurted. "Quinten killed himself... he and Espen were best friends. There were rumors Quinten was in love with him, but his love remained unrequited, and so he took his own life."

"And what do you think?"

"Quinten was a troubled soul. If he could, he would have carried the sorrow of the entire world. Every insignificant problem got magnified in his head, and it usually got so big he fell into a depression. Multiple depressions since he was a child."

"Quinten committed suicide in the house you squatted. What happened that day?"

"Jussi had scored some hash and Marie wanted to get high, but Quinten wasn't in a good place, and he didn't want to be with us. He'd had a big fight with Espen a few days before."

"Why?"

"I don't know, but it was bad. They hadn't talked for days."

"And then?"

"Then we got high and when we woke up, Quinten was dead. He hanged himself."

She said it without emotions.

"And the police came and brought us home. But..."

"What, Ms. Ljungman?"

"It's weird. I hadn't thought about Quinten for a long time, but before her disappearance I remember that one evening Marie suddenly started talking about him. Out of nowhere. She asked me if I had seen anyone the day Quinten died."

"Who?"

"She was talking about a face she'd seen, someone staring at her. She was babbling, confused. She wasn't making any sense."

"Did something trigger this?"

"No, nothing I can think of. It was about six months ago."

"And Espen Frisk?"

"I don't know too much about him. He's studying engineering or something in Stockholm. We lost contact. I sometimes see him when I visit my parents, but he usually ignores me. I guess he doesn't want to be reminded of that time."

"One more thing, Ms. Ljungman. This isn't a cheap apartment. How could someone like Marie afford it? Where did the money come from?"

She shrugged. "She had jobs. And she didn't have to pay that much. Daddy supports me. I was surprised though when Marie suggested moving in together two years ago. I didn't complain. My dad and I had a big fight and he cut me off temporarily. But I didn't understand why Marie would want to live with me. She had just changed courses. She wanted to do economics, and it didn't really suit her. She passed her first year, but it took a lot of her energy."

"And the designer dresses?" Isa asked.

"She got them from me," Teresa said quickly. "Throw-aways. I didn't use them, anyway."

"Thank you," Timo said and got up.

She held out her hand and said, "Give my regards to your mother. She's a lovely woman."

* * *

"Your mother must have made quite an impression," Isa said as the elevator descended.

"Leave it," Timo said with a straight face, "Teresa Ljungman is a dangerous woman."

"You know her?"

"No, but I know her father. And she's just like him. Manipulative. These people think they own everything and everyone. He's been in the news lately, with some scandal about an affair."

He sighed. "Marie Lång is a woman of contradictions. Traditional girl who runs away from home and lives in a crack house with four friends. She's in a steady relationship with a man who completely clashes with her ambition to be part of the high society. And why would Ms. Ljungman take Marie in? It's for sure not charity."

"Keep your enemies close," Isa said.

Timo turned to her. "Yes, Marie was competition, but for what? Teresa didn't trust her."

"I think Quinten Hall has something to do with it."

"Maybe. But I agree, we need to dive a little deeper into that case."

The elevator door opened, and they stepped outside into the cold air. The weather was a lot worse than the days before. Rain was coming.

"You drive," Timo said, and tossed the key.

She had kept quiet, but now she couldn't hold it anymore, "So, how many cars do you actually have?"

She looked at the convertible. Nice looking car, flashy, almost new. And then she remembered the shiny big BMW he'd driven when he'd visited the Långs the other day. Expensive cars. Not exactly what she had in mind for an inspector's salary.

"Many," Timo said.

"Many? Stockholm must be paying very well! Maybe I need to get myself a job there. Or maybe it's a leftover from the beau monde days?"

He said nothing but kept a straight face as he stepped into the car. There was a story behind it, but something told her he would only make her part of it when the trust was there.

"Just don't hit anyone!" he said suddenly.

The frown on her face forced him to explain a little more, "You have a certain reputation."

They drove to the station in silence. The trip lasted more than an hour. She loved the car, which made up for the nasty remark he had thrown at her. Feeling the power of the engine as the car thrusted forward, the ease with which she changed gears, the maneuverability, she had to stop herself from speeding. It was a welcome distraction. She still struggled to focus on this case. Marie Lång deserved better, but the only thing she could think of were the Sandviken files lying on her living room table.

Timo broke the silence. "I want to go back to the lake."

"Why?"

"I can't put my finger on it. There's just something about that place... the house."

"Oh, you're one of those," Isa said while keeping her eyes fixed on the road.

"What does that mean? Are you always that disrespectful to your superiors? Or is it just me?"

She kept her eyes on the road.

"I see our little conversation the other day didn't help," he continued.

"You need to earn trust and respect."

"Why?"

"What do you mean?" she said.

"I'm your boss."

"And? That doesn't give you a free pass to do or say whatever you like. You Stockholm guys are all the same! You come in here and think you own the place. You think you know better; you think you have to teach us."

"Lindström, I don't think that's the problem. You just don't like me interfering with what you're doing. Anders left you on your own. No control. I'm not Anders."

"Indeed, you're not."

Isa drove to the parking lot of the police station.

"Ah, one more thing: I think you still need to bring back the files you pulled from the registry... it won't be long before the Uppsala team starts looking for them, so...," Timo said before getting out of the car.

As if she didn't know!

"I need more time," she said as they walked to the entrance.

"You have no more time. I need them tomorrow, otherwise I can't protect you."

She didn't need his protection; she needed a new set of eyes to look at the case. Bringing back the files was a detail. Irene Nordin was still her prime suspect, but she was desperately looking for the evidence that could put the old woman at the crime scene.

"Have you looked at them?" she asked.

His expression showed no emotion. "No, should I?"

Should he? Yes, he should. But did she really want him to get involved? This was so personal. He would be her conscience, he would get her out of this tunnel vision, but did she really want that? He was right. His meddling could set things in motion. So far nobody and nothing had torn down the perfect image of Alex, but what if...

"You just have to ask," he said.

Was this an invitation? He looked sincere. So far he just had been annoyingly right about everything, but making him part of her quest was a step too far. The jury was still out on him.

"I'll get you the files by tomorrow," she said.

"Perfect."

* * *

Magnus was sitting on her doorstep. With the streetlamp barely giving enough light to distinguish anything, Isa didn't recognize him until she was a few meters away from him.

He was edgy, fiddling with the strap of his coat, eyes jumping from left to right.

Was he there?

By now his vision was adjusted to the darkness. His nemesis had followed him the entire day. He found no peace. The voice had stopped, but the image of Alex followed him everywhere. His conscience, his guilt. A few months ago, he'd been carefree. His confidence and arrogance had been boundless. But now... Did he regret killing a human being? No, he regretted what it had done to him. He regretted the overwhelming guilt he had to deal with and couldn't. People, his own family looked at him with suspicion. Why had Anna asked if he had ever killed someone? Did she know anything?

"Magnus, what are you doing here?"

He smiled when he saw her. God, she was so beautiful! But almost immediately he felt shame take over. If she only knew.

Isa, I have to tell you something. I've done something so awful there are no words to describe it. I wish I could turn back time; I wish I had ignored that phone call; I wish I had never gotten in that car and driven to Mats' house. I wish I had never picked up that gun and pulled the trigger. Two seconds, only two seconds. I killed Alex, the love of your life. I took him away from you.

"Can we talk?" he said.

"Sure." She turned the key and invited him in.

The hallway and living room looked strange. The furniture was new, and the walls had been repainted.

"I love what you've done to the place," he said and threw his coat over the back of the couch.

"Well, I had to do something with my free time," she said and threw the keys in the porcelain bowl on the cupboard next to the door.

He sighed. What was he doing here?

"What's wrong?" she said.

"I just... Toby. Am I doing the right thing?"

"God, I don't know. You shouldn't ask me."

He threw himself on the couch next to her. "You are the only one I can trust."

"You know, I really admire you," she said, "the way you deal with your son's illness is so incredible. The way you believe in him, that it will all work out when everyone around you is saying it's a lost cause. I think you need to face the fact it takes a superhuman to cope with it. You have to talk to someone and it isn't me. A professional, a psychiatrist."

He put his head in his hands. A psychiatrist would be bound by professional secrecy. It could work if only he found the courage.

What are you going to tell the psychiatrist? How you killed me and then tried to take the love of my life?

The voice was back.

"I'm scared," he said, hands still covering his face, "I hear voices... voices of people who aren't really there."

She breathed sharply and for a moment her mouth fell open in a dumbfounded gaze.

"And what do these voices say?" she said and let her hand run over his back.

Goosebumps. It felt so familiar.

"That," he took a deep breath, "I'm a terrible person."

"Magnus, this is all in your head."

"Is that how it started for Toby?" he cried and then continued, "Sorry, I shouldn't bother you with this."

"No, you should, you aren't well," Isa said.

He wanted to put his head on the pillow and close his eyes, slowly being engulfed by the warm sleep. He hadn't slept in days. The mere thought he would only find peace again if he confessed, terrified him.

"Can I stay? Anna is at her mother's... and I don't want to be alone."

Well played.

"You can sleep on the couch," she said, got up and came back with a few blankets she threw over the backrest. "I hope this is okay."

"It's fine," he said and let his hand run over the blankets. It felt soft and warm. He stared at her, and for the first time he realized how sad and lonely she looked. It looked like she had been crying.

Crying? Over that loser again. Every bit of remorse and pity for Alexander Nordin was gone. She didn't know what he had sacrificed for her. Until then, he had never been angry with her. Now he was. It was her fault.

Why don't you just take her? She should give you something.

The tone of the voice had changed. This was no longer Alex in his head. This was evil. This was the true Magnus Wieland.

"It's late. Maybe we can talk more tomorrow. Then I'll check if we can take you to a doctor. Does Sophie know?"

He shook his head.

"Okay, I'll be in my room... if something's wrong, let me know," she said and left him alone.

She wants you. Go after her!

Oh, God, this wasn't him! He removed his watch and put it on the table next to the couch. He took the blankets and started to set up his bed, but his attention was drawn to the pile of papers lying on the edge of the wooden table, between the used coffee mugs and half-eaten sandwich.

He looked around to check if she was gone, and pulled the files toward him.

It was Irene Nordin's statement and the forensic report of the crime scene where the bodies of Annette Norman and Alex had been found. Panic overtook him. Isa couldn't read this. She might find some inconsistencies. Quickly he flipped through the pages. Where was it?

Suddenly she was standing in front of him, looking down at the files he was holding. She closed the folder and took it out of his hands.

"What's this?" he said. "Why do you have these files? Issie, what are you up to? What if they find out? Your career will be over."

"It's okay. Don't worry! It's not your problem."

"But it is my problem. I'm your partner, your friend. I want to take care of you."

He put his hand on the file as if he wanted to take it from her, but she brought it closer to her body, then turned and walked away from him.

"I'll see you tomorrow," she said and went upstairs. She disappeared with the papers in her arms. It was too late. Eventually she would figure it out.

* * *

She closed the bedroom door and kept her hand on the key, unsure of what to do. Was it the right decision to let him sleep here? He was Magnus, her friend, but what he had just told her made her uneasy. He heard voices. Could she still trust him? The handle of the key felt cold and smooth, and she ran her finger over it.

No, she couldn't. He was acting weird, and she couldn't get the images of psychopathic killers out of her head. She turned the key and the familiar click assured her the door was locked. One last yank to verify it, and then she turned her attention to the files. The laptop on the bedside table was started by now. She placed it on the bed and then stretched out in front of the screen.

She opened the folder on the computer. If Irene Nordin had helped Mats Norman kidnap the victims, she had left traces. She had been at the Maritiman when Katrien Jans disappeared. Here it was, the statement of Irene Kirkegard, maiden name of Irene Nordin.

Mrs. Kirkegard had witnessed the quarrel between Josip Radić and Katrien Jans before the girl went missing. She testified how she had seen the young man follow the girl outside until they both had disappeared.

She had been there with her husband.

Husband? Isa scrolled down, looked at related links, but nowhere there was a transcript of the husband's interview. His name was not even mentioned.

Was it Peter Nordin or Mats Norman? She continued reading: date, place of the interview. There had been no follow-up conversation or confrontation with the suspect Josip Radić.

"Mmm, this is interesting," she said.

The interview with Mrs. Kirkegard was recorded. Other than that, there was nothing interesting. She was about to close the file when she suddenly cramped up. This couldn't be right. She skipped through the pages of the file lying next to the computer until she held the paper she was looking for in her hands and pressed it to the screen next to the file that was open on the laptop. The signatures didn't match. Irene Nordin's signature was distinctly different from Irene Kirkegard's scribble. Round letters, sloping left in one case, pointy, straight, and large on the other page.

"My God," she said. These were not the same people. She was convinced the paper in the most recent file had been signed by Irene Nordin. Then, who was the witness in Göteborg?

CHAPTER

6

WHEN ILAN ARRIVED, the garage was plunged in darkness, apart from a faint orange light at the entrance. The door was unlocked, and he entered without thinking. Frank, the mechanic, had an excellent reason not to draw attention to his late-night activities, but inside the warehouse it was as dim as outside, and Ilan had to navigate his way to the office by touch.

As his eyes slowly got accustomed to the darkness, his lungs filled with the pungent smell of oil and battery acid. The grease stained his fingertips as he ran his hands along the shelves and racks to find a grip. A screwdriver lying on a bench was sticking out and scratched the palm of his hand. He could barely contain a cry of pain.

"Frank, are you here?"

An hour ago, he had received a text message to meet the illustrious Frank in the garage where he fixed cars under the counter. Frank was in for about everything. No questions asked. That was why Ilan had brought the car to him a few days ago, to replace the bumper and hood. The message had stated that the car was ready and that he could pick it up.

He finally found a light switch by the door leading to the next compartment of the warehouse. The light wasn't strong enough to illuminate the entire room, but it gave Ilan an overview of the racks and the tools scattered across the benches and floor. The enormous doors to the parking lot were closed, and his car was nowhere to be seen. The intoxicating odor of exhaust gasses, still very present, triggered the onset of a migraine.

"Frank?"

There was still no reply, and he went to the next room. As soon as he opened the door, a strange scent sharpened all his senses. This wasn't the typical fusty smell of a poorly maintained, moldy workshop. From behind the metal tool racks, a little too high to glance over, dividing the room in two, a faint glow came and illuminated part of the place. The stench grew stronger, sharper and more recognizable. The smell of sweat and vomit mixed with the iron scent of blood and starting decay.

In the background, he heard the calculable rhythm of fluid hitting the surface. He remained stock-still. As he exhaled, he heard the air come out in short shallow breaths. His legs felt weak and numb, unable to move, as if someone had nailed them to the floor.

His voice trembled. "Frank?"

He jumped up when he suddenly felt the phone vibrate in the pocket of his pants.

He took a few more deep breaths before he moved closer to check what was behind the cupboards. The phone rang again, and a second time he ignored it.

There, in the light of a small fluorescent lamp that hung against the wall above the narrow wooden desk, among the papers, in a pile of blood, lay a motionless body, with a nasty cut running from ear to ear, exposing part of the trachea. The face was frozen in a panic-struck gaze, eyes wide open, looking straight at him. Frank.

A beeping sound.

What should he do? Call the police? Explain what he was doing here? No, this was out of the question.

Another beep.

He suddenly realized this was important and he looked at the screen. The text message was clear: "Answer your phone!"

He held his breath. A repeat of the first message. And then the phone rang again. With trembling hands, he had a hard time pressing the accept call icon on the touch screen.

"Yes," he said, with the dead eyes still staring at him.

The metal voice, twisted by the modulator, said, "Look what I've done for you."

What was this? What twisted, perverted game was this?

"Who are you? What do you want from me?"

"All in good time," the voice replied calmly.

There was no way of telling whether this was a man or a woman. There was another beep. It was a picture. His car. But the background looked strange. A barn or a warehouse?

"I have your car," the voice said. "Frank was about to call the police. I couldn't let that happen. Say thank you! I saved you."

"What? Frank would never do that. He would never risk exposing his business," Ilan said.

"Say thank you!"

"You killed Frank!"

"SAY THANK YOU!" the voice said. The loss of control and the threat that emanated from the tone terrified him. The headache pounded in his head. The nausea he had felt until then had subsided and been replaced with a fight-flight feeling for preservation.

"You don't get it... if you don't listen and do as I say, Frank won't be the only one paying for your disobedience with his life! You're mine now."

"But what do you want?" Ilan said.

The stress, the panic. His life was in danger, and there was nothing he could do.

"If I were you, I'd hurry and run... the police are coming," the voice continued, and the conversation was over.

The police? Think! Did he leave fingerprints or DNA? He turned and walked back. In the dim light, he saw how he left footprints on the dusty floor. He had to be quick.

* * *

Berger stared at the whiteboard. It looked good, better than usual. More structured. He was glad Isa hadn't interfered. It was time to show what he was worth. Secretly he hoped that this case would be his ticket to become chief inspector and even superintendent further down the road. There was no harm in thinking big and being ambitious, but he was cautious. A new boss, new ways. He liked Anders Larsen, the former superintendent. Anders had been tough, but respectful, and he'd always given his team the freedom to do what they did best: finding the culprits.

But Anders had been a ghost boss at times, leaving the team alone to deal with their nuisances, little tensions and avoidable fights and arguments. They sometimes looked like a bunch of amateurs. And what would Mr. Stockholm think? Everyone agreed: inspector Paikkala was there to test them. He couldn't be trusted.

With a deep sigh, Isa came in, didn't give her colleagues another look, and sat down in the chair furthest from the man in the front.

"So, where are we?"

Timo threw himself in the front-row seat, took a long gulp of the black coffee that had been fuming for half an hour, and looked at the whiteboard. The frown showed he wasn't pleased with what he saw. And when he turned to face the team, he looked straight at Ingrid Olsson who, still in doubt, stood in the doorway.

"Dr. Olsson," he said, "come in!"

"I'm not sure. Should I be here?"

"Yes, you should," Timo said, "you are part of the team."

Ingrid took a seat a few meters away from Isa. Obviously, she was still angry with her friend.

"Marie Lång, twenty-two, university student, run over and strangled. Her body was found in the lake near Strömsbro."

"Home of the rich," Lars interrupted.

"Is that right?" Timo said.

"Yeah, I mean... never mind!"

Timo ignored him and continued, "She was barefoot and probably held captive close to where we found her."

"So, the assumption is that she escaped and to catch her, her killer hit her with his car, strangled her when she wasn't dead and threw her body in the lake."

"Even if the area isn't that densely populated, he took a huge risk to kill her there. There was an immediate need to dispose of her."

Timo moved closer to the whiteboard and ran his fingers over the photograph. He was close enough to see the green and brown spots in her eyes.

"Why, Marie Lång, were you a target? Why did you have to die?" Then Timo turned suddenly and said, "Dr. Olsson, any news on the car and the shoes the mother brought in?"

Ingrid jumped up from her chair. She was nervous judging by the way she first scanned the room and took a deep breath before saying,

"DNA swipes from the shoes were sent to the lab. Other than DNA from Bengta and Marie Lång, we found nothing."

"And the car?"

"We are checking all CCTV in the area for a dark-blue car, but so far no results."

"The twig in her mouth," Timo continued, "bears a significance... any ideas?"

"It probably means something personal to the killer," Ingrid said.

"Yes, but what?"

It stayed quiet in the room.

Timo shook his head and then turned to Berger. "What did you find out about Jussi Vinter?"

"No criminal record... surprisingly. He ran away from home at fifteen, and a month later was found in an abandoned store together with Marie Lång, Teresa Ljungman, Espen Frisk and Quinten Hall. He was placed with foster parents after he got home and was almost beaten to death by his father. Mr. Vinter lost touch with his father, but he still sees his mother and siblings regularly."

"What about the others?"

"Very different stories. They are all children from established, stable families. Now students at the university in Uppsala and Stockholm, except for Quinten Hall. He died in 2011."

"He took his own life." Timo stepped aside, took a seat, and leaned backward so he could have a better look at his inspector, who put the picture of the teenager on the whiteboard. Blond hair, soft features, but with a sad, melancholic look on his face.

"He hanged himself in the bathroom of the house, but the others were too stoned to remember what had happened."

"There was an investigation, but it was ruled a suicide. All the children returned home, and that was it."

"It might have something to do with Marie's murder," Lars said.

"Maybe we should talk to Teresa Ljungman again," Berger suggested.

Timo started pacing around the room in a way that showed he wasn't pleased.

"There is a tradition in German hunting where the hunter sticks a twig in the dead deer's mouth as a sign of respect. It's called 'Brüche', twigs of cervine fair trees. Then the hunter takes a twig, puts a little blood of the deer on it and attaches it to his hat."

Timo looked at Ingrid in surprise. "How…"

"Don't ask me how I know. My father is a little obsessed with… anyhow. It's probably too far-fetched."

Timo shook his head. "Well, it's the only theory I heard so far. So, our killer is a hunter?"

Isa sighed. "Wait a minute! Are you saying the killer collects twigs with the blood of his victims?"

"And what is your explanation, inspector Lindström?" Timo said.

"Marie was the wrong girl in the wrong place, at the wrong time. She saw something, got caught, tried to get away, but was captured by her killer."

"She disappeared two months ago. There's more to it than this simple generalization."

Isa frowned and said, "So, since we're in Gävle, you think we're dealing with a serial killer. We don't have them running around in every street and corner of the city."

Timo shook his head. "That's not what I said. I want you to keep an open mind."

She threw her feet on the empty chair next to her and pouted her lips like a child who didn't get his way.

Timo gave her a quick glance of irritation and then turned to the rest of the team. "Lars, look into this hunting angle, and check if any similar cases have been reported in recent years! Broaden the search to the entire country."

With shock in his eyes, afraid of the gigantic task ahead, the young man nodded.

"Berger, Lindström, we're going back to the lake, and pay the Forsbergs a visit."

"Forsberg? Like in Gerard Forsberg?"

"Yes, your richer than rich guy," Timo said.

* * *

The team dissolved after another lecture by inspector Paikkala about teamwork and respect, pro-activeness, and professionalism.

"As soon as I get the forensic report of Marie Lång's apartment, I'll send it to you," Ingrid said.

The boss was still grabbing the papers from the table and the empty cup he would refill with the worst coffee he had ever tasted. He turned to the woman who looked at him with big green eyes.

"Thank you. And as always, my door is open. Don't hesitate to discuss it in person!"

She smiled. "I will."

"And Dr. Olsson," he said with a calm voice. The tone was so soothing and melodic. It was the first time she noticed it.

"Yes?"

"Well done. I told you … you are just as much a part of this team as any of them. You should come to our briefings more often."

She was a practical woman. She did her job, and tried to distance herself from the drama, unprofessional friction, and ego-tripping of many of her colleagues, but this felt right. Appreciation. Being noticed and acknowledged. Her ideas were considered.

"Then you should invite me."

"No problem. Consider it done."

"Sorry to interrupt," Isa said, "you wanted to see me?"

Timo's smile folded into a stern, disapproving line and disappeared like the glowing twinkles in his eyes. "Yes, Lindström. We have a few things to talk about."

* * *

"I am discrete," Isa said.

"I disagree," Timo said calmly.

He didn't yell. He never did. Usually a stern glance sufficed, but not on her. She knew it irritated him.

They were in his office. He had done little to give it a personal touch. It was just as minimalistic as before, when Anders had been the main occupant.

"Well, Finn Heimersson of the Uppsala team asked me why you requested access to the recordings of the 2002 Göteborg police interviews in the Katrien Jans case."

"Of course, Heimersson had to stick his nose in it."

"Inspector Heimersson is a decent man and... a friend of mine. We should be happy to have him on board."

"He is a pain in the … you know," she said.

"Lindström, I'm trying to avoid getting you suspended again or worse... losing your job."

"Shouldn't you find reasons to get rid of me? I don't understand you."

"You don't need to understand me," he answered with the same cool calmness as always. The man never seemed to lose control.

"If Heimersson is such a wonderful friend, you know what to tell him."

"Sure, as if I have nothing better to do than to babysit you," he said and sighed, "why do you need those recordings, anyway?"

She knew it. Deep down, the case interested him. Not just to get her off his back, but he simply couldn't bear injustice.

By now, the entire Gävle police department had contacted someone in Stockholm to find out everything about Timo Paikkala, and so had she, but the only information she had received was disappointingly boring. There should be more than the polite praises of efficiency and brilliance. He was a mystery.

"There is an inconsistency between Irene Nordin's statement of a few months ago and the interview taken in 2002."

He looked at her in surprise.

She continued, "We assumed the witness was Irene Nordin, but the signatures on the witness statements don't match."

"It's easy to forge a signature. Maybe she didn't want anyone to know she'd been in Göteborg?"

"Then why would she use her maiden name?"

"Okay. So, what does all that mean?"

"I don't know yet, but the interview has been recorded, and I want to check if it's her."

"I assume," Timo replied, "they checked her identity."

"No, they haven't. She wasn't considered a suspect, only a witness."

"Even then, they would have checked it. So she never testified?"

"Josip Radić was never formally charged."

"Very well," Timo said, "I'll see what I can do."

"I don't need your help to get the recording," Isa said indignantly, "I need you to get the Uppsala team off my back."

He calmly opened the desk drawer and put a new file on the table. She shook her head. He got on her nerves again. That was how the dynamics worked. Respect and irritation. Most of the time, she couldn't figure out what he was thinking or where even the most straightforward conversation with him led to, but it had a purpose. Everything always had a goal in Timo Paikkala's mind.

"I want your opinion on this," he said and pushed the file across the table to her.

"What is it?"

"Frank Harket, 42 years old, divorced, two children. He was found murdered in his workshop four days ago, throat slit. Mr. Harket was no stranger to the police. Drugs, arms trafficking, theft... he was a fixer. So, it's not surprising he would end up dead sooner rather than later."

"What is so special about the case?" Isa leaned over, picked up the file and opened it.

"Page four."

Page four showed the picture of dark-blue flakes. The report talked about chips found at the crime scene, in the room next to where they had found Frank Harket.

"You think it's the same car that hit Marie Lång?"

"Maybe. Dr. Olsson says the flakes match those found near Marie's body."

"Did she?"

Timo looked up. "Is there something wrong?"

"You like Ingrid."

"So? She's good, and I value her opinion, and she could use a little more appreciation."

"She's married and has two young sons," Isa said.

He leaned back, still staring at her with furrowed eyebrows. The chair balanced on two legs and the backrest was continuously bouncing against the wall. Another one of his lectures was coming, and she already regretted making the remark.

"What does that mean?" he said finally.

"Nothing," she replied and pivoted her attention to the file, but he wouldn't let go.

"Are you trying to tell me something?"

"No... just leave it," she said.

The chair landed on its four legs, and he continued, "You may have a different opinion, but I can assure you my actions and motives are purely professional."

She nodded. Still, she wondered if that was truly the case. Why did he feel the need to tell her that? Professional demeanor. It applied to him as much as it applied to her.

"And how is inspector Wieland?"

Of course, he had to move to that topic.

"He's home. He'll be back at work soon. It was just a matter of not getting enough sleep... with his son and all."

"I understand that. But I hope our dear inspector doesn't run off and disappear like he did a few months ago. We don't have enough people as it is."

"He didn't run off. It's not like that. His son is badly injured. He doesn't know what to do."

"Well, you know my point of view. I'm always willing to look for solutions together with him, like taking a sabbatical or reduce his working hours, but I haven't even seen him. He's hardly here. This behavior is unacceptable. I'm running a police department, not a charity."

"Coming back to this case," Isa said, "any fingerprints or DNA?"

"Plenty... I'm sure we can match a lot of them with prints and DNA we have on record, but that doesn't mean they belong to his killer. The light switches were wiped clean, and we found blood on a screwdriver."

"We need to find that car."

"I agree," Timo said.

"Sorry, to interrupt." The policewoman standing in the doorway hesitated to enter.

"What is it?" Timo said.

"Inspector Lindström, this was brought for you," she said and handed Isa a small package.

Unwrapping it didn't take very long. It was a USB stick accompanied with a short letter.

"Already," she exclaimed in surprise.

"They brought it this morning, special delivery," the young police officer said and left.

It was a copy of the police interview conducted with Irene Kirkegard in 2002. The file was uploaded to the computer, and, with Timo next to her, she watched the footage. The video image, taken from a high angle, showed a small room, with a table and two chairs, a woman on the right-hand side and a police officer sitting close to the door.

"The quality is terrible," she said.

She hardly recognized the woman. The woman's head was turned away from the camera, looking only at the policeman. The woman resembled Irene Nordin. She had the same physique, hair color and manners, but there was something wrong. Was it her voice? It sounded much lower than Irene's high-pitch tone. The interview lasted approximately ten minutes. The questions were curt and objective, but the woman continuously wanted to steer the conversation to Josip Radić and his involvement in the girl's disappearance. She had seen him run after Katrien just before the girl went missing. Why hadn't other people reported this? Was she the only one who had witnessed it?

"Is it Irene Nordin?" Timo whispered.

"I think it is… although." She wasn't sure and felt disappointed the tape hadn't given her more to work with.

And then the interview was done. The woman stood up and looked straight into the camera. For one second, she had forgotten it was there. A mistake.

"Oh, my God," Isa cried out. She recognized the woman, and it wasn't Irene Nordin. This took a bizarre turn. How could they have been so wrong? Those two seconds of carelessness. If she hadn't seen the change in signature, if she hadn't asked for the recordings, they never would have discovered this.

"What's wrong?" Timo didn't see the relevance.

"This isn't Irene Nordin."

She turned to him. He still didn't understand.

"It's Annette Norman, the wife of Mats, our serial killer. They have been working together all this time. That's why she had to die."

CHAPTER

7

THE AIR WAS FILLED with the scent of spring. For a second, Irene wasn't the woman who had lost her husband and son, who had been betrayed by the people she had called her friends for more than thirty years. For a second, she was allowed to feel happy and marvel at the budding blossoms on the trees and the smell of young flowers as she walked past the small urban gardens in front of the colorful houses.

The shopping bags felt heavy. She could have taken the car, but these days she preferred to walk to the department store herself, to feel connected to the world. Lately she'd been feeling more and more secluded. An old woman in an old house, surrounded by painful memories. No one to talk to, no one to take care of. To the outside world she seemed strong and arrogant, almost unaffected by her husband's tragic death and the murder of her only child, but Irene Nordin was insecure, devastated and worried about her own future. She strolled down the street to the house. Deep in thought, she hadn't noticed the woman in front of her home. When she got closer, she recognized who it was. The slender, tall figure, the light-brown curly hair. Yes, it was her. Irene stopped a few meters before reaching the door. Neither of them knew how to start the conversation.

"What are you doing here, inspector Lindström?" Irene said. "You want me to file a harassment complaint with your superiors... it's not too late to do it."

"I need to talk to you," Isa said.

Irene walked past her, put the bags on the floor and pushed the key into the lock. What would Isa Lindström have to say to her she didn't already know? She was done listening to another recital of allegations about killing her son.

"Irene?"

No yelling, no threats. It made it so much easier if they could continue with the same hostility as before. But Irene didn't care. Isa Lindström was irrelevant. It wouldn't bring Alex or Peter back.

"Annette Norman," Isa said.

Irene turned. The name sparked something more than surprise. It resonated through her mind and body like a tsunami, ready to destroy everything in its path. Isa knew. She had finally figured it out.

"Come in," Irene said.

* * *

They were sitting in the same living room as they had many months ago, looking for the killer of nine teenage girls, interviewing the wife of a suspect, mother of the witness. The same impersonal, cold and empty room. The pictures were gone. Pictures of Alex. Removed from her life, forgotten. Irene put herself in the one-seater. She felt exhausted even before the conversation started.

"You knew she helped her husband," Isa said.

Irene quietly stared at her hands.

"Why didn't you say something?"

"I didn't know, not until that day," Irene said.

"What day?"

There was a lengthy silence. Should she really tell her everything? Her feelings about Isa Lindström hadn't changed.

"The day Alex died."

The day Alex died, everything changed.

"Annette called me in the morning. She couldn't come on our shopping trip. Her mother's health had taken a turn for the worst, and she had to stay with her."

"So, what happened next?"

"That would have been it until I remembered that I urgently needed her to sign a book club document. She was president of the club and… anyhow, I called the hospital and her sister mentioned she had gone home to pick up clothes. If it was urgent, I could probably catch her then."

"You drove to their home?"

She wished she hadn't.

The conversation was tough, with endless pauses, words to be sought and found, emotions to be suppressed to complete the story. What she had seen that day in the home of Mats and Annette Norman had undermined her confidence and the foundations of everything she believed in. She knew what Mats was capable of. But Annette? She had always been a victim until she hadn't.

"When I arrived, it was quiet. In the driveway, I saw two cars: Annette's car and a red, old Volvo I didn't know. It looked so much like our old car. That should have triggered suspicion, but it didn't. The front door was open, and I heard someone talking. I still don't know why I entered. I should have called or rang the bell."

"Who was there?"

"Mats was standing by the window, and Annette was sitting on the couch, leaning over the body of a teenage girl... Sara. She was sleeping."

"Probably drugged. This was just after Sara's abduction."

Irene nodded and stood up. The room looked so empty, as if nobody was living in the house. She still remembered Alex sitting on the play mat by the window when he was a child. The Legos in front of him, nicely categorized according to color and length. Usually there was a period of five to ten minutes in which he continued to stare at them, before he started building the most fantastic things. Castles, hospitals, churches, bridges. Buildings he had seen in books. Such a weird child!

And Peter sitting on the sofa, reading and occasionally looking at his son out of the corner of his eye. A son that wasn't his.

"Irene?"

Eyes watery with tears, Irene turned to her. "I can't..."

"There's no point in withholding this from the police. We'll figure it out, eventually."

"How did you find out?"

"She was a so-called witness against Josip Radić when Katrien Jans disappeared, pretending to be you. I saw the recording of the interview. She could easily pass on for you. You have the same posture and body type. It took me a while to realize it was her. And then all pieces nicely fell into place. It was so simple. She must have known about the girls. The perfect accomplice."

Irene sighed. Yes, it had been that simple. Why hadn't she thought of that?

"So, you caught them red-handed?" Isa said.

"Yes. They tried to deny it at first. And I was too shocked to realize I could be in danger."

"And were you in danger?"

"Annette tried to convince me it was something futile, that they all needed to make sacrifices to please Mats. I couldn't say a word. It was just so disgusting. All these years, thinking she had been a victim! I felt sorry for her and her children. But it was a setup from the start. I screamed, I cried, I told them to stop and surrender to the police."

"And then what?"

"Nothing. She laughed and told me how stupid, weak and gullible the Nordins had been, how perfect scapegoats we were and how easy it would be to get rid of us. She had tried before and succeeded."

"Succeeded?" Isa said, surprised.

Irene's voice broke. "They killed my husband. They killed Peter."

The silence that followed was needed to put Irene's thoughts straight, but the flood of emotions was creating chaos.

"They killed him when he questioned Mats' involvement in the disappearance of those girls. Peter didn't know Annette was involved, and he talked to her about it. But with that, he signed his own death sentence."

"Who killed Annette?" Isa asked.

She had expected that question.

"The gun was on the table next to the couch. I assume he had used it during the assault. Please understand I don't know what came over me. It isn't me!"

"Did you kill her?"

"I wish I had," Irene whispered, "but no."

"Did Mats kill her?"

She nodded.

"Why?"

"I grabbed the gun and pointed it at them. I wanted to call the police, but then Annette started laughing, saying I would never pull the trigger, how weak I was just like my son. And then she went on to talk about

Alex. How sorry she was that our son, Mats' and mine, a mistake, hadn't died so many years ago at the hands of Nikolaj Blom while she had planned it so perfectly."

"It was Annette who brought Alex to the bunker where Nikolaj assaulted him?"

"Yes. I just lost it. I pulled the trigger and shot her. It was confusing, but I regretted it the moment I put my finger on the trigger. And then Mats took the gun."

"Was she dead?"

"No, she wasn't, but she was shouting at Mats he should kill me. But then he pointed the gun at her and fired twice. She fell on the couch. Dead. I ran out of the house as fast as I could, afraid he would come after me."

"And did he?"

"No," she mumbled, "I think he knew I wouldn't go to the police."

"Why did he kill his wife?"

His facial expression had changed the moment his wife explained how she had led the toddler to the bunker and locked him up with Ida Nilsson. It had been a calculated move to get rid of Ida and Alex. The sexual predator Nikolaj Blom would take care of them. She had done it for Mats. Ida was replaceable, and Alex had been a mistake that needed to be corrected. Only, Mats didn't see it that way. Alex was the son he loved the most, result of the greatest love he had experienced in his life. It was his son, his and Irene's. How could Annette have done this?

Isa looked at her. "And who killed Alex?"

Irene hid her face in her hands. The next moment, Isa heard her sobbing like a child. The haughty Irene Nordin showed a side of her most people rarely got to see.

"I don't know, I don't know," she cried, "I think he did. My God, Mats killed my beautiful son, my son, my Alex."

Isa sighed. "Alex was Mats' son. Why did you deny it? Even when you were confronted with the DNA results you didn't want to admit it. Why?"

Irene looked up, tears trickling from her face, falling on the hands she had held in her lap.

"We always assumed you and Mats were in a relationship and Alex was your love child, but I think we were wrong, weren't we?"

Still no answer. For years, Irene had kept it to herself. Now the words were lacking. How could she talk about it? Talking was reliving one of the most devastating things in her life aside from her mother's death. Those two moments had defined her.

"Yes," the word came out as a relief, and while she wiped the tears from her face she continued, "it's complicated."

"You were his first victim?"

She turned her head sideways. It was time to tell her story. Perhaps then inspector Lindström would understand why she had behaved the way she had. Why it had been such a struggle to love her son.

The story began more than thirty years ago. She was an administrative clerk at the University of Uppsala. She had known Peter since secondary school and they had been best friends first, and then lovers. He was her first and greatest love. He knew her family's history. How her father had murdered her mother and how she had been raised by foster parents. They were loving and decent people, but the trauma her father had left behind was harder to mend than she had imagined. Peter was patient, and he gave her the protective and secure environment she needed to forget a trauma that had destroyed the childhood she had been entitled to. They dreamt of a life together. Children, many children, and she would do so much better than her parents. She felt safe and confident with him. It would be a life far from any violence and abuse. Until she met Mats. Dazzling, handsome Mats was a young PhD student in the physics department. He had passed by the office a few times to sort out the issues with his fellowship. She had noticed him, and he had noticed her. She was a beautiful young woman. He was married, but she interested him. They became friends, but he wanted more than that. He had this way with women. He knew exactly what they wanted to hear. But she saw through his charming facade, hiding a more sinister and darker core that was terrifying and was capable of unimaginable atrocities. She told him she would marry Peter and they only could be friends. He seemed to accept it and even befriended her fiancé.

She married Peter, and everything settled down to a friendly way of interacting, a friendship between two young couples, savoring life. This went on for a few years. Until that day...

How could she know that his infatuation with her had become such an obsession he had started stalking her, that he had broken into her apartment, that he had tried to sabotage her marriage to Peter by trying to run him over with his car? How could she know that in his mind a plan had taken shape to possess her? A plan, largely nurtured and encouraged by Annette, after she had discovered her husband's perverse fantasies. It was one of those things Annette had confessed to when Irene had confronted them after Sara's abduction.

That fateful day, Irene had been working late, and she was alone in the office when he came in. He locked the door before he started a chitchat about the summer holidays. They would rent a cabin in Sandviken, and Annette and he would love it if they could join as well. Almost instantly she knew something wasn't right. He came closer and before she could react, he had pinned her against the wall. She couldn't move and then...

She couldn't say it. This couldn't have happened to her. She, the woman, who had vouched she would never let a man control her, never let a man force her to subject to his will, she had been submitted to his perversities.

"He raped you," Isa said.

"Yes."

Although for years, she hadn't given it a name, at least not that one. It was confusing. Maybe she had wanted it, maybe she had sent out the wrong signals. She couldn't deny she longed for him and dreamt of him. Hot, wild dreams. At least in the beginning, when he pretended to be Prince Charming, the ideal son-in-law, before she felt that darkness in him.

"Did you tell anyone?"

"Yes," she said, "but I wish I hadn't."

Instead of helping her, the university board had suggested her to find another job. Mats Norman was a rising star in the field of nuclear physics, and they couldn't allow the slander harm his career. She had probably provoked it.

And Peter. She had told Peter, but he didn't believe her either. He questioned her motives. He thought they were having an affair. Instead of supporting her, he distanced himself from his wife. Their relationship deteriorated, and that had an enormous impact on his state of mind. With a long history of mental health problems in his family, he was receptive to succumb to the doubts and fears about his marriage.

"Why didn't you go to the police?"

"Who would have believed me? It was his word against mine. The university didn't believe me. Peter didn't believe me. Why would they? Times were very different, and even now the woman's behavior is usually put under a microscope, questioning her actions. They treat her like a criminal, rather than seeing her as a victim."

"And then Alex came?"

"A few months later, I found out I was pregnant. It's supposed to be the most beautiful time of your life, but it was horrible. I cried every day. Peter kept quiet. He tried to convince himself it was his child, but I knew very well it was Mats'."

"Did Mats know?"

"It didn't take long, and he demanded to be involved as if nothing had happened. For him, the baby was the result of our love. I didn't know what to do."

"What did Peter say about it?"

She shrugged. Peter had said nothing. He had let it happen. He should have intervened; he should have protected her.

"You kept the baby. You could have..."

"What? Abortion? Give him up for adoption? Give him to Mats?"

Those first days, Irene could barely look at her son. And she had been so relieved when the baby had disappeared the day Mats had taken him to persuade Clara Persson, his first official victim, to get in his car.

Irene bowed her head.

"Alexander. I didn't know how to love him. He was the result of violence, abuse. Whenever I looked at him, I saw the face of the man who had violated me. Loving Alex was like loving the man who had done this to me; it was like agreeing with what he had done. I couldn't cope with that. So, I defined some ground rules to behave around him, to look like a loving mother, but it was hard. I couldn't let myself care and love him. At first, when Alex was young, it was okay, but as he got older, I got scared he would turn out like his father. A rapist, a manipulator who hated women. I couldn't let anyone go through the same ordeal."

"And then the abuse began," Isa said.

"What abuse?"

"I can't imagine what you've been through, but that doesn't justify the mental and physical abuse... torture..."

"Torture? What are you talking about? I just wanted him to behave."

"Has Alex ever given you reason to worry?"

"Do you think Mats' parents ever realized they were raising a rapist?"

"I ask you again: did you have any reason to be concerned?"

"Alex was weird! Not normal!"

"You made him weird," Isa said.

Irene clenched her fists. "I've done nothing wrong."

"Really? Tell me about the suicide attempts! Are you absolutely sure you have done no harm to your son?"

What did Isa Lindström know? She had poured her heart out over the trauma that had defined a large part of her life, and now this woman questioned the loyalty to her son.

"The suicide attempts. I wanted to give him at least a way out. He chose to..."

"And you did nothing to help him? You left the bottle of pills on the table. You saw how he slowly bled to death on that bathroom floor, and you did nothing."

"That's what he wanted," Irene said and jumped up.

"No. It was a cry for help. He didn't want to die. Luckily, Peter saved him twice. But as a mother, you should never accept the death of your son. How could you?"

"How could I?"

Yes, she felt guilty. The chance to make amends had been taken from her, but even if Alex had been alive, it would have remained a difficult, complicated relationship that nobody but the two of them would ever understand.

"Did you kill Alex?" Isa asked.

"No, I didn't kill Alex. Mats did. This is my final answer and now I want you to leave."

CHAPTER

8

MAGNUS STOOD in the middle of the room. The light was so bright he could barely see where he was. It looked like a theatre. Red curtains, a wooden floor beneath his feet, the orchestra, the balconies. He was the performer who took the stage and entertained the audience with a story that wasn't real. Others were hiding in the shadows, watching him. He felt their presence. But whichever direction he moved, the light was fixed on him, making it impossible to see beyond the ray of light.

"Who is there?"

He could hear the slow, steady breathing. It came from everywhere.

"Show yourself!"

Slowly a figure emerged from the darkness and approached him, while he was still struggling to adjust his eyes to the light.

Toby? It couldn't be. His son was in a hospital bed, unable to move or speak.

"Toby, how..."

Toby just stared at him, with those dead eyes following his every move. This wasn't his son. This was dark and evil.

Another ghostly apparition stepped into the light. Alexander Nordin.

What was this? Judgement?

"Magnus." The soft voice sounded familiar.

"Isa? Where are you? Where am I?"

He couldn't distinguish her from the darkness. "Isa?"

He looked at Toby. What wouldn't he have given to talk to his son again? This was a delusion, an image fabricated by his desperate mind.

Then he turned to Alex standing next to Toby. "This is your doing. Is this another attempt to make me confess?"

Still no response. The stress spread through his body and mind.

Calm, be calm!

This wasn't real. His mind was telling him something. Maybe he should listen.

Suddenly Toby raised his arm and pointed to something behind him. And Alex did the same.

"What? No!"

Behind him, on the floor, lay the bloody corpse of a girl. How could he have missed it? She wasn't there before. He came closer.

"Oh, my God, Anna!"

He leaned forward to touch her face. Part of it was gone, blown off by a gunshot. So much blood! It was everywhere.

"Anna, Anna!"

And then he woke up. His heart was racing. His T-shirt was soaked with sweat, and he was shaking. This was new. He remembered every detail of the dream. Anna. Why was Anna there? And Toby? What did it mean?

* * *

The young woman, who had let them in after they had introduced themselves as the police officers investigating the lake murder, looked at them with confidence and maturity, as if she owned the place.

"Lise Forsberg," she said, and held out her hand.

She signaled them to come in and take a seat on the brown leather sofa in the living room. The room was gigantic. At least twice the size of her own living quarters, Isa thought. The entire room exuded a sense of finesse and elegance. The floor-to-ceiling windows and the magnificent stone fireplace in the center of the room gave it a rustic feel, while the architecture forced the residents to fully immerse themselves in the landscape. The rough concrete of the walls gave it a rocky appearance as if they were sitting outside.

"Is your father here?" Timo asked.

"Yes, I'll get him," Lise said.

She got up and walked through the sliding door to the patio. Through the open door, Isa saw the father standing at the edge of the terrace, with his back to them. Lise exchanged a few words with him and then placed her hand on his shoulder. Mr. Forsberg looked exhausted. He gave her a faint smile and followed his daughter as Lise walked in with steady step. He, on the other hand, almost sauntered across the wooden floor from the patio to the sitting room, occasionally glancing into the distance.

"Mr. Forsberg, we are investigating the murder of a young woman who was found in the lake nearby," Timo said as the man took a seat next to his daughter.

"Marie," Lise said.

"You know her?"

"Well, yes, we both studied economics, and I know her from primary school. We were in the same class for years."

"Why didn't you come forward?" Isa said.

"Why should I? There is nothing I can tell you. The last time I saw her was more than three months ago, at a party here. And then I heard she went missing. Terrible. I need to talk to her parents."

"You met at school?"

"Yes, but we lost touch years ago until Teresa told me she was studying in Uppsala, and we started to hang out again."

"She came here often?"

"Rarely. But she liked the parties."

"Which parties?"

"My brother Henrik likes to throw parties. He's a bit of a..."

"Wild boy," Gerard said with a deep sigh. "I gave up on him years ago. Drugs, alcohol, women. Whenever I say yes, he says no. So, we came to an agreement. If he resumed his studies in economics, I would continue to give him an allowance. The only thing I requested was that he kept his parties... private. I'm a public figure and whatever he does affects my reputation."

"And Marie frequented these parties?"

"Yes, she liked the company of the rich and reputed."

"Ambitious girl?" Isa said.

"Yes, she was," Lise replied, "and Henrik didn't mind."

"Why do you say that?"

"Well, I think they were lovers."

Gerard turned to her. "Why... how?"

"Daddy, you are so oblivious of everything. It was clear Henrik had a thing for her. I've seen them many times, whispering in secret, jumping up whenever I caught them. There was clearly something going on between them."

"Marie was pregnant when she died," Isa said and looked at the older man, who shook his head in confusion.

"Good God, you think it's Henrik's?" Lise said.

"We don't know, Ms. Forsberg. She had a boyfriend."

"Jussi? Yes, I know him. It's a good-for-nothing. I was glad she dumped him."

"So, you knew about that?"

"Yes, I advised her to get rid of him. He mistreated her. And if she wanted to climb up in society, she had to make choices. He would never be the man to advance her career."

Lise Forsberg gave her a 'Teresa Ljungman'-vibe. Until then, she had been the girl next door, but there was a certain bias in the way she spoke of Jussi Vinter. She felt privileged and better than him.

"And she said nothing about the pregnancy?"

"No. Maybe you should ask Henrik?"

"It's quite a coincidence Marie was found close to your home," Isa said.

"What do you mean?" Gerard said.

"Have you seen anything suspicious the past few weeks?"

"No, I can't say I have," Lise said and then looked at her father, who confirmed by shaking his head.

"And Henrik?"

"Henrik has been in and out the past few weeks. I don't know where he is right now, but you can probably reach him on his mobile."

"And is there a Mrs. Forsberg?" Timo asked and turned to Gerard.

Lise took her father's hand.

"Linda left me years ago," Gerard said.

"I'm sorry to hear that."

"My parents had an open relationship," Lise said.

"Linda had," Gerard interrupted, "it was never my thing, but I tolerated it because I loved her."

"What happened?"

"She had many lovers, but she always came back to me," Gerard said with tears in his eyes, "until two years ago."

"Where is your wife now?"

"Since she left, I haven't seen or spoken to her. The last message she sent me dates back to the day she left us. God knows I've left her plenty of messages over the past two years, but she refuses to talk to me."

"But I talk to her," Lise intervened, "well, she sends me messages on my birthday, Christmas... but like my dad, I haven't seen her in two years."

"You don't seem to be that heartbroken about it, Ms. Forsberg."

"I'm at peace with it. She has always been like that. She will come back, eventually. After a while she gets bored anyway."

"And do you know the man she ran off with?"

"No," Gerard answered. "A mystery man. There were rumors it was Harald Müller, but he claims not to know where she is. Lise and Henrik think she's in Stockholm. I've often thought about looking for her, hiring a detective, and tracking her down, but my children convinced me she'll come back to us, even if it has been two years. But she's never stayed away for so long."

"It's strange how the media hasn't picked up this story," Timo said.

"I spend a lot of money and time to keep my private life out of the press."

"With success, obviously."

Gerard sighed. "But this... people will find out eventually. They already know."

Lise took her father's hand again. A touching scene, but somehow it felt like something wasn't quite right. Only Isa couldn't quite pinpoint what. Was it Gerard or Lise?

After the interview, Mr. Forsberg offered to accompany them to the exit.

111

"You're a hunter, Mr. Forsberg?" Timo pointed to the stuffed deer head that adorned the wall at the entrance.

"No, my father was, but I keep it there to remind me of everything I shouldn't be."

"I see," Timo said.

"My father was a terrible man. He was cruel to animals and people."

"We should have put his head there, dad," Lise grinned, but the remark, intended as a joke, was not appreciated by the rest of the party.

"Do you own a weapon, Mr. Forsberg?"

"Yes, a handgun. A few years ago, I received some threatening letters. My entourage advised getting protection. I keep it in my office, in the vault. I've taken shooting lessons, but I've never used it against anything or anyone."

And then Gerard sank back into the same state of apathy and fatigue as at the beginning of the interview.

* * *

The walk to the car was, as always, an occasion for reflection, and Isa found herself alone again with Timo. She had to admit the case intrigued her. Isa had been so occupied with the Sandviken case that she and Timo had hardly spoken about Marie Lång. Her boss wasn't always so thrilled with her obsession, but she had made progress. Annette Norman was an exciting new lead, but Timo was worried now the Uppsala investigation team had arrived. Heimersson had requested an urgent meeting, and the commissioner wanted an update on his progress. Above all, he didn't want to draw attention to the fact that he had reinstated the most compromised detective in the entire department and that, on top of that, he had put her on a high-profile case. Everything had to be handled with care and a certain discretion. And keeping his best investigator under control was a gargantuan task that took up too much of his time. They needed to have another conversation about her unofficial activities, but not now.

"That was interesting," Isa said. "Why did you want to check that house?"

"Gerard Forsberg has been watching us ever since we found Marie's body. He's worried about something. We just need to find out what."

"His son?" Isa said and looked at him. She had underestimated him. He had a trained eye for detail and a decent knowledge of human nature.

"Maybe. But it's clear we need to do background checks. On all of them. And I wonder what really happened to his wife."

"Yes, they didn't seem to care."

"Mothers can sometimes be too much. Linda Forsberg clearly had a particular lifestyle her husband and children didn't like. See what you can find out about her! And we need to talk to the son."

"Do you still believe in this hunting thing?" Isa asked.

"Either this angle is real, or it has been staged to make us believe this isn't personal, this isn't about Marie. I need..."

"What?"

He shook his head and then turned to her. "And good to know I have your full attention on this matter, inspector Lindström."

Full? Maybe that was a stretch too far, but her interest was sparked.

***

"When are you coming back?" The woman's voice on the other end of the line sounded serious and not what he had expected.

Kristina Rapp. Timo hadn't talked to her since his move to Gävle. He still remembered the dinner at their favorite restaurant in Stockholm, where he had laid out his plans. She had reacted with surprise and disbelief. Why? She had said that word about ten times and had received no proper answer. He had told her he needed something new. He needed to get away from Stockholm, where everything had become familiar and painful at the same time.

"I don't know when I'll be back," Timo said.

She sighed. "Timo, you can't seriously consider staying there. It's a rathole. You will never make a career there. They'll bury you."

"We'll see."

"Jesus, what the hell are you doing there?"

He interrupted her, knowing her lamentation could take a while. "I need your advice on a case."

"I'm all ears," she finally said.

He told her about Marie Lång. All under the pretense, he hadn't heard her concerns. He was a coward. There was so much more to her polite questions and comments. She had confessed her love for him years ago. He had taken her hand and had looked into her eyes, telling her he wasn't ready for a relationship. She had nodded, baffled more by the fact she'd told him her most embarrassing secret than by his answer. There had been no one. Thirty-five years. No husband, no children. She had been waiting for a man who could never reciprocate her love. He respected her as a colleague and friend, but it could never be more than that. At that time, he didn't really know what he wanted.

"I agree he has done this before. It was audacious to put her in the lake, knowing it's a public area with many people hiking there, with the Forsberg's villa so close. He wanted her to be found. He's confident. He thinks nothing or no one can stop him. And the twig... I need to check a few things, but it was put there deliberately, and it sends a message."

"One of my team members said it's a German hunting tradition."

"Oh, so you know. Yes, it is. Very clever team you have there."

"But is it a single case or..."

"Are there more victims?"

"Yes, exactly," he said.

"And are there more victims?"

He sighed and said, "No."

"Then it's speculation, but if this is a pattern then he has done this before and he will kill again. He has left traces for sure."

"Though, it feels personal and impersonal at the same time," Timo said. He opened the files, took the autopsy photos, and put them side by side.

"The scratches on her arms and face. Like she was running, trying to get away... hunted like game."

"Timo, give me some time. Send me the file and I'll have a look at it. And you owe me dinner."

He let out a sigh of relief. Kristina Rapp and he went a long way. They had started working for the Stockholm police around the same time. He as a rookie cop, she as criminologist. She had studied in the US and learned about offender profiling. And much later, they had teamed up on a first big case involving a serial rapist.

"Okay, no problem."

"A decent dinner in a nice restaurant! Not one of your trials."

"What's wrong with them?" he said indignantly.

"I don't have enough time to explain," she said, and he heard her laugh.

She told him she would call back in a few days, and he said goodbye.

* * *

"Isa?"

When Isa failed to respond, Ingrid put the file under her nose.

"What's this?"

"The blood found on the handkerchief," Ingrid said, almost out of breath.

"What about it? It's Marie's."

"Yes, Marie's DNA was found on the handkerchief, but the blood belongs to someone else."

"Who?"

"Oliver Pilkvist, the boy who disappeared two months ago."

Isa jumped up and looked at her. "What?"

"I'm almost a hundred percent sure. I also don't understand how these two cases are connected."

"If this is true, this gives the case a whole new dimension."

CHAPTER

9

"**THE BLOOD IS DEFINITELY OLIVER'S,**" Ingrid said, handed Timo the document of the blood analysis and threw herself in the chair on the other side of the desk. This was nice. Just the two of them. She watched him flip through the document, stopping now and then to read the text. She still didn't understand where the strange interest came from, but he intrigued her. There was something mysterious about him.

With an audacity so unlike her, she let her eyes go over the black T-shirt he was wearing. She hadn't seen him wear anything else since he had arrived in Gävle. It was nothing special, but it contoured his athletic upper body so perfectly.

Jesus, Ingrid, get a grip! You are a married woman!

Where did this come from? Was she that frustrated? There was nothing wrong with her marriage. She was happy, even if life revolved around the boys these days, her two young sons. No time for herself, not enough quality time with her husband, but that was a normal part of life and marriage. Her strange interest in Timo Paikkala would disappear, eventually. All she could do was leverage the boost in energy and creativity it gave her, and the thoughts were hers and hers alone. She wasn't Isa, who needed to jump on every man who showed interest.

Isa. How she missed her best friend! They hadn't really spoken since the incident. Maybe she needed to call her and talk it through?

"Tell me about Oliver Pilkvist," Timo said.

"Okay. Thirteen-year-old boy, disappeared two months ago on his way home from school."

"Two months ago? The same time Marie disappeared?"

"Yes, and he disappeared near Stromsbrö."

"Where we found Marie. Tell me more. Was there a suspect?"

"To be honest. This case didn't get the attention it deserved. We were so busy with the Sandviken killer. That poor woman!"

"Who?"

"Oliver's mom. A widow. She drops by every day to check if there is any news about her son. She didn't stop looking for him."

She turned her head to the window. The office was on the ground floor. Police officers were passing by, cars driving away. Everything seemed so normal, so every day. She sighed. It made her nostalgic and sad.

When she faced him again, he was looking at her with a strange expression on his face, almost like he had seen a ghost.

"Anything wrong, inspector Paikkala?"

She looked straight at him. He shook his head.

"Are you sure? You don't look well."

"Uh... just a migraine," he said.

"So, you are a migraine sufferer? If you need..."

"I don't want to talk about migraine," he blurted.

"Oh... sorry."

Timo closed his eyes as if he wanted a reset, and then took a deep breath. "My apologies, it's just the pain talking."

Ingrid said, "Anyway... a suspect? Yes, Mark Lisberg, soccer coach and teacher."

The conversation turned to normal, but she knew this was more than a physical pain she had seen in his eyes.

"But he was never charged?" Timo turned his attention back to the paper on the table.

"No, circumstantial evidence. His car was seen in the neighborhood at the time Oliver disappeared. CCTV images. His house was turned inside out, and his whereabouts were checked, but nothing."

"Do you think we need to talk to him again?"

"Are you asking me?"

"Yes, I'm asking you." There was no escaping his gaze, which now seemed to have recovered from the momentary lapse.

"I am not an investigator. I bring the evidence. It's up to you and the team to connect the dots."

"So, you don't think your ideas and opinions matter?"

"That's... not what I said," Ingrid said.

"But that's what you think."

In addition to the amazement, an increasing degree of irritation was creeping up on her. A conversation with inspector Paikkala could take your emotions to all the corners of your psyche: sadness, happiness, irritation, anger. As if he was flirting with the boundaries, testing how far he could go.

"You have an analytical mind. I don't want to put people in boxes. Inspectors do the investigative work, forensics gather evidence. This works, but never lifts anyone beyond what they can do. It never pushes anyone to the next level."

She hesitated, but then said: "Yes, we should talk to Lisberg again. I think he knows more than he told us."

"Okay then."

Aimlessly he turned around on the swivel chair. It was a funny sight. This was something her sons would do, not a grown man in his thirties.

"How is Isa doing?" she said calmly.

He tilted his head slightly while he looked her straight in the eye, as if he was processing the question and deciding what to answer.

"What part of Finland is your mother from?"

"Uh... what?"

"Where is your mother from? I don't think that's a difficult question."

"No... but why?"

He kept looking at her, expecting an answer.

She sighed and finally said, "You wouldn't know it anyway: Masku."

"I do know it. My father is from Turku."

Where was this conversation going? Half an hour ago, she had longed to be in the same room with him. Now it felt like an interrogation, and she wanted out of there as soon as possible.

"How did your parents meet?"

"Shouldn't we talk about the case instead of my parents?"

"Did I upset you?"

"No, but..."

She took a deep breath. Maybe she was overanalyzing this. It wasn't the first time she heard colleagues complain about inspector Paikkala's strange way of starting a chitchat. Like the others, she found herself answering the weird questions that seemed to come out of nowhere.

"My mother was working in a hotel near Helsinki, and one day my father showed up. A business trip. He was thirty-five. She was twenty. But he claims he had never seen such a beautiful woman before in his entire life. Love at first sight. They started talking, and that's how their story began. What about your parents?"

"My mother was an actress, not a particularly good one, who desperately wanted to leave Russia, well—the Soviet Union, and my father was the victim. I don't know when and how they met, but she succeeded."

"Wow, that's not..."

"Very romantic? Yeah, I know, but it's the truth."

She didn't know what to say. It was honest and cruel, which was okay, but sometimes people needed to hear the sugarcoating.

"But it must have been hard," she said.

"Uh... what? Why?"

"To leave your country and family behind to be with the man you love."

His mouth fell open and his eyes stared in the distance as if to let the idea sink in. It took a few seconds for him to react. "I guess... anyway, would you like to have a coffee with me?"

Talking about her parents was one thing. A bit of flirting was fine too, but openly tapping into the tension that was floating around the room was another.

"I'm not sure that's a good idea," Ingrid said.

He smiled. There it was, that radiant smile, matching the twinkles in those beautiful blue eyes.

"It's just coffee, Olsson. Not a marriage proposal."

"It's just," she said, "why me?"

There was another flirty grin on his face as he almost seductively swung his body against the back of the chair. "I make you nervous."

"A bit."

"I need your advice on something," he said.

"What about?"

"I'll tell you when we have a coffee."

"Why me?"

He sighed. "I'm new here, and I don't have any friends, and you are kind. You were the first one, and maybe still the only one who doesn't see me as the enemy. It's really nothing urgent. I understand if you don't... just forget about it!"

He walked to the door. She couldn't stop watching him move. So elegant, yet with such a determination and strength. And then she heard herself say, "When?"

He turned around and smiled.

*   *   *

Two days later, they got some quality time in a small café near the police station. The café had been modernized and expanded a few years ago when it became apparent it could no longer handle the influx of police officers who came mainly in the afternoon for a quick bite to eat and a cup of warm coffee. The establishment was modern but hadn't lost its old-world charm. The wobbly wooden chairs and tables had been replaced by more robust metal versions, which strangely seemed to blend in with the wood paneling and Baroque-style decorations on the doors and ceiling. Upon entering you were welcomed by the smell of freshly ground coffee beans. While the coffee-making process may have been a little too automated by Italian standards, the owner regularly boasted that he could serve his customers an authentic cappuccino or espresso like no other in Gävle.

"So, tell me, why did you become a doctor?" Timo said, lifting the cup of warm coffee to his mouth.

Ingrid couldn't take her eyes off the second cup he had ordered almost immediately when they had entered the café. In fact, he didn't have to say anything. The waitress knew what her most valued customer wanted. Two large black coffees, sometimes a third one depending on the time of day.

"Do you always drink that much coffee?"

He took a long sip and then said, "Yep, I live on coffee."

"Since when?"

"Since always. So, why doctor?"

"I think I've always liked being one."

"Behind every choice is a reason," he said, "it can be a good reason or a bad one, but there is a reason. What's yours?"

There he was again with his psychological stuff. The conversation was going to be tiring. But there she was, sitting at the small table, facing the man who was a mystery to her. He probably knew more about them than they knew about him. Surprising. It was still him and them. No one really considered him as the captain. He was an intruder, someone who would test them and then decide who to kick out.

"Okay, if you must know," she said in a neutral voice, trying to hide her irritation.

"My grandmother had this enormous bookcase, at least it seemed huge when I was six and there was that one book on the bottom shelf that always intrigued me. It was old and damaged. Brown cover, some parchment-like pages sticking out, and when I pressed my nose against it, it smelled important. I asked my grandmother to take it out and look at it, but she said I was too young, and I needed to wait to get older to understand what was in it. And then she died when I was eight. Marvelous woman. I loved her very much."

She hadn't thought of her grandmother for a long time. It felt good. Sweet memories. As much as she wanted to deny it, Timo Paikkala got people to talk about their most personal things without realizing it.

She said, "I still remember walking around the empty house after her death. My father had packed all the books in cardboard boxes and had sealed them, except one. The lid was open and there it was—the book. I picked it up and hid it under my jacket, to open it at home."

All the time, he was slowly sipping his coffee, saying nothing, but with a face full of emotion, as if he had told the story himself. She could have sworn his eyes filled up with tears when she mentioned the death of her grandmother.

"An amazing world opened up to me. The book was one of the early editions of the Medical Handbook for Households. Looking back now, it was so outdated, but the drawings, the descriptions... it felt important, and I wanted to be part of something important."

The book. It was standing in her bookcase now, on the bottom shelf like it had been in her grandmother's living room. Maybe one day, her children or grandchildren would notice it and just like her, be marveled by the world of medicine.

"That was my story. What about you? Why did you join the police force?"

He smiled. "Okay, fair enough, but my story isn't as beautiful as yours. Just promise me you won't laugh!"

"I won't," she said, "your secret is safe with me."

"Miami Vice."

"The flashy police series from the eighties?"

"Yep."

"Tell me more," she said, "I am intrigued."

"My father was a huge fan. I think he must have seen all the reruns. We loved the show so much, my father, my older brother and I. It was our family evening on Sunday. When my father switched on the TV, everything went quiet and we were all looking at the screen, mesmerized almost. I was still young, and I didn't understand most of the storylines, but it was so great. This was glamour, coolness in every way! My God, there was a Ferrari, beautiful women, bad guys—what more did a young boy need?"

"So who did you want to be?" she asked. "You must have a favorite character?"

"I'll disappoint you," he said, "but Sonny Crockett!"

"Don Johnson?"

"In my family, I am the only one with dark hair. I just wanted to be the blond God that had the fast cars, got Sheena Easton, and caught the bad guys."

"Sheena Easton? That's your type?"

He froze. What had she said to upset him? He looked at the coffee mug and took another gulp.

"Tell me about your husband," he said.

"Anton? There isn't much to say. He's a lawyer. We met at university, moved back to Gävle after our marriage, and then our two children were born."

Why was he so interested in her husband?

"Criminal lawyer?"

"No, corporate. He specializes in acquisitions and mergers. He works for Global Law in Uppsala... well, actually in Gävle, they have a small office here."

"How long have you been married?"

"Thirteen years."

"And you have two boys?"

"Yes, eight and eleven, a handful," she laughed.

"Eight," he said, and his expression turned gloomy.

"Was he your first boyfriend?"

She frowned.

"Look," Ingrid said, "I don't know where you're going with this... what about yourself? Girlfriend, wife, boyfriend even?"

"Okay. I have no girlfriend or wife. I only had one long-term relationship in my entire life. One and only one, and that one ended rather dramatically."

She looked at him, first puzzled, then with a certain pity and sympathy.

"I'm sorry," she stammered, "what happened?"

"She died eight years ago," Timo said.

"What happened?" she repeated and for a moment she wanted to take his hand, resting on the table, but then changed her mind.

"It took me eight years, thirty or more therapy sessions just to be able to say this to you," he started with a voice that was about to break, "and it will probably take even longer to tell you what happened. Maybe one day, but not now. It's not important, anyway."

Who was she, the woman who had broken his heart? For a moment, she thought of tracking down the terrible history herself. But everybody needed privacy and their own way to deal with the pain of loss. He wasn't ready to share, and she should leave it at that.

"You wanted my advice," she said softly, breaking the silence.

He tried to regain the energy the story had drained. It had been a peculiar conversation, swinging between pleasantries and drama.

"Two things, Olsson," he said and pushed the two cups aside so he could place both hands on the table.

"I'm thinking of buying a house here," he said, "any suggestions of areas where the quality-price ratio is still decent?"

"It depends on what you want. Where do you live now?"

"Hotel."

"What? I thought you were at least renting an apartment or something. A hotel, that must be expensive?"

"Let's say money is not a problem."

That explained the cars. She had seen him show up in at least two different ones. And they didn't look cheap. How could he afford them?

"My parents are pretty well off. My father was a diplomat. When my brother and I were young, we travelled the world. I got to meet lots of important, fascinating people. Hey, I once saw Don Johnson at a party at the embassy in the US... from afar. It was fun."

"But in reality, you didn't like it."

"You're right. It was like you belonged everywhere and nowhere. I had no real home. When we came back to Sweden, I was so happy. I was thirteen, my brother sixteen. But it was tough those first months. My native language is Finnish. I knew a bit of Swedish... since we lived in Stockholm before, until I was four, but I basically had to learn it all over again."

"I didn't notice it," she said.

He smiled. "I can hide it very well."

Then he turned around and signaled the waitress to get the bill.

"I'm actually a bit of a failure and a hypocrite," he said.

"Why do you say that?"

"I detested my father's job and the money that came with it, but here I am using the substantial inheritance he left me when he died, too soon."

"So, why do you use it then?"

"To taunt my mother and my brother. We just don't get along."

"How did your father die?"

"A car accident. He was only fifty. My parents were coming back from a gala dinner. My mother survived. She now lives with her sister in St. Petersburg. My brother is in politics. I hardly see him, but that's okay. And I am just a mere police inspector. I could have done so much more with my life. At least that's what my mother says."

"But you're good at it." she said.

"How do you know?"

His stare was so intense, that she would have looked away if the waitress hadn't brought the bill.

"It's what everyone says," she answered after he threw a 100 SEK note on the table.

"I haven't done anything yet. I still need to earn the respect of the team. So, to come back to my question. Where do you think I could find some interesting property?"

"There are a few good real estate agents in Gävle. I can give you their names. Maybe it's best to talk to them. What's the second thing you wanted to ask?"

"I need to go back to Stockholm, to a funeral."

"I'm sorry to hear that. Is it family?"

"No, the mother of a friend," he said. "But I'll be gone for a few days. Isa will be in charge. Can you have a look at the disappearance of Linda Forsberg and Oliver Pilkvist? Are there any incidents that show resemblance to those cases and Marie's death? Work with Lars."

"I'll do my best, but I'm not sure."

"It's just going too slow," Timo said with a voice that gave away a certain level of irritation. "And Ingrid…"

"Yes?"

"Talk to Isa," he said in a calm voice. "Make it right. You are friends."

* * *

In the five-minute conversation, the noise level at the other end of the line had gone from normal to overly agitated.

"What are you getting at, Paikkala? This is not what we agreed."

"I don't know what you mean," Timo said in his most innocent voice.

"Don't be cheeky with me! You were supposed to fire her, not reinstate her."

He had just put the travel bag in the trunk of the convertible when Timo had received an urgent call from the commissioner. A moment, he had hesitated and let his finger hang over the accept button, but he had finally given in.

"Are you questioning my actions?"

"I am, Paikkala. I hear you'll be spending some days in Stockholm. We need to talk."

"But…"

"Just be there!"

What had he expected? Sooner or later, the news would reach Stockholm and he needed a good explanation. If he had to be honest, he still didn't have one. There was something about the place and the people that had made him instantly fall in love with Gävle. A sense of belonging. Something he had been looking for all his life. And maybe he had come here with a different motive, but in the few weeks he had been there, he had never felt so alive. The heavy burden of his past was still there, but it felt like he could handle it so much better.

Buried deep in his wallet, behind the credit and useless membership cards that nearly made the leather explode, there was a picture, he dreaded to look at. He still did, but for the first time it felt like he was close to taking the next step and letting go.

He opened the car door, got in and drove off direction Stockholm, back to his old life.

CHAPTER

10

HENRIK FORSBERG. Lise's twin brother and enfant terrible of the millionaire's family. He had a reputation Isa had learned after talking to his family and acquaintances. When the young twenty-something wasn't partying with his friends, smoking hash, having sex with the first girl who showed an interest in him, or hanging out at the racetrack squandering his dad's money, you could find him at the shooting range, practicing his killer skills. Unlike his father, Henrik was an avid hunter, especially moose. His ultimate dream was to go trophy hunting in Africa. A few years ago, barely eighteen, his uncle had invited him to South Africa, but his father had blocked the trip. Henrik had sulked for weeks, had refused to talk to Gerard and on a moonless night a few days after receiving another lecture from his dad about the immorality of killing animals, he had, with fake ID in his hand, gambled 250 000 SEK in a Stockholm casino and had lost everything.

When Isa met him at the shooting club, he was cleaning his rifle after a frustrating round of practice and had only looked up when the inspector told him she wanted to talk about Marie Lång.

"Marie? The girl is dead. That's what I know. And?"

"Your father and sister told us you are the man to talk to about Marie."

"Why? I have nothing to do with her. Sweet, little Marie. So normal, nothing special. So not my type."

"But she seemed to come to your parties quite often."

"She might have ended up on a list. God knows, I don't keep track. I know hundreds of people."

"She was pregnant," Isa tried.

"Oh, really? And you think I was the father? Like I said: not my type. But in some way, she was fuckable though. She had this kind of innocent, naïve look. At most, I would have slept with her once."

"Then you wouldn't mind giving us your DNA. To exclude you."

"I would mind," he said with a straight face, "if you want my DNA, talk to my lawyer."

"Fair enough, Mr. Forsberg. That's your right, but I always get my way. And it doesn't do your case any good."

"Is that a threat?"

Isa smiled, but kept quiet. By now, Henrik had reassembled the rifle and should put it back in the case, but he ostentatiously pointed it at Isa, under the guise of checking the scope. It was bluff. Isa wasn't sure what it would buy him, and he wasn't the first suspect to play that game.

"Russian roulette," Henrik laughed as he kept the focus on the woman standing only a few meters away from him. The bullet, traveling at more than 2000km/h, would blow her head off in less than a second.

"Is that a threat?" Isa said calmly. Not a sign that a reckless, spoiled brat like Henrik Forsberg could penetrate the steel walls of inspector Lindström. But deep down, her anxiety was growing.

He put the rifle down. "Relax, no bullets."

"So, to go back to Marie. They told me you had a fight with her, just before she went missing. I would say you knew her better than you claim."

"Who says?"

"Your friends, your sister."

"Most of the time I was so wasted, I can hardly remember what I did or said. Although..."

He looked up and stared at the window behind Isa, as if he suddenly remembered something.

"What, Mr. Forsberg?"

"Uh, nothing... I thought... Nothing."

"You don't like your sister and father. Why is that?"

"I'm okay with Lise, as long as she doesn't get in my way. But she always follows me around. Like a puppy. I went to study economics; she wanted to study economics. My friends are her friends now. Ridiculous! That girl needs to get her own life!"

"And your father?"

"I resent him not doing anything to stop my mom from leaving, that he allowed her to carry on with all those men. He's weak and stupid. He should have been a real man and made it clear to her he wouldn't put up with that."

The man clearly had a mommy issue, although Isa wouldn't think he was the type. She recognized the reckless, almost destructive behavior. She had been there herself.

"Were you close to your mother?"

His expression turned gloomy. "Do you know what it does to a teenage boy when he hears his own mother through the walls of his bedroom... well, having sex with men who aren't your father? And the next day to see that pathetic look in your father's eyes when she let them out of the door?"

"I can't say I do."

Henrik stared at the window again, and for a moment, she hesitated. He looked like a lost and lonely little boy.

"So most of your mother's relationships were short-lived?"

"Most. It was all about sex. After a while she got bored with them. But not all of them. Her last one... actually her last relationship was with Harald Müller, a drunk and a nobody. I still don't know why she liked him... maybe his looks, maybe the sex, but they were together for almost a year, just before she left us. Anyway, I thought she ran off with him, but obviously not."

"Your sister is still in touch with your mother. You too?"

"I get messages from her now and then, wishing me happy birthday, asking how I am, but it all seems so fake."

"Why?"

"It's a pro forma answer. I don't know how to explain it. It's like it's not my mother on the other side."

"Have you recently talked to your mom?"

"Not recently. Just before she left."

"It was her? You're sure?"

"It was her, but she sounded agitated, almost scared. She told me she loved me and that everything would be okay. It was strange. I tried to call her again, but she didn't pick up."

"Have you ever wondered something else was going on?" Isa asked.

"Like what?"

"That she was running away from something or that she was afraid for her life?"

"I don't think so," Henrik mused. Then he put on his jacket with another smug grin on his face, raising the hairs on her arms, and he picked up the case with the gun.

"It was nice chatting with you, inspector, but now I have to go. I need to spend some of my father's money on useless things."

And he almost looked proud of it.

"No worries... I'm sure we'll meet again," Isa said, looked at the man and left. In any case, she was more than determined to get that court order and get the man's DNA.

On her way back to the car, she became irritated again. Not about the twenty messages Magnus had left her, but about the messages that weren't there. Timo had sent her a cryptic text in the morning that he wouldn't join her for the interview, but that she could just go ahead without him. After that, everything had gone silent. No reply to her messages. She knew he had seen her Whatsapp texts, but no reply. What was the man up to?

* * *

Kristina threw her arms around him, showing no trace of the difficult conversation they'd had over the phone a few days earlier.

"You look good," she said and sat down.

Timo had kept his promise and had invited her to an Indian restaurant in central Stockholm.

He loved the smell of herbs, the flavor of the exotic. It took him back to his childhood. His father often traveled to Asia. And he had been lucky enough to accompany his dad on many of these trips. It had molded his character. It had sparked his interest in other cultures and societies.

"Do you have something for me?" Timo said.

"Hold on. Not that fast! Let me scan the menu for the most expensive dish."

He laughed and said, "I'm just a mere police inspector, so take it easy."

"A police inspector with a huge inheritance! I think you'll survive."

They checked the menu in silence for a while and then ordered.

"He might be a hunter," she said after the waiter had left them alone again.

"So you think this might be more than an isolated incident?"

"Let me finish. There is indeed a tradition in German huntsmanship where the hunter puts a twig in the dead deer's mouth as a sign of respect. But so far you have only one real case. However..."

"However?"

"I found two similar cases from a few years ago. One case from three years ago, in Valbo."

"Why do you think these cases are related?"

"Because of this," she said, turned to the bag she had carelessly tossed on the floor when she had entered and pulled out a file.

"You took the file with you?"

"No worries. They don't know it's gone, and I'll bring it back tomorrow."

The photo showed the head of a young woman, taken at the autopsy, pale, eyes closed and with the twig sticking out of her mouth.

"Who's this?"

"Ebba Horn. She was found death in the woods near Valbo together with her boyfriend. The case was classified as a murder and suicide. Presumably her boyfriend shot her and then killed himself. The rifle was found next to him, with only his fingerprints on the trigger. There was a history of violence."

"How did the police explain the twig?"

"They didn't," Kristina said, "the case was clear to them, and they didn't investigate it."

"And the second one?"

"Uppsala, five years ago."

The couple sitting next to them gave them a terrified glance as she threw another file on the table and displayed the horrific pictures of the dead father and son. Not the best conversation to have in a crowded restaurant.

"Arnar and Knut Olander, father and son. They went missing five years ago on a hiking trip near Uppsala. Their bodies were found in the river a month later."

"Another twig?"

"Yes, but only the father."

Timo picked up the boy's photograph and stared at it. The boy was barely ten years old.

"He takes pairs," Kristina said, "a young couple, a father and a son."

He shook his head and then said, "Marie Lång and Oliver Pilkvist? It's not the same. These people were connected. Marie and Oliver were not."

"Maybe he had to change plans unexpectedly. They were the unfortunate victims at that moment."

"This is cruel. Who does such a thing?"

"That's a good question, and I have no answer for you. I've learned a lot over the years about what drives a killer. Profiling only gives a brief glimpse into the mind of the vilest human beings running around on this planet. It's hard to predict. But what I can say is there are always hints... even since childhood. Torturing of animals, arson, and bedwetting."

He sighed. "Regardless, if he's a serial killer, he must have prepared it very well. He had everything under control."

"Yes, he did. We can assume Marie didn't escape. Not really. This was just a game. The hunter needs a challenge, but a controlled one. In the 1970s and early 1980s, Richard Hansen killed at least seventeen women, and probably even more, in the desolate areas of Alaska. He tortured them, raped them and then released them in a deserted area to hunt and kill them."

"But Marie wasn't tortured or raped."

"It doesn't have to be sexual. It usually is, but anger can be a motive, just like the thrill of taking a human life. They're addicted to the adrenaline rush the killing gives them. For these thrill-killers, the victims are usually strangers, but he has to follow them for a while to get to know their habits before abducting them."

"So, he stalked her."

"Maybe, unless it was an inspiration of the moment. What did her friend tell you?"

"Nothing much. Marie is a mystery to me. The more information I get, the more confused I am. She made a few decisions in her life that seem out of place."

"How?"

"She ran away from home when she was fifteen. Why does an introverted, unremarkable girl do such a thing? It seems to me her group of friends had their own reasons for leaving. Teresa rebelled against her father, Jussi wanted to escape an abusive dad, Quinten had problems getting accepted by his family. We still need to talk to Espen Frisk, but according to his file, he was the victim of sexual abuse by a teacher. What was Marie's reason? The family seems normal."

"You're right. There is always a trigger. I haven't spoken to the parents. What did they say?"

"Bad friends. They blame Jussi Vinter."

"It's always good to have a culprit, and it prevents them from having to look at the possibility that it could have something to do with them as a family."

"Marie was bullied early in her high school career."

"It's difficult to say why? Lack of self-esteem, but she could also have been a threat to the popularity of her bullies. Girls often target other girls when they may impact their own social status. Was she a popular girl at school?"

"No, she wasn't. Quite the opposite."

"Smart?"

"Not exceptional from what her parents told us."

"So, she was introverted and submissive. You're right. That clashes with the confidence she showed later in life. It's not impossible, but people rarely change that quickly. It's a long process, over many years. However, Quinten Hall's death could have something to do with it."

Kristina observed him as he carefully pushed the pieces of chicken aside and started with the vegetables and rice. She put the fork down, leaned back like she was done eating and then said suddenly, "Are you happy?"

He looked straight into the dark eyes that stared at him with a certain compassion. This change of topic was unexpected, but he knew where the conversation was heading, and he wasn't ready to show her the inner sanctum of his soul.

"As happy as I can be," he said.

"What does that mean?"

"That's all you'll going to get," he continued and took a bite.

"I heard about... I'm sorry."

"Thank you. The funeral is tomorrow."

They ate in silence, followed by a conversation where she did most of the talking, trying to ignore the drama that was lingering in the background. She told him stories about his Stockholm colleagues. How they already missed his witty, weird remarks and his drive to solve a case. How suddenly there had been a new way of working after the Sandviken debacle, where everyone had started to tiptoe around ticklish matters. New rules had been implemented, burying everyone under a pile of useless paperwork. All because of the mistakes of one police department: Gävle. And how, in the midst of it all, everyone felt he had abandoned them.

The last sentence felt like an attack, a finger pointing.

"It's not like that," he said.

"Then what is it? You could have left eight years ago. Everyone would have understood. But why now?"

"Maybe I need something else."

"Is it because of me? Because of what I said?"

"Kris, no, of course not! You are one of my best friends."

She lowered her eyes, opened her mouth as if to say something and then closed it again.

He sighed. "But we haven't really talked about the other issue you've managed to dodge so carefully. It must be hard for you. You don't look happy."

"Not because of that," she said.

He put the fork down and took her hand. She grabbed it so tight that he could feel the tension build in her body, when she said, "I'm thirty-five, the same age as when my mother became ill. I'm just scared."

"Why haven't you done the test yet?"

She sighed. "Would it matter?"

"It matters a lot. Knowing what will or won't come."

"Would you like to know?"

He didn't have to think about it. "Yes. I would like to know. Because I think I would make different choices. If I knew my life would spiral down in a concatenation of degeneration, depression, and I would probably die at a young age, I wouldn't hesitate for a moment. I would take every day to the fullest. I would quit my job, I would travel the world, I wouldn't endlessly doubt my decisions."

"It's easy for you to say. You're not in that situation. I don't want to know. I want to live in the blissful ignorance that I won't have my mother's faulty gene and…"

"But the uncertainty keeps you from living," he said in a stern voice. "Suppose you'll get through this year without symptoms, but what about next year, and the year after?"

"Leave it! It's my choice. And I'm trying to live my life as best I can.

That's why I told you about... my feelings." The last sentence she had said in a soft tone and with a tear glistening in her eye. "Was it because of this? My disease?"

"Kristina... no. I love you as a friend, but I can't be what you want."

* * *

As Timo walked through the streets of Stockholm that evening, he felt the cold cut through his clothes and numb his limbs. The fresh air was rushing through his lungs. The conversation had ended on a too emotional note, and he needed to put the balance back into his head.

In the distance he saw a few youngsters walking unsteadily and talking loudly as if they were drunk. Other than that, there weren't too many people on the streets. The rain had left a slurry of mud and dirt behind, and he felt the soles of his shoes lose grip as he walked toward the hotel at a determined pace.

Hotel rooms. He had seen way too many of them these days. He had sold the house, perhaps a little too rashly, and now it was time to find another home. And the way it looked right now, it wouldn't be in Stockholm anymore.

Though, he liked the small streets, barely lit. He always thought there was an unexpected treasure hidden behind every corner. A marvellous piece of art, a special architecture.

He had walked for ten minutes before noticing the strange echo of footsteps through the empty alleys. It couldn't be the rubber soles of his boots.

He turned around but saw no one.

The sound stopped for a moment and then started again when he continued his way.

He was being followed. He didn't feel safe. His gun was lying in a safe in Gävle. When it came down to it, he only had his fists and legs, and he had never been good at one-on-one combats.

Or maybe this had all been in his head. He was a little tipsy from the wine.

Why would anyone follow him? He had discovered nothing.

And what would they do?

He felt threatened, and the feeling persisted all the way to his hotel. Even in the safe environment of his room, he kept looking outside. Apart from the few men and women passing by in the dim light of the street posts, there was nothing suspicious.

CHAPTER

11

CREEPY SIVERT WAS flashing his eyes at Isa, nearly undressing her with every glance he threw her way. Would he have done the same when Timo was there? Of course not.

Sivert, IT expert, would have stayed in the corner of the room and he would have only spoken when addressed. But with the boss absent, Sivert had taken far more liberties than he was entitled to and crossed the boundaries of professional decency. The whole #metoo movement had passed him by and he had tried several times to talk to Isa about going out with him. Like a stalker he had followed her even to the ladies' room, and it was hard to get rid of the clingy young man.

Timo was supposed to do the briefing, but he had sent Isa another last-minute message to take over. What was it with men these days? Isa had seen the disappearing act with Magnus, and now with Timo. She wasn't pleased.

At least Magnus had shown up this time. He looked good, throwing jokes back and forth with Berger. And was he flirting with the young policewoman in the back? Who was she? Blond, slim, smooth skin, and looking fashionable even in the dark-blue police uniform.

Isa had been in that situation more than two years ago, the center of his attention and flirtatious looks. On the one hand she was glad he seemed better and dared to move on without her, but in the back of her mind she wished she was the only one. She needed the attention of men to feel worthy and complete. Drama, passion, and pain, drove her, though she'd overdosed on it these days.

She turned to the other people in the room. Lars was unusually quiet. Rough night, given the bags under his eyes. She had to admit she didn't know the man that well, except that he was friends with Berger and he often irritated her with his lengthy descriptions of case files. The man just couldn't get to the point.

Ingrid hadn't shown up. Timo was right. She needed to make amends with her best friend.

"We have a special guest today," Isa said. Giving arrogant Sivert a stage for his ego might not have been the best move.

He pushed the glasses higher on his nose, gave his audience a look of superiority and started: "CCTV when Oliver went missing shows the boy took a shortcut through the forest area."

With a certain disdained air, he pressed the key on the laptop, standing on the table next to him. Instantly the blue screen, projected by the beamer, changed and showed the high-angled footage of the traffic camera. The resolution was poor, but the image showed a boy with backpack walking on the sidewalk. He was jumping around like a kid, excited school was over for the day, until he disappeared from view.

"His mother told us it was cold that day. It had snowed, and she had told him to take that road. She saw no harm for it was about noon."

Sivert continued. "The camera images show he entered the area around 1:00 p.m., and then disappeared. After that, no trace of him. The CCTV at the other end of the road never picked up his image."

Isa walked to the screen and stared at it for a few seconds. Strange. She remembered Timo looking at Marie's picture with the same intensity. Almost instinctively, she was mimicking his behavior. She took a step back and then said, "The driver of the school bus, Gabriel Landvik, said he saw Oliver at 1:10 p.m. when he drove by. He couldn't remember seeing any other car drive by. But at 1:25 p.m., Mark Lisberg's car pulled into the alley. It takes about five minutes to bridge the distance. It took Mr. Lisberg more than thirty minutes. He was questioned but denied everything."

"How did he explain the time lapse?" Magnus asked.

"He stopped to take a short walk in the forest. He didn't see the boy."

"That's bullshit," Berger hissed.

"Be careful," Isa said, "don't spread these accusations without evidence. The man already lost his job."

"But...," she started again, "I think he must have seen more than he realized, and so we'll talk to him again."

"I'll join you," Magnus said.

She hesitated. He looked fine. He behaved like Magnus Wieland, but there was a gnawing feeling in the back of her mind, telling her something wasn't right.

"Are you ready?" she said.

He nodded.

"Very well then. Anything else?"

She turned to the man who had been watching her throughout the briefing and who had come a few centimeters closer each time she had opened her mouth, to the point where she had moved to the other side of the table.

"Yes, I have something more," Sivert said and turned to her with a 'I am that brilliant' kind of look. Like a virtuoso he pressed the keys of the computer and suddenly a new set of camera images appeared on the screen. The black-and-white image showed a young man and woman approaching an ATM.

"Who's that?" Berger asked.

"It's Marie Lång and…"

"Henrik Forsberg!"

"Ah, the lady inspector has an eye for detail," Sivert said.

Lady inspector? After the briefing, she should have a serious discussion with him about his attitude toward women.

"When was this taken?"

"The day she disappeared," Sivert said. "He withdraws five thousand SEK and gives it to her, and then they leave."

"Where?"

"Near the Uppsala hospital."

"What were they doing there?" Isa asked.

"I checked. Marie had an appointment that day at the gynecology department."

Isa sighed. "Why wasn't this mentioned in Marie's file anywhere!?"

"I don't know," Lars said, "but it's clear the Uppsala guys neglected the case. Sloppy work!"

"They were too busy getting their hands on the Sandviken killer," Isa said.

"Do we have the footage of the hospital?" Magnus said.

"We see Henrik and Marie enter the hospital and leave together an hour later."

"And then?"

Sivert shrugged.

"Any trace of Marie on the Stromsbrö footage?"

"No. Nothing."

Isa stared at the frozen image on the screen. Henrik Forsberg and Marie Lång.

"Mr. Forsberg clearly didn't tell us everything. It's time for another chat with the black sheep of the family. I'm not sure this is enough to get a warrant to collect his DNA, but we need to try."

"The Forsbergs will fight that by any means possible," Magnus said.

"Possibly," Isa said in a stern voice. "I want Henrik Forsberg in that interrogation room as soon as possible telling us what happened to Marie that day."

"Okay," Berger said, "but maybe we should wait for inspector Paikkala to return?"

She turned to him and frowned. "Why? Do you miss him? And why are you still sitting here? Get on with it!"

Suddenly it was dead-silent in the room. She regretted the outburst almost immediately, but she had enough of the constant doubts about her investigative skills. She could perfectly lead this investigation, with or without Timo Paikkala. She was in charge now, and this was nothing compared to the Sandvikén case. Fair enough, a case she had messed up in her own Isa-like way, but they had caught the serial killer in the end.

She turned to the rest of the people in the room, who were, open-mouthed, staring at her.

"Well, what are you waiting for? I expect to see results!"

* * *

As the people left the room, Magnus walked up to Isa and gave her his most splendid smile, but she wasn't amused.

"Well done."

Really, Magnus, you too?

Was she waiting for a pat on the shoulder? Patronizing.

"So, you are back," she said and gave him a stiff nod.

"Yes. Full-time. And it looks like I have a new partner. Berger Karlsson."

"Well, maybe you should help your partner then," she said.

"We have been instructed to help you."

"By whom? Paikkala? Jesus, does he really think I can't handle it?"

"Are you going to solve this case on your own then?"

Isa bit her lower lip. She felt like a child being corrected.

"Issie, what's wrong?"

"It's inspector Lindström," she said curtly. "Sorry, it's just... I don't know where Timo is and he's just so..."

"So you need help. I'm here for you."

"Magnus..."

"And maybe we can go out this evening and get dinner?"

She sighed. "I have things to do."

Half an hour ago, his flirtation with the young police officer had sparked a tinge of irritation, and now that he was all hers again, she couldn't accept his invitation. She didn't understand. Why was she acting so erratic?

"Like what?"

"I found something. Annette Norman helped her husband kidnap the girls, but I still don't know if Irene Nordin had anything to do with Alex's death. I need to..."

"What? Are you still working on that? Why can't you just let it go? The man is dead. You should concentrate on the people who are still alive and love you."

"I know you care about me. But I told you I need more time."

"No, you need more of this," he said and pressed his lips to hers while he ran his hands over her body.

"Magnus, no, stop," she said and pushed him away. "I can't do this."

He scared her. The Magnus she knew would never act like this. In all those years as her partner and lover, he had treated her with respect, unlike many of her male colleagues, who still believed that a woman had no place in a world where violence was commonplace. It always amazed her how conservative and ego-tripping men could be. Had Magnus finally shown his true nature, disguised under a declaration of love? She felt as if she were an object he could appropriate just because they had a history together and he claimed he still loved her.

"What's wrong with you?" she said.

"Inspector Lindström, are you okay?"

Sivert. Weird Sivert, who had continuously eyed her during the briefing, was only a few meters away from them. Did he see the kiss?

"I'm fine," she said, "but you and I should talk more about the footage."

And off she went, leaving Magnus alone in the room.

* * *

Espen Frisk looked at him with big brown eyes. A handsome, bright but timid looking young man, who was fiddling with the ribbon of his dark blue hoodie with the Stockholm university logo printed on it, eyes darting from side to side as if to make sure they weren't overheard. Meeting a police inspector could be intimidating, but Timo wondered if it wasn't just his nature to be suspicious about everything. They met in a pub across the street from the Stockholm police station, where Timo had visited his former colleagues.

"Are the police finally taking Quinten's death seriously?"

"I don't understand, Mr. Frisk."

"I thought you wanted to talk about Quinten," Espen stammered.

"No, Marie Lång was found dead two weeks ago. Murdered."

"Marie? I didn't know. What happened?"

"Didn't you know she disappeared two months ago?"

"No." The young man shook his head. He stared at Timo with disbelief and genuine concern.

"I've lost contact with Marie and the rest of the gang," he said.

"Why is that?"

"They belong to a past I don't want to think about anymore."

"But you still think about Quinten Hall?"

"Yes. Do you know what I do, inspector?"

"You are a student. Engineering, someone told me."

"No, I study criminology at the University of Stockholm. And do you know why?"

Timo shook his head and said, "No, tell me."

"I want to find my best friend's murderer."

"Murderer? It was suicide."

Espen Frisk sipped his coke and took a deep breath. "That's what everyone says. Quinten was a sensitive boy; he wasn't emotionally stable. He struggled with his feelings."

"People say he was in love with you, and you turned him down, and that was the reason for his suicide."

"I refuse to accept that," Espen said.

He had said it calmly, with compassion, but at the same time with a certain level of common sense.

"So, what is your explanation then?"

"Quinten was gay, and his family refused to accept him. They had spoken about sending him to a youth camp, to correct him. That's why he ran away."

"Camp? Is that even legal?"

"They are not advertised as such, but they do exist."

"And that's why Quinten ran away from home?"

"We were friends. He understood what I had been through, and we had many long conversations about his feelings and doubts. He may have seemed weak to others, but he had accepted what he was and what he had to offer to the world."

"That's all very nice, but what evidence do you have to suggest that he was murdered?'

"The weeks before it happened, he was scared. He thought someone was stalking him. Like you, I thought it was all in his head."

"Did he ever say who was following him?"

"No, but I think whoever it was had something to do with his death."

"I've read his file," Timo said in a stern voice, "he left a suicide note."

"Exactly. He would never write a note like that," Espen said, out of breath. "His idea was that words could never describe thoughts or passions."

"That's awfully circumstantial," Timo said and gestured the waitress to bring him another cup of coffee. Since he'd gotten out of bed that morning, a haze had been clouding his mind. He found it difficult to connect the dots and try to understand what this man wanted to tell him.

The funeral and the difficult conversation with the police commissioner hadn't helped. For ten minutes, the man had yelled at him. How irresponsible he had been lifting Isa's suspension, how he had disregarded every one of his superior's requests and orders. The report on the desk was abysmal, and he had disappointed him and the entire police force. He shouldn't think that because of his reputation the commissioner would go easy on him. Timo had listened to it, unsure of how and whether to respond. And when he left the room, he still didn't know what to make of it. Had he convinced the commissioner or not?

"Inspector, please help me," Espen said. "I only want justice for my friend."

"You had a big fight before his death. What was it about?"

"I wanted him to go back home. If he was that frightened, he'd be better off with his family, but he refused."

"Teresa Ljungman told us you were high when it happened."

He looked at his hands and nodded.

"Tell me about Marie, Jussi, and Teresa. Were you good friends?"

"I wouldn't say that. Teresa is... well, I truly believe she was only there to make a statement to her parents, and she hated the rest of us. She didn't want to be associated with bums like us, as she used to say. And Marie, sweet little Marie, at least that's how she often presented herself, but that woman slept around with everyone and poor Jussi let it happen."

"He knew?"

"Of course, he knew, but he didn't say a thing because he was afraid of losing her."

"And you? Why were you there?"

He jumped up. "I... I...," was the only thing he could utter. "There is a part of my life I don't want to talk about."

"The sexual abuse?"

Espen froze at the words, took a few seconds to regain his posture and then said, with a dark look in his eyes, "Janusz Haugen destroyed my life. Running away was a way of coping. Not a particularly good one. A new drama to replace the old one. So, if you don't mind, I'd like to change the topic."

Timo let out a sigh. He had to let it go. "When was the last time you saw Marie?"

"At the police station, after we found Quinten."

"You haven't seen her since?"

"Maybe now and then in Gävle. But I never felt the need to talk to her."

"So, you lived together for weeks, months even, witnessed the suicide of a friend, and then you cut all ties with those people. Why?"

"I wanted to move on," he said with tears in his eyes, "I needed to move on, and they would hold me back."

Timo wanted to believe him, but there was something he couldn't quite pinpoint. He had felt it with Teresa and Jussi too.

"Teresa told us Marie had spoken of someone she had seen that day. What was this about?"

Espen shrugged. "I know nothing about that. She never told me. Maybe it was the same man who was stalking Quinten?"

"Okay," Timo said, took a last sip of the coffee and stood up.

"Inspector, please think about what I said. Quinten didn't commit suicide. He was murdered."

CHAPTER

12

"**ARE YOU STILL THERE?**"
"Yes, I'm here," Ingrid said.

Isa had texted her that afternoon asking to talk. A vague text message, way too long and full of typos. Not knowing what to think of it, Ingrid called her in the evening.

Isa needed advice on the Marie Lång case, but before she realized it, the conversation had turned into a litany of words about Magnus. Isa liked to talk about herself, and usually Ingrid made the effort to listen, but this time Dr. Olsson was distracted. Why couldn't she focus? The entire day, her mind had wandered off to coffee breaks and dark-haired inspectors. She could swear she had been dreaming about him. Stupid. Just a stupid schoolgirl crush of an almost forty-year-old woman. It wasn't the first, and it wouldn't be the last. Her interests usually faded after a few days, but her obsession with Timo Paikkala was getting stronger by the minute, especially after that weird tête-à-tête.

"So, what do you think?"

"Uh," Ingrid stammered.

"Should I give it another try with Magnus?"

"He loves you."

"So he says, and before you know it, he's running back to that slob Sophie."

"I thought we were going to talk about Marie?"

Through the half-open door, sitting in her husband's office, Ingrid saw her youngest son Kjell running down the hallway to the kitchen.

She usually avoided taking work home with her, but this time there was no escaping it. She heard the creaking of the leather as she leaned over to get a better view of the hallway. Through the door she could see the marble steps of the stairs and the metal railing. The desk itself was big, way too big. Her husband sometimes received clients at home, and he knew he had to impress them. Therefore, the room had been designed with that only goal in mind. The oak desk dominated the room and was supposed to make him shine when he sat there. To her right was a sitting area with dark leather seats and a small glass table, and behind her the floor-to-ceiling windows overlooking the garden. For sure, Anton had style.

She heard the hasty footsteps in the background and sighed. The children were still running around. It was way past bedtime. Her husband hadn't followed her instructions to put the children to bed by nine o'clock.

"Anton, Anton," she shouted a few times, but there was no reaction from her husband. A deep breath. He was getting on her nerves these days. A lot.

"Sure, we can talk about Marie," Isa said.

"Sorry, it's just... I'm short on time."

For a moment Ingrid thought the line was cut, until she heard Isa say: "Yeah, I know I got an entire list of things to do from mister Timo. Where is the guy anyway?"

Just hearing the name was enough to make her shuffle back and forth. And while Ingrid heard her friend rattle on, she tried to calm herself. Timo, Anton, the children. It was too much.

"Seriously, if this is another of his tests, I'm..."

"Isa."

"I've had enough of these patronizing little games and rebukes that need to teach us something," sounded Isa's voice through the loudspeaker.

"Isa, he had to go to a funeral."

It became silent on the other side of the line.

"Oh well, why didn't he tell me?"

"I don't know," Ingrid replied.

Timo had confided in her, and only her. Why was she the privileged one?

"He doesn't trust me!"

"He does. Otherwise, he wouldn't have put you in charge," Ingrid said. "Can we talk about the case now?"

"It's easy for you to say, he likes you."

"Who likes you?" a deep voice said, and Ingrid jumped up. Her husband was standing in the doorway.

"Uh, nothing," she said. "The boss."

"The new guy? He'd better," Anton said with a straight face. "Rumor has it that he's out to fire people, so you better be on his side. And what

155

do you need me for?"

"The children," she answered and gave him an angry look.

"Oh, right." And Anton ran off to fetch the two boys.

On the other end of the line, Isa had noticed the tremble in Ingrid's voice. "Ingrid, are you okay?"

For a moment, Ingrid doubted. She had always been the reasonable one in their friendship. The serious one. She still needed to be. She couldn't stray down in a spiral of drama and love triangles, heartache and jealousy as she had seen with Isa over the years. She just needed to stay away from Timo Paikkala, and then everything would be fine.

"I'm fine."

"Are you sure? Is something wrong with Anton?"

"We're okay. So the case: I checked with my sources and Marie Lång indeed had a hospital appointment before she disappeared. The appointment was for an abortion."

"Abortion?"

"She arrived that day accompanied by a man but left before the procedure was done."

"So she didn't go through with it."

"Obviously. She was still pregnant when she died. And it looks like we're getting that warrant to collect his DNA."

"That's good news. Anything else on Forsberg's alibi?"

"That's your job."

"Right," Isa stammered.

Maybe it was time her friend turned her full attention to this case instead of trying to chase Alex's killer.

Ingrid said, "Let me help you: Henrik Forsberg has no alibi. He never mentioned he saw Marie that day, and no one remembers where he was."

"But are we sure Marie disappeared that day?"

"That's why we need to narrow it down. I hate to say it, but Sivert has done a great job in tracking down her whereabouts using the camera footage."

Ingrid saw her husband pass by the study again. Thumbs up, showing her he had done his duty. He hurried to the living room, but she still wasn't happy. The boys were probably playing games on their smartphones or reading under the covers. He needed to check up on them.

Isa said, "Anyway, we need to talk to Henrik Forsberg again, and we need to review the timeline. Do we know anything about the car that hit Marie?"

"Not much." Ingrid took another file from the stack of papers on the desk. "We have a list of potential candidates, based on camera images in the area where Marie was found. Unfortunately, there are no surveillance cameras on the road itself where she was found, and I had to make an estimate about the time window. That might be off."

"How many candidates?"

"Forty-seven."

"Jesus, that many?" Isa said.

"If we find the car and the driver, I'm not sure what useful information this will give us."

"Even if the driver is not the killer, he could have seen something."

"Maybe," Ingrid said.

"My feeling is that the Forsbergs are up to their ears involved."

"Can we continue this tomorrow?" Ingrid asked. "I have to check on the boys."

"Sure, but Ingrid, before you go, I need to ask you something about the Sandviken case."

Ingrid let out a long sigh. Last time Isa had brought it up, it had ended in a fight. Timo might have given his blessing for this unofficial investigation, but she hadn't.

"Okay."

A plain, emotionless okay.

"The file mentions a footprint they found in the Norman house, close to where Alex was lying. A footprint in blood. Anyway, I can't find a picture or scan of it. It was filed, right?"

Ingrid looked up and frowned. "That's strange. I remember adding it to the file, and there should be a digital copy in the folder on the main drive."

"It's not there."

"Let me check tomorrow. I discussed it with Nina Kowalczyk. We even compared the print with the shoes found in the house."

"And?"

"To be honest, I haven't followed up. The best person to talk to is Nina."

Isa sighed.

"Is that all?" Ingrid asked. She suddenly noticed how quiet it was in the house. Had she been too presumptuous to think she was the only one who could put the children to bed? Sometimes her husband surprised her.

"Alex's cell phone?"

"We didn't find it."

"That makes no sense," Isa said, "if Mats Norman killed him, he didn't have time to ditch the phone, and why would he?"

"We have a list of the people Alex called that day. You were the last one."

"Then where is the phone? Why did it have to disappear?"

"Isa, it's late. Let's talk tomorrow."

They said goodbye. Strangely enough, the conversation had also raised a few questions with Ingrid. Maybe Isa was right. These were details they should never have overlooked. She closed Marie's file, stared at it for a moment, while going over Isa's questions about the Sandviken case in her mind, and then shook her head as if to make the strange ideas disappear. No, there was probably a good explanation for everything.

She had decided for herself she wouldn't be sucked into another typical Isa-drama. She still didn't understand why her friend was so obsessed with Alexander Nordin. Isa had only known him for a few months and had already called it a relationship. This couldn't have been serious. Maybe it had been in Isa's head. Yes, she and Isa were different in almost every way. Maybe that was why the friendship worked, but now and then she'd had enough. Having Isa as a friend was like raising an extra child, who unfortunately never listened and kept pushing her opinions.

And yet, she admired the freedom Isa commanded, the courage to show the world who she was, without compromise, while Ingrid was only too eager to hide behind the perfect picture of mother and wife. She secretly longed to color outside the lines herself.

*** * ***

"Let's go over the timeline," Isa said. There were only a handful of people in the room: Berger, Magnus, Lars, and Ingrid.

On that rainy Tuesday afternoon, Isa had gathered the team in one of the shabbiest conference rooms in the entire police station. In the room, it was a lot darker than the overcast sky outside, full of clouds that could pour their fresh load of rain at any moment. She missed the large, modern meeting rooms in Uppsala where she had temporarily been stationed months ago, searching for the Sandviken killer.

She sighed as she looked at the board filled with incoherent notes. How many times had she complained about it? Everything they, as police officers, did was sensitive, and she didn't want to find confidential information on a whiteboard about a case she had nothing to do with. She ran the wiper over the painted metal, relieved that Timo hadn't shown up yet. She wanted to enjoy her status as case lead a little longer.

"Is this our new workspace now?" Berger said. "Why did narcotics have to claim our room?"

Ignoring Berger's whining, Isa watched Lars roll in the tripod with the flip chart, where he had copied the notes and structure from the old room's whiteboard. While Lars put the post-its on the whiteboard and started to draw the timeline, Berger couldn't hold himself and let out another complaint, "Flip charts? We're back to the Middle Ages."

Isa said, "Let's do a quick recap. Teresa Ljungman reported Marie missing on January 29. This was after the weekend that Ms. Ljungman and her friends were skiing in Åre. Marie's body was found on April 4 in the lake near Stromsbrö."

"In the backyard of the Forsbergs, so to speak," Lars said. "She was strangled and dumped in the water. She also showed signs of being hit by a car. On-site evidence shows it was a dark-blue car. We are still looking for the driver. No results yet. On Friday, January 26 at 10:00 a.m., Marie was seen with Henrik, the son of millionaire Gerard Forsberg, at an ATM near the General Hospital in Uppsala. He withdrew five thousand SEK, and the footage shows he gave the money to her. At 10:30 a.m. she had a hospital appointment for an abortion, but she leaves an hour later."

"Is Henrik with her?" Isa asked.

Lars nodded. "Yes. The traffic camera shows his car heading north, towards the E4."

"It takes a little over an hour to reach Gävle."

"Why would he drive to Gävle?" Ingrid asked. "We don't know when Marie was kidnapped or where she was held captive."

"The current theory is that the paths of Marie Lång and Oliver Pilkvist, the missing boy, crossed that same day. Marie's killer is the same person who kidnapped Oliver. And the timeline of Oliver's disappearance is clearer. He disappeared near Stromsbrö around noon. So, if Henrik is the killer, he had to be there at that time."

Ingrid said: "But there is no evidence that he drove to Gävle. His car wasn't seen on the E4, neither in Gävle. Marie's apartment is located outside the center, in the north. He could have just taken her home."

"Sivert is checking the CCTV from that day to see if any of the

Forsberg cars were spotted near Stromsbrö."

"Isa, they live in that area."

"So, they could have seen something," Isa said.

Why did Ingrid question everything she said?

"Tomorrow we have the interview with Henrik Forsberg. Let's be prepared. We have the warrant. So, we'll soon know if he's the baby's father."

"I find it hard to believe he's a serial killer," Ingrid continued.

"I'm not claiming he's a serial killer," Isa said, surprised. "I don't believe that theory. Marie had to die because she was pregnant. She refused an abortion, and he killed her. He tried to get rid of her body, but Oliver was a witness and he too had to die."

Ingrid shook her head. "So, he held on to the body for two months and then dumped it in the lake? This means he must have kept it in a freezer. There is no sign that this was the case. And what about the hit-and-run?"

"Paikkala's idea of a serial killer makes little sense either," Isa hissed.

"But you have to admit there are similarities with the files he sent us."

"The only similarity is the twig and anyone with any knowledge about hunting can mimic this."

"I contacted the teacher," Lars tried to interrupt the conversation that was gradually turning into a yes-no debate. "It took a while to reach him because..."

"And?" Isa sighed, exasperated by Ingrid and her urge to undermine her leadership, and trying to cut off an unnecessarily lengthy description of Lars' train of thought.

"Mark Lisberg claims he didn't see Oliver that afternoon."

"I'll talk to Lisberg myself," Isa blurted. "Just focus on finding the evidence we need to lock up Henrik Forsberg!"

"What about Quinten Hall?" Lars said. "Timo wants us to look into this case."

Maybe Ingrid was right. The case was more complicated than she had expected. That morning, they had received an email from the boss with a long list of questions and requests. He had given them a summary of his conversation with Kristina and his interview of Espen Frisk.

"Tell me," she said and threw herself in the chair near the flip chart. Her mood had plummeted, and so had the energy level. Just like Magnus, who had been standing quietly in the corner of the room, as if he wasn't part of the team.

"He died seven years ago, age fifteen. Suicide. One evening his friends got stoned, and he hanged himself."

"And there was no reason to doubt that story?"

"No. There was a suicide note. It was handwritten and verified to be Quinten's handwriting. The case was closed."

"But his friend Espen doubts that?"

"Yes, Espen Frisk. He is regarded as a very intelligent young man, but with a tragic story. At the age of thirteen, he was assaulted by a teacher at his school. The guy was never convicted, and he has always maintained his innocence. However, Espen's parents started a petition and because of the intimidation that followed, the man had to leave Gävle. He lives somewhere in Börlange. Espen went into therapy for years. At the age of fifteen, he ran away with Teresa, Jussi, Marie, and Quinten and lived in the crackhouse for a while, until Quinten's death. They were best friends since elementary school. Espen had confided in Quinten after the assault. And finally, it was Quinten who told his parents what had happened to his friend."

"So, if Quinten didn't take his own life, he was killed. Why?"

"Espen talked about a stalker? Quinten was scared. Can we verify that with Teresa Ljungman and Jussi Vinter?"

"I've tried," Lars said, "but they're not returning my calls."

"Quinten was bullied at school, especially as a teenager. Maybe it was a joke that went wrong?"

Magnus had woken up. He was acting strange. Continuously looking around, his eyes jumping from left to right, shaking his head like he was talking to himself. Isa was worried.

"Has anyone ever wondered why these five people were friends?" Ingrid said.

"Why?" Isa asked.

"The friendship seems artificial. They don't match."

"Maybe they don't match now," Magnus said, "but at one point they had a common ground. They were all troubled teens."

Isa looked at the whiteboard on which Lars had meticulously jotted down notes during the discussion. Five people. All so different. How was it all connected? And how did Oliver Pilkvist fit in?

* * *

After Berger, Lars, and Magnus left, Ingrid was the only one still sitting in the room. She was deep in thought.

"What's wrong?" Isa asked and sat down next to her. From where Ingrid was sitting, she could see the whiteboard with the new structure. The schematic, linking the different players and the events, was more structured than before. Lars had done a great job.

"What was that?" Ingrid said suddenly.

"What?"

"I've never seen you cut so many corners."

Isa frowned. "I'm just focusing on the most likely scenario and refuse to go off in these ridiculous stories of serial killers, stalkers. One serial killer at the time. You'll see that the story is pretty simple. And Timo is wrong."

"As far as I understood he isn't taking a position, but merely tries to keep an open mind."

"Yeah sure, open mind! Everyone seems to take his side these days."

Ingrid threw her hands in the air. "Isa, there is no good or bad side!"

"He came here to fire me!"

"But he didn't, and more than that, he even gave you the freedom to continue that ridiculous witch hunt."

"Ridiculous?"

It was out in the open.

Ingrid sighed. "Stop this. The only reason you want this case to be closed as soon as possible is to go back to your own unofficial investigation. Mats killed Alex. Accept it!"

"I can't. Alex deserves a decent investigation."

"He had one. Isa, you are basically saying we—Magnus, Nina, Berger, and I—did a terrible job finding his killer."

Isa stared at the whiteboard. "You all think the same thing. That he was a fling, nothing serious. But I loved him, in my own way. I loved him so much."

It was easier to think Alex had been a nobody, replaceable, insignificant. But maybe he had been Isa's greatest love. True love.

A hug was all Ingrid could give her best friend. It wasn't enough, but it felt good. And as Isa laid her head on her shoulder, Ingrid said, "I'm sorry, but for your own sake, let it go."

Isa lifted her head and wiped a tear from her face. "Ingrid, I can't. It feels like I let him down."

***

There was this feeling again. As if she was being followed. Teresa had turned around a few times but had seen nothing and no one suspicious. As she continued her nocturnal walk through the streets of Uppsala, now deserted and dark for most of her journey, Teresa got scared. She'd heard the echoes of footsteps that weren't hers: stopping when she did, starting again when she did. The feeling had been there ever since she had said goodbye to Jussi Vinter. He had called her and told her he was in Uppsala for a few days and that they should talk about Marie. He had talked, and she had listened, but not for long. Soon they had taken the conversation to the bedroom and had made love. Jussi had realized it wasn't Marie but Teresa he had longed for all these years. And Teresa, after years of denial, had finally admitted she was interested in him.

He asked her to stay, but she told him she had class early in the morning. She needed to be fresh and rested, but it was a lie. That morning, a mysterious letter had arrived, requesting a meeting. She didn't know from whom, neither what the meeting was about. Tonight at 11:00 p.m., in a park near the university campus. At first she doubted she would go. She should have told Jussi. Since the police had spoken to her about Marie, she had felt an unrest. There was something lingering in the back of her mind. A word, a sentence, but she couldn't quite grab it. Something Marie had told her, or maybe not. But it was important.

She increased the pace. The sound of footsteps grew louder.

Whoever it was, he or she was catching up with her.

As the panic rose and the heart rate increased, she told herself it was just her imagination.

She turned the corner and found herself in a small alley. The darkness seemed even darker. The walls of the buildings were so close together that if she stretched her arms, she could touch the bricks on either side, and they were so high she could barely see the stars in the dark sky.

This wasn't a good idea. She was vulnerable here. It only took one person in front and behind her to block her.

Midway, she stopped. It was quiet.

Then she heard the footsteps again and felt a hand on her shoulder. She screamed, but the sound was lost between the cold, and wet stones of the houses. In the distance, she saw the orange beams of the lampposts.

"Ms. Ljungman, I'm sorry. I didn't mean to startle you."

The voice was calm and polite.

She turned, out of breath, ready to lash out, when she saw the old man.

"You don't know me, but I need to talk to you. It's important."

"I know who you are," she said.

CHAPTER

13

"**MR. FORSBERG, WELCOME.**" The young man shuffled in his chair. Beside him sat his lawyer, leafing through the file with an irritating calm, briefcase on the floor and glasses halfway up the bridge of his nose. Like a skittish animal, Henrik looked around the room and jumped up every time the door was opened. He had met the woman before, but not the older man, who hadn't taken his eyes off him ever since Henrik had stepped into the interrogation room.

"I hope this can go fast," Henrik said.

"Do you need to be somewhere?" Magnus asked.

"I have a full social life," Henrik said, and then felt his lawyer's hand on his arm. A sign he would take over from now on.

"My client is here of his own free will. He is willing to cooperate. I hope you respect that and don't treat him like the next criminal or..."

"Or he'll tear you apart," Henrik hissed. He felt another pinch in his arm, but he didn't care.

"I see daddy is useful for something," Isa mocked, "as you brought his expensive lawyer."

Henrik struggled to suppress a sarcastic smile on his face.

"But let's get right to the point. Who is this?"

Isa put a photo in front of him.

"For the record, I'm showing Mr. Forsberg a printout of the CCTV footage taken at the ATM in Uppsala on January 26 of this year," she continued.

Shock. Pause. His brain in shutdown. He had never noticed before how subjective and relative the concept of time was. He hadn't expected this. When Marie's body was found, he had gone through the events of that day, one by one, hour by hour, minute by minute. What had he done? Where had he been? He could explain it all, but he'd been stupid to think he had left no traces.

No words came. He tried to think, but it seemed as if the access to any logical reasoning was blocked.

"So, let me help you. This is Marie Lång, and this is you. The timestamp shows that this was taken on January 26 at 10:00 a.m. You told us you hadn't seen her. In fact, you told us you had nothing to do with her. But this paints a different picture, doesn't it?"

"It's me," he said in a frail voice.

"So, you knew her better than what you told me?"

He sighed, looked at his lawyer, and then turned to the inspectors sitting on the other side of the table.

"Yeah, I knew her. She was a friend, and she needed help."

"A friend? I think she was more than a friend. You were lovers."

Think! What else did they know?

"Mr. Forsberg?"

"If you say so," Henrik said.

"How long have you been involved? Where did you meet?"

"I met her at a party I hosted last September. Teresa brought her as a guest. It just clicked."

"You told me she wasn't your type," Isa said.

"I lied. We started hanging out. She dumped that loser, and we became a couple."

"And you were the father of her baby?"

Henrik shrugged.

"What happened? You were seen in the hospital where Marie was scheduled to have an abortion, but she didn't go through with it."

"She wanted help, and I helped her," he said. As he pushed the words out of his mouth, his eyes turned watery, and a single tear ran down his cheek. He had always been good at faking emotions.

"She wanted to keep the baby, but you disagreed. The nurses told us you had an argument just before she decided to leave and cancel the procedure. Did it get out of hand?"

He took a deep breath. "No, you're wrong. She wanted the abortion, and I convinced her not to go through with it."

"And what happened then?"

"I drove her to the apartment. Teresa wasn't there. She had left on a skiing trip with friends."

"And it escalated?"

"No, no! Why would I kill her? Sure, she was angry with me about persuading her to keep the baby. She told me to get out. When I left her she was fine."

"You're the last person to see her alive, Mr. Forsberg. You have no alibi for the rest of the day. Your car was seen in the neighbourhood of Stromsbrö."

Henrik jumped up, his arms swaying in all directions. "I live there for God's sake! I was driving home."

"Henrik, sit down," his lawyer said, stood up and tried to calm the young man.

"And I wasn't the last one to see her that day," Henrik said.

"Who?" Isa said with a calm voice.

"She got several text messages during our argument in her apartment. She was distracted and almost seemed upset."

"Did she say anything else?"

"No, but I think she planned to meet someone later that day. I think that's why she wanted me to leave."

"Her phone records show that she didn't receive any calls or messages that day."

He laughed. "So, you don't know. Marie had another phone. Prepaid. Unregistered. She was a girl with a double life."

Isa quickly looked at Magnus.

"What double life?"

"Didn't you know Marie worked as an escort girl? That's how she could afford her life of luxury. The apartment, the clothes, the parties. But she stopped when we got involved."

"Where is the phone now?"

"How am I supposed to know? Lost. In the lake. Maybe the killer has it? Maybe the killer is one of her former clients."

"Do you know her clients?"

He shook his head.

"Does Teresa know?"

"I wouldn't be surprised Teresa put her up to it. I found out by chance."

"Maybe she continued her old ways. You got angry and killed her."

He sighed. "And I first held her captive for two months? Really? That's all you can come up with?"

"Very well, Mr. Forsberg," Isa said and took another document from the file in front of her. "This is a court order to collect your DNA."

"What? Why? I told you I am the father. Why do you need my DNA?"

She handed the paper to the lawyer and motioned the police officer at the door to get Dr. Olsson, who didn't take long to enter, armed with the DNA toolkit. As Ingrid opened the box, Isa kept her eyes locked on the young man.

"It's valid," the lawyer said and put the paper on the table.

"Please open your mouth," Ingrid said and held the cotton swab in front of his face.

"I... I don't...," Henrik stammered. These were the only words he could say before the swab touched the inside of his cheek.

"I assume my client is free to go," the lawyer continued.

"For now. But I'd stick around if I were you."

* * *

"You went over my head!"

The voice was familiar. She hadn't expected her boss back so soon. There he stood in the doorway. He had watched everything from behind the glass wall.

"Inspector Paikkala," she said and tried to put a smile on her face. "I had to. You weren't here, and we had to move fast."

"You could have called or emailed," Timo let out. "And you knew I'd be back today."

"Did I?"

She saw a glimpse of frustration on his face as he walked out the door and followed her into the hallway. "Do you ever read your email or check the messages on your phone?"

She couldn't tell him she had scrolled through his text messages and had ignored them. The idea of getting another to-do list was too much to bear.

"It worked, didn't it", she said with confidence.

"Yes, he was scared, very scared. Why was that?"

"He gave us something, but he's hiding so much more."

"He's afraid his DNA is going to show up implicating him in so much more than the fatherhood of Marie's baby."

"We just need to know what," she said.

"And escort girl? We need to find out who her clients were."

"Teresa Ljungman knows," Isa said.

"Yes, pay her another visit. And I'm going to talk to Patrik Mikaelsson."

"Who's that?"

"The last person who saw Linda Forsberg."

"Linda Forsberg? Why?"

"Linda's disappearance could be an important clue. I'm going to talk to him this afternoon. I'd like you to be there."

"No," she blurted.

He couldn't hide the surprise on his face.

"I need to see someone," she said.

"Who? What is more important than this?"

"Nina Kowalczyk."

"Why?"

"Just something I need to check with her," Isa said and tried to be as casual about it as possible.

"Lindström, we had an agreement. The Lång case must come first. Yesterday, I spent an entire afternoon trying to convince the commissioner not to fire you. At least you owe me an explanation."

"Okay, okay," she said and took a moment to sort everything out in her head. She lowered her voice as if she expected someone would eavesdrop on their conversation. "I think someone tampered with evidence found in the Norman house."

"What?" he said, took her arm and pulled her in one of the interrogation rooms.

"Are you sure? Why do you think that?"

Isa looked at him in surprise. This was a slight overreaction on his part.

"I'm not hundred percent sure, but pictures taken at the scene have disappeared and more peculiarly a footprint that was found in the living room near Alex. It's mentioned in the report. That final report was written by Nina. I need to check with her what happened to the evidence. The pictures were never sent to the forensics team. Nobody investigated it. This could tell us something about the murderer."

He let go of her arm and straightened his back. "This is bad."

"I know that. That's why I want to make sure I'm right about this. And... you shouldn't be involved."

His blue eyes struck her again, just like the first time she had met him.

"Okay," he said and walked to the door, "but let me know what you find out."

She nodded.

* * *

"Yes, I know Linda Forsberg," Patrik Mikaelsson said.

"You were friends?" Timo asked.

"No, not really. She was an acquaintance. I knew her, and sometimes spoke to her," the man said, and he poured another cup of coffee.

"According to her family, you were the last one to see her. Lise Forsberg said she had an appointment with you that day?"

"Has something happened to Linda?"

"Why? Do you think so?"

He shook his head. "No, no."

"But two years ago she left suddenly. Do you know anything about that?"

Patrik glanced at the window, where the raindrops had left their mark. The last few days had been so gloomy, as if it was autumn again. He needed the sun to fade the sense of dread and sadness that always came as the date approached. The day, his life had changed.

"I know. I met her at the pub a few days earlier. It was a school reunion. She was there with Harald Müller, one of her new lovers."

"Müller?"

"Everyone knows the kind of marriage the Forsbergs have. Harald wasn't the first and he wouldn't be the last."

"And what happened?"

"We started talking."

"About what?"

"Oh, about everything. Work, life, family. Jonna."

"Who's Jonna?"

"My daughter. She's dead."

"I'm sorry to hear that," Timo said. "How did she die?"

Jonna. Patrik wanted to talk about her and then again not. The sharp pain of realizing she was gone had become manageable over the years. He had it under control, put in mental boxes, contained. But now and then, when someone dropped her name, a smell, a word, a phrase, it broke down those thin walls and everything came flooding back. And occasionally he initiated it himself. He had to. Otherwise, her memory would just fade.

"She drowned. They found her in the lake close to where the Forsbergs live. It was an unfortunate accident. She was only thirteen. My wife died a year later. Cancer, but people sometimes say shock can be a trigger."

"So, you were talking about Jonna?"

"Yes, Jonna was in the same class as the twins Lise and Henrik."

"What about Jussi Vinter, Teresa Ljungman, Quinten Hall, Espen Frisk, and Marie Lång?"

"I don't know Jussi, but the others were all in the same year as Jonna. I'm not sure if they were in the same class."

"And they all knew each other?"

"Yes."

"Was there anything strange about your conversation with Linda?"

Patrik stared at his hands, trying to recall the conversation. It had started as a polite inquiry about his well-being and had ended with him remembering the most difficult moment in his entire life: when the police officers had rung the bell and had told him and his wife they had found Jonna face down, lying in the icy water of the lake, six hours after she had disappeared. Linda Forsberg had listened to the stories about his daughter. He had pulled the long-forgotten photograph from his wallet and shown it to her while telling her how great Jonna had been.

"The strange thing was Linda suddenly showed up at my doorstep a few days later, the evening she left."

"To talk about Jonna?"

"Yes. That was a weird conversation. She wanted to know everything about Jonna. Who were her friends, whom she talked to, whom she confided in. Something was bothering her, but she never said what. She stared continuously at the pictures over there."

He pointed to the photographs on the mantelpiece by the fireplace. It was covered with the pictures of his wife and daughter. Patrik often glanced at them before going to sleep at night, as if he took them with him, as if they were still there. Only the good things.

Timo walked over to the fireplace in the corner of the room. The girl in the photograph was smiling at him. Short brown hair, dark eyes, but with a twinkle showing how proud and confident she was. A bright blue sweater decorated with an elegant golden necklace showing her name.

Lovely girl.

"She was interested in the photos. Are you sure?"

"It looked like it."

"Did she say why?"

"No, but she really insisted on talking about Jonna's friends."

"And who were those friends?"

"Jonna was a popular girl. She had many friends, but Teresa Ljungman was her best friend, and she had a crush on Henrik Forsberg."

He couldn't stop smiling as he remembered how the thirteen-year-old blushed every time Henrik was mentioned, how she stammered that he was just a good friend, nothing more. Henrik Forsberg. Not exactly the best choice, his wife had said. Apart from the money and the good looks, there was nothing going for the young man. A little bastard who took everything and everyone for granted, who thought he owned the people around him. As if he was entitled to.

"We went through Jonna's photo album. I talked a little about my daughter. And then she left."

"How was her state of mind?"

"She was calm and rational at the start, but she got agitated. I don't know if I interpreted it correctly, but I saw fear on her face."

"When was that? Do you remember?"

"At the end of the conversation, when I started talking about her son."

Timo walked over to the couch again and sat down.

"Mr. Mikaelsson, was there anything suspicious about Jonna's death?"

"It was an accident," Patrik stammered, "that's what the police…"

"Forget about the police! What is your instinct telling you? As a father."

Silence. Those thoughts, those suspicions he had put in a mind box years ago. He was told repeatedly it had been an accident. There were doubts. He had struggled to accept it, but he finally had. Why would they want to ruin it now? Now, there was no more energy to fight.

"I... you can't ask me that."

Tears, tucked away for years, found their way back.

Timo leaned forward and looked straight at the man.

"I know it's painful, but you owe it to your daughter."

"Really? For years, I was told it was nonsense. I was told I was imagining things, that my mind was clouded by grief. And now you're asking..."

"To tell me about the nagging doubt," Timo said.

"She wouldn't have come near the water."

"Why?"

"She wasn't a good swimmer, and there had been an incident when she was eight. While on a boat trip, she fell into the water and nearly drowned. Her anxiety went through ups and downs. At times she seemed to be over it, and then there were moments when even looking at a glass of water triggered an episode of irrational fear. I told the investigating officer, but he couldn't do anything. There was no proof. Maybe it was an accident, maybe she had been too close to the edge."

"Would she have gone there alone?"

Patrik stared at him for a moment.

"No. Probably not."

"So, either she wasn't alone, or someone brought her there on purpose."

"What are you saying?"

"That her death wasn't an accident," Timo said. "And Linda Forsberg knew it."

"You think something happened to Linda?"

"Could be. When did she leave your house that night?"

"Uh, it must have been around 9:00 p.m."

"She went home, packed all belongings and ran, never to be seen again."

"Her husband must have seen her that evening," Patrik said.

"Why do you say that?"

"She got a message from him while she was here, asking her to come home. She told me they'd a fight about Müller."

"Are you sure?"

Patrik nodded.

"What was the fight about?"

"She didn't say, but she left shortly after she got the message. As I told you she was agitated and after receiving the message, she seemed even more concerned."

"And you never saw her again?"

"No. Maybe deep down, I knew something could have happened to her, but I told no one, not even when the superintendent asked me. What was his name again?"

"Anders Larsen."

Timo leaned back. It was clear now. Linda never left her family to be with her mystery man. She had disappeared, and Gerard knew a lot more than he pretended.

* * *

When Nina stepped outside, it was already dark. She was the last one to leave the lab. With arms full of case files and a heavily loaded bag, it was impossible to lock the door without putting some of it on the ground. When she had called professor Riksand months ago about her decision to leave the police department and pursue a career in forensics, he had immediately offered her an internship bridging the time between her resignation and the start of the academic year. The job was great. It was a better learning experience than any of the courses she would take at the university.

"I knew where to find you," the voice said.

Nina jumped up, dropped the key, and turned around. Every fiber in her body trembled until she saw who it was.

"Good God, Isa," Nina said, out of breath, "never do that again!"

"Didn't anybody tell you it is not safe for a young woman to be here alone, at night, in a quiet, ill-lit place?"

"But you are here, alone," Nina remarked and bent over to take the key. She put it in the keyhole, turned it and then picked the papers and bag from the stone floor.

"I can manage, but I doubt you can," Isa said.

Isa hadn't forgotten how her former protégé had turned against her. Little, promising and ambitious Nina had written a letter about her relationship with Alex Nordin to the police commissioner, triggering the internal investigation. It hadn't been Irene Nordin; it had been someone in her own team. An act of betrayal she didn't understand. By then, Nina had already left the police force. Was it a twisted belief that justice would be served if she reported this indiscretion? Why couldn't she leave it alone? The temporary suspension Anders had given her would have been enough.

Nina had problems with her way of working. Isa had always seen procedures and rules as something that could be bent or broken if the end goal justified it. Nina would never consider flirting with those boundaries. Isa couldn't deny Nina had talent, but she had always worked within the limits set by the system.

"There is no need to be sarcastic," Nina said and walked past her former boss.

"What do you want?" Isa heard her say as she increased the pace but the pile of documents, she was carrying, slowed her down, and soon Isa caught up with her.

"Let's put our differences and grievances aside for a moment," Isa started, "I need to ask you something."

"I'm not the one with the insults," Nina said.

"The forensic report of the Norman house..."

Nina frowned. "I thought you were off the case."

"Obviously, I'm not. The forensic report talks about footprints that were found in the blood near Alex's body. When looking for them, I found the entries in the evidence recovery and photo logs, but I can't find any of the actual pictures, scans or any processing of the prints back. It's just gone."

"No, that can't be. I remember examining them myself and I...," she said and then halted as if she had seen a ghost passing by.

"Nina?"

"I... let me look into it," she said slowly. The color of her face faded, confused as she was.

The last person she had entrusted the evidence to was Magnus. Had he been careless?

"And his phone?"

"We never recovered it from the scene. He didn't have it with him."

"Where is it? If Mats killed him, why would he take it? He barely had time to remove it. Between shooting Alex and the police intervention was maybe half an hour, maybe a bit more. And the phone records?"

"Nothing special. The last phone call was to you."

"Then why did the phone have to disappear?"

Nina shrugged. Suddenly there was so much going through her head. A seed had been planted. Something important, but something she couldn't quite grasp yet.

CHAPTER

14

"**M**ICHAEL?"

There was no answer from his eldest son. After his arrest, Mats Norman had tried to get in touch with his children, mostly through his lawyer, but they had refused to talk to him. Now he had mixed feelings about seeing Michael. He longed to see his children, but he was afraid of the reaction. He had been their father, their hero, the one they respected and looked up to, and now he was a mere criminal. Not just any, the worst: a child murderer. He had grandchildren, almost the same age as the girls he had abducted, raped and killed. How could they come to terms with the fact their grandfather was one of Sweden's most notorious serial killers?

Michael put his hands, palm down, on the table. He took a deep breath and looked at his father, lips pressed together in a grim expression, trying to keep the oppressed anger in.

"Michael?"

Mats reached out to take his hand, but his son pushed it away. He didn't insist and leaned back. Perhaps his son needed time.

Michael took another deep breath before he said, "The police came to our house to talk about mom."

Mats froze. "Mom? What did they…"

"Shut up," Michael said and clenched his fists. "You don't talk. Don't you dare to say anything!"

With a voice full of sarcasm and disappointment Michael continued: "I didn't get it. For months this has been playing through my mind. That we didn't know, fine. We were just children, but I didn't understand how all those years mom had never noticed anything. And now we know. She did. She helped you. Unbelievable! All those years, we pitied her, we felt sorry for her, not just us, but everyone. I can live with the fact you are a womanizer, an adulterer, but a rapist and murderer? That's impossible to bear. And now mom! How could she have done this to those girls? She had a daughter herself. Why?"

Michael stopped and stared at the cramped fingers of his hands. With every word he had folded them into the clenched fists that now lay on the table. "You don't understand how you screwed up your children!"

Another pause before he said, "Simon is back."

"Why? What's going on with your brother?"

"Did you really think this wouldn't ruin our lives? Seriously?"

"What can I say?" Mats said. "You've made up your mind about me. I'm obviously to blame for everything that has gone wrong in your lives."

"And aren't you to blame? You and mom. My life, my brother's life, my sister's life. Tessa checked into a psychiatric hospital. Depression, suicidal tendencies. I have to wonder: did you practice on her first?"

Mats jumped up. "How dare you!"

The sudden movement alerted the guard, and he approached them. But Mats just stood there, staring at his son.

"I actually just came here to tell you I will no longer be Michael Norman. I've started the procedure to change my name. I want to erase you from my life. You and your wife don't exist to me anymore. You were never my parents. At least then I can try to fix the destructive and negative spiral that ripples through what is left of this family. I just hope there'll be no trace left of you. I'll burn all the pictures, I'll try to wipe away all the good memories, because they are tainted. I'm glad you killed her; I only regret you didn't die with her. I don't know what Simon and Tessa will do. I'll try to help them, but if they choose to be on your side, they'll be out of my life as well."

"You think you can escape your gene pool, Michael, but you can't. We'll always be a part of you. We made you. And maybe one day those urges will surface too and then you won't be able to resist them. You'll be me."

Michael got up.

"And why exactly did you have children? To use us in your perverted plans? Like you did with Alex? Or to create your successor? What was it?"

"No, Michael," Mats said, desperately holding back the tears. The tears were real, but to his son they were just instruments of manipulation.

He never wanted to involve his children. He wanted a normal life for them. But how could he explain it? Those impulses, ever since he was a child, had always been so much stronger, difficult to ignore, and he had lost sight of what was moral and respectable. He wanted to be normal. He wanted to be average and lead a mediocre life until he finally had given in. Annette had fueled his desires and had encouraged him to follow them. He had never met a woman like that. An invisible force had brought them together to do great things.

Great things? That was the wrong way of putting it. She had been a girl with the same dark urges, hidden for years, restricted by the ordinariness of a family that didn't understand her. Her little brother was the first victim. He had been an experiment. To this day, her mother and sisters still hadn't a clue how he ended up under the wheels of the car in the garage, legs crushed, beyond saving. The handbrake had been easy to release and the slight slope in the floor had done the rest. She had made sure her brother had been playing behind the vehicle. As he was lying there, eyes open, looking at her in confusion, she stared back at him. What was it like? Knowing that you were about to die?

Her father blamed himself for the accident, and he took his own life when she was fourteen. Victim number two. Annette learned quickly that by subtle manipulation you could make other people do what you had planned. His wife was a master puppeteer. He knew it, but every time he fell for it until she broke his heart.

Annette rarely talked about it, but his obsession with Irene made her insecure. And when a child came in the equation, her jealousy was boundless. Irene became secondary; Alex was the nail in her coffin. She channeled her rage, invisible and tempered most of the time, to the most diabolic plans that sometimes took years to carry out. But she was patient. As the hatred continued to fester, she devised a plan to get rid of Nikolaj Blom, the nobody who had dared to blackmail her husband, and Alex Nordin, the favorite son, the secret love child.

But the plan hadn't been completely successful. Nikolaj was dead, but Alex wasn't. Damaged, but not dead, and that wasn't good enough. The years that followed, Peter Nordin became the instrument of her devious attempts to destroy Alex. She had fed Peter's unstable mind with lies and doubts about Alex.

But as years passed, Peter grew increasingly suspicious about his confidante. He had trusted Annette, the only one he deemed innocent and standing above the drama that had been going on. Irene had been disappointed with his reaction when she had told him about the rape and the pregnancy. While he had doubts, he started to stalk Mats. He knew Mats had something to do with missing teens, but he was too much of a coward to do anything about it. He felt sorry for Annette, he wanted to support her, maybe he had even fallen in love with her, but there was nothing left of that affection that afternoon when he confronted her with the documents, he had found implicating her in the disappearance of the girls, the death and disappearance of Nikolaj Blom, the impeachment of Josip Radić, and the assault of Alex and Irene. He wanted to go to the police. Annette had grabbed the first heavy thing nearby and had hit him with it. Her mind had worked quickly. She called her husband and together they staged it as a suicide.

Mats threw a final glance at his eldest son as the guard took him away. He remembered how his wife had stood there, in their living room, laughing, bragging about how great and unscrupulous she had been in her attempts to ruin the Nordin family, including his youngest, most beautiful son.

Irene, with the gun pointed at Annette, pulled the trigger, but she wasn't brave enough to finish the job. Taking a life was hard, at least the first time. Her hand was shaking wildly. Annette kept yelling at him. In that moment, he knew what he had to do to protect his family. Irene and Alex would never be safe. He came closer, put his hand on Irene's, as if they both were holding the gun. It happened so fast. His index finger touched hers. He pulled the trigger, and shots were fired. A shot to the head and another to the heart. Irene just let him. He did what she couldn't do. They had done it together. Then he had taken the gun from her hands, had wiped off the fingerprints and had told her to go home. He would take care of it.

But he hadn't killed Alex. How could he? He had loved him more than his other children.

A few days later, the confrontation with his son still fresh in his mind, he thought he was ready to confess to murdering his wife Annette and his son Alex Nordin, but he couldn't. It would have been too easy. Irene had killed Alex, and she had to pay.

* * *

Isa Lindström came to see Mats the next day. The conversation lasted only ten minutes. In those ten minutes he said nothing, gave her nothing. Her mind couldn't reconcile the love of a father with the cruelty of the murderer. And she was right, but he had no answer for her.

That evening, she had a breakdown for the first time in months, just like after Alex's death. She listened repeatedly to his voice mail, the YouTube movies, the pictures, the papers he had written. She wanted something that belonged to him. His pullover next to her in the bed. Why couldn't she leave it behind her? Why did he still affect her so much?

The answer to solving his murder was somewhere in the file, but she just didn't see it. How she missed Magnus! It was the first time in weeks she really longed for him. He was her rock in the surf.

But Magnus wasn't well. After his first mental breakdown, they had released him from the hospital and sent him home with a bunch of meds, but the problem wasn't solved. The dreams about Toby and Alex were so vivid he always found himself somewhere else in his apartment when he woke up. Sometimes with a knife in his hand, about to strike. Sometimes crying, sometimes his heart was racing so much that it felt like his chest would explode. It became increasingly difficult to concentrate on his work.

"I hurt someone... really badly," he had told the psychiatrist.

The psychiatrist wanted him to elaborate, but all he could talk about was how he had let Toby down. How, in hindsight, he had done wrong to let him suffer so long. He should just end it. Why hadn't he listened to Sophie and Isa to let his son go quietly? He had only thought of himself.

But confessing to murder was a whole different ball game. He couldn't take that step. He hated Alex Nordin even more than before. The delusions about his victim prevented him from focusing on his son, on his family, on things that mattered. And Alex was still standing between Isa and himself.

* * *

Magnus still felt invincible until his first real conversation with Timo Paikkala.

"I've heard you disagree with my decision, and you have been helping inspector Lindström instead of assisting inspector Karlsson."

In his no-nonsense way, Timo opened the first face-to-face with his senior inspector.

"To be honest," Magnus said, "it surprised me... I have nothing against Berger, but he is a junior."

Babysitting a junior was boring and demeaning for an inspector like him. He wanted to be Isa's partner again. It felt like they had replaced him, thrown him away. And who was Timo Paikkala to tell him what to do? He was at most an interim, an outsider who had been so audacious to take his place. Slowly but with an unstoppable determination, his attention had shifted from Alex Nordin to Timo Paikkala, the man he had seen only once before. Why did Timo want to be with Isa? Maybe he wanted her all for himself. Dark hair, blue eyes, the same category as Alexander Nordin.

"And training a junior is beneath you?"

"No, I wouldn't say that, but I can do a lot more useful stuff with my time. Maybe I can help inspector Lindström with her investigation into Irene Nordin."

"How do you know about that?"

"Uh, she told me."

"Of course, she did." Timo sighed and turned his head to look at the window, seemingly contemplating Magnus' suggestion. "Okay, let's do the following. You can help inspector Lindström with her unofficial investigation, but you have to keep it quiet. There are some anomalies that have popped up."

Fear. It had lasted less than a second, but there had been a flash of terror going through his entire body. And judging by the furrowed brows and narrowed eyes with which inspector Paikkala had locked his gaze on him, Magnus knew his boss had noticed the momentary loss of control.

"Uh... what anomalies?"

Timo said with an icy coldness in his voice. "Evidence is missing. Do you know anything about that?"

"What evidence?"

"A footprint, mentioned in the file but missing from the log."

The hatred and jealousy, so targeted at Alex Nordin, had found a new victim. Timo Paikkala was a dangerous man.

Timo continued. "This is serious. Very serious. You were in charge, together with Nina Kowalczyk. I ask you again: do you know what might have happened?"

"Uh, I really don't know. If you want, I can try to find out what went wrong. There is probably a simple explanation for it."

Timo's compelling gaze told him that the man wouldn't let go, as if he already knew everything, and the conversation was just a deception to gauge how far he had to go to break him.

Then Timo said calmly: "Okay then, but I trust you can keep it quiet. If someone is undermining this investigation, I want to know. Rest assured, whoever is responsible, will pay."

"Of course," Magnus stammered.

* * *

"You are so quiet," Isa said, "didn't your talk with Timo go well?"

Magnus had thrown himself in the chair at her desk after the conversation, without saying a word.

"Tell me," she said. "Is there something wrong?"

"No, I can work on the case," he mumbled.

"That's great, isn't it?"

"I guess... sorry, I'm just tired."

"Toby?"

He shrugged.

"Are you feeling okay? You haven't heard those voices again, have you?"

"No, no, they're gone," he said annoyed.

"Anyway, I am glad you're on the case and..."

"He said something about tampering."

"Yes, a footprint is mentioned in the file and..."

She reached out to open one of the drawers, but at that moment, the ringtone of his cell phone sounded. An unknown number. He quickly looked at Isa as if he wanted her blessing to answer it.

"Take it," she said, "no problem."

"Magnus Wieland."

"Magnus, it's me, Nina," the woman said.

He hadn't talked to her in months. Why would she call him?

Nina immediately came to the point. "Do you remember the footprints we discovered at the crime scene in the Norman house?"

For the second time in less than an hour, fear ran over him like a tidal wave, temporarily freezing every muscle in his body, stopping his breath for a tiny millionth of a second, flushing the blood to his brain, depleting it from his face.

"What's wrong?" Isa asked.

"Nothing... I need to take this," he said and went outside.

As he walked down the hallway to find a quiet room to take the call, he replied, "Footprints? I can't remember. Why?"

"Magnus, seriously? You can't remember? We reviewed the pictures and scans together. You even wanted to investigate it further. Remember, you were going to talk to the forensics team."

"You must be mistaken. Are you sure it was me? Why are you asking about this?"

"I gave the photos to you," but she suddenly stopped.

There was a long silence. In that silence, her mind was going over all the options. And suddenly she understood. Not the why? But what he had done. He was thorough, a good and experienced detective. His perception and sharp memory had always amazed her. The only explanation was that he had deliberately removed evidence. But why? Her first reaction was he must have wanted to protect his partner Isa, but then why would Isa have inquired about it? The other option was too inconceivable. He wanted to protect himself.

She tried to recall the events of that day.

He hadn't answered his phone.

Isa had called him from the car. He hadn't answered. Why? It had been such a crucial moment in the whole intervention. Why hadn't he been reachable? She hadn't thought much of it and neither had Isa.

It couldn't be. He was on his way to Sandviken.

But he could easily have passed by the Norman house.

People must have seen him. Why hadn't anyone noticed? No, there must be a good explanation. He wasn't a murderer.

And he was the one who had taken care of the phone records. Had he also tampered with those files? She wasn't sure of anything anymore.

"Nina?"

He heard her breathing on the other end of the line. Slowly at first, then increasingly faster as if she were having a panic attack.

Then silence superseded the gusts of air. She had hung up.

* * *

When Magnus rushed by after the phone call with Nina, Isa, now sitting in Timo's office after the boss had asked her to provide an update on the Lång case, paused for a second.

"How is Magnus?" Timo said it without looking up from the laptop.

"All right, I guess. Looks like you're allowing him to work on Alex's case."

"Any new breakdowns?"

"No, he's okay. You talked to him. Do you think he's not?"

Timo's eyes were still fixed on the file.

As she got no response, she continued, "Of course, his son is still in the hospital, and he is under a lot of pressure."

"Don't make excuses for him! Do you think he's a liability?"

"Why would he be a liability?"

It was silent for a while, before Timo said, "Don't you think it's strange?"

"What?"

"That sudden mental breakdown."

"His son is braindead; his marriage is gone. I think it's only natural."

"Every one of us has dealt with loss in one way or another, and for sure everyone is different in dealing with that, but... take you for example."

"What about me?" she said.

"Did you experience such a downfall after Alex's death?"

"That's kinda personal," she said and frowned.

"The first weeks and months you can't stop crying, and you wallow in pity. Why them, why me? Every morning, you have to drag yourself out of bed and tell yourself why that day is worthwhile living without them. Time eases the pain a bit, but every small thing, a word, a sound, a smell can remind you of them and it rips the wound open again like it was in those first days. And it will always be like that. Forever. Does that sum it up?"

With open mouth she stared at him.

"But there are no delusions or paranoia in the picture," he continued.

"Everyone is different," she said, "some people reside to drinking and drugs."

"Is he drinking?"

"No... I... I don't think so."

Timo closed the laptop and leaned backward. "You broke up with him, because of Alex."

"Correction. He broke up with me."

"He broke up with you because of his son?"

"I knew he had children, but he kept his son's disease from me. He thought I couldn't handle it."

"But he still loves you."

She didn't feel comfortable talking to him about it. She had a reputation. A woman of free sexual morals, who didn't care too much about the feelings of others, but it bothered her Timo only got to see that side of her.

"What are you exactly implying?"

When he still didn't answer, she repeated, "Timo, what were you implying? What aren't you telling me?"

"Nothing," he said. "You still don't believe Mats Norman killed his son?"

He was lying. The boss was holding something back. She could feel it. A suspicion, a thought.

"What more can I say than I already said before? I'm telling you he's not responsible for Alex's death. There are so many questions unanswered. Where is the phone? What happened to the scans? And the biggest question: why? Why would he kill Alex?"

"Uppsala thinks he did. What do you want me to do?"

Since he got back from Stockholm, the bond between them had grown stronger. She started to trust him, even if he hadn't shared everything with her.

"Help me. If it's not Mats Norman or Irene Nordin, then who is it?"

"Okay," he said. "What do you need?"

"Can you talk to Nina? She doesn't trust me."

"Do you think she's hiding something?"

"I don't think it's her, but she knows more," Isa said. "She won't tell me."

"She was your protégé?"

"A long time ago," she said quietly, "but you could say we had different views on things."

"She was Magnus' last partner," he said with a straight face, and then turned to the papers lying on the desk next to the laptop.

Why would he say that?

He was now flipping through Oliver's file. She wouldn't get anything more out of him. The opportunity was gone.

But why was this important? He never said anything for no reason.

CHAPTER

15

"**MARIE LÅNG?**"

She had repeated the name at least five times in the past two minutes. Mrs. Pilkvist was a frail, ordinary-looking woman whose world had completely collapsed five years ago after her husband's sudden death. From then on, her life had revolved solely around her son. She didn't care what happened to her. She herself no longer had any ambition or desires. But two months ago, her son was also taken from her. She ended up in the darkest place she'd ever been. It had been a struggle to get out of bed those first weeks. She loved to linger in the dreams where her family was still complete and happy, but little by little she realized Oliver would never stand a chance if she didn't do something. She had to be there for him.

Like Bengta Lång, she had knocked on every door and had visited the police station every week to inquire about her son.

"You know her?" Isa said.

Sitting in Mrs. Pilkvist's living room, Isa and Timo had told her about Marie's death and the possible link to her son's case.

"Yes, of course. She was Oliver's babysitter. I'm a nurse and sometimes I have difficult hours: evenings, weekends. She wasn't the only one, but Marie took care of him now and then, whenever she could. The last years, mostly during the weekends."

"So, Marie and Oliver knew each other?"

She nodded.

Isa leaned back and turned to Timo, who hadn't moved a muscle. "Marie could have gotten the handkerchief on one of her visits?"

"But there is blood on it," Mrs. Pilkvist said. More than anything else, that red stain on the photograph hadn't left her field of vision. "Marie never mentioned anything happened during her visits. Where does the blood come from? Besides, we haven't seen Marie in over a year."

"Why?"

"It's not that I didn't want her to come, but…"

"She declined?"

"Yes, as if she didn't want to come anymore. There was always an excuse, a reason she couldn't make it."

"Do you have any idea why?"

"No, but I wonder…" She turned her head and looked at the window. The sunlight was pouring in. Brighter and warmer than expected. Only an hour ago, the rain had lashed in gentle waves against the glass. Darkness and light. Pain and happiness. "Maybe it wasn't Marie, but Bengta."

"Bengta?"

"I don't want to spread rumors, but it felt like it wasn't Marie's decision. Bengta told me, and that woman always scares me. The way she looks at Oliver, the way she treated Marie. So overprotective and controlling."

Timo leaned forward and let his eyes run over the woman.

She was nervous and tired. Tired of worrying. The daily tasks had been such a chore for the past months. Cleaning, washing, eating. It could only distract her mind for a moment. But then the fear took over. The fear she would never see Oliver again.

"Did Bengta do anything to make you worry?"

"Nothing concrete, but she's just weird."

"Weird? That doesn't help us."

She sighed. "Ask her family! Oskar always defends her but ask the children! Something strange is going on with that family."

"Mrs. Pilkvist," Timo said, "can you tell us anything more?"

She shrugged.

"What about Mark Lisberg, Oliver's teacher?"

"Oliver liked him, but you never really know. People often hide their true selves." Then she sighed. "I just want Oliver back."

"Mrs. Pilkvist..."

She shook her head. "No, he's not dead. I refuse to believe that! What about the people who claimed to have seen him? Greta Claesson told me an old woman saw him with a man and a woman near Stigslund."

Timo said, "We checked that, but the woman couldn't identify him. It was a dead end."

Isa said calmly, "Mrs. Pilkvist, we'll try everything we can, but you have to be prepared. The blood on the handkerchief is Oliver's. He could be injured or..."

"No, no. Find my son! You've wasted too much time already!"

* * *

Timo had called Isa and Sivert in the conference room. There was silence. Only silence as he let his blue eyes jump from one person to the other.

"I found something," Sivert said. He slid his right hand across the keyboard, while spinning the ballpoint pen between the fingers of his left hand. Sivert, all hyper from the dozens of coffees he had consumed throughout the day, was jumping up and down in his chair. Timo didn't know what it was: the fact that he couldn't stay in one spot for even a second or the weird glances he was throwing at Isa as if he had never seen a woman before, but every time the man opened his mouth, Sivert annoyed him.

"Well, what did you want to show me?"

"Patience," Sivert said.

"Which I don't have," Timo answered.

Sivert stroke a few keys on the desktop, and a camera image appeared on the screen.

"I found out that there could be another witness to Oliver's disappearance," he said.

"Who?"

"Well, that's the thing. This is half an hour before Oliver disappeared."

Sivert drew the attention of his audience to the car passing by the traffic camera and entering the long road through the forest. The road Oliver had taken, going home from school. The road where Mark Lisberg, soccer coach and teacher, had stopped to take a break.

"It takes about five to ten minutes to bridge the distance between the cameras at both ends of the road. But this car passed by the same traffic camera only an hour later. Mark Lisberg mentioned he had seen a car, parked between the bushes next to the road, slightly hidden from sight, not so far from the area where the bus driver had last seen Oliver, but he couldn't see if anyone was in the car."

"How could we have missed this?"

"The time frame and the fact that Mr. Lisberg wasn't regarded as a credible witness," Sivert said. He stopped the frame and enlarged the picture on the screen.

"I was able to trace the car until Hille, then I lost track."

"And the license plate?" Timo asked.

"Well, that's the strange thing. The car was registered a year ago to Linda Forsberg."

"Linda Forsberg? How?"

Timo turned around and looked at Isa.

She shrugged and said, "Either it's her or someone pretending to be her."

"Can you identify the driver?" Timo said, leaning forward, trying to see if he could recognize the blurred image on the screen.

"I can enhance it, but I'm afraid that's as good as it's going to get," Sivert said.

Timo kept looking at the screen.

"Timo?"

Then he got up and turned around. "I want to know everything there is to know about Linda Forsberg. Finances, phone records, where is she registered... everything."

"Timo, you know it isn't her, right?" Isa said.

"I know but finding Linda or what happened to her might be the clue to solving Marie's murder."

He left the room, but the way he walked down the hallway seemed almost like he was kicking an invisible enemy. He felt an inexplicable irritation and anger.

"Timo," Isa said.

Suddenly he stopped and turned around. "You should have known... you should have checked this earlier! And you should have checked the connection between Marie and Oliver! Do I have to do everything myself?"

Where was this rage coming from? Everyone made mistakes.

"I... I didn't realize," she stammered.

"You never do because your head is always somewhere else! Maybe they're right, and you are all a bunch of amateurs!"

And then he suddenly realized he had lost control, that he was pouring all his frustrations about Magnus on her.

"Oh, I see," she said. "Well, these amateurs are all you have. Take it or leave it!"

And then the voice of wisdom took over, his inner voice, saying a powerful leader should be able to admit his mistakes, that a strong person should never let his emotions take control.

"I'm sorry," he said.

"I know you're stressed. This is a complicated case, but I've had enough of these insults that have been thrown my way in recent months."

"I told you I'm sorry."

She gave him a faint smile. "Okay then."

"So, what do you make of Mrs. Pilkvist's remark about Bengta Lång?" he said.

"We ran a background check on the family. Nothing unusual. Besides a few parking tickets and fines for speeding, all of them have a clean record."

"But something triggered Mrs. Pilkvist to tell us that. Talk to the neighbors and friends of the family! Perfect families don't exist."

"Yes, boss!"

He frowned. "And be thorough!"

* * *

The green lasers drew a maze of straight lines on the ceiling. Then they turned orange and red. Like mystical patterns, they were dancing through the air, almost igniting the smoke. The techno music was loud, but so invigorating. Isa held her hand up to touch the eerie mist. How she had missed that! The adrenaline rushed through her body. The high was so overpowering she could hardly control herself. Isa felt sexy, and she needed a man, fast.

With the dark make-up and red lips, none of her colleagues would have recognized her. After Alex, there had been no one, but that evening she was looking for the next lookalike to take home with her. Sex was the only thing on her mind; it was the only thing she couldn't control when her mind went in overdrive. Around her, young men passing by gave her an appreciating look. They were at least ten years younger, but that was okay. Even the bartender in his simple white T-shirt, young, handsome and probably willing, would do. She ordered a cocktail, took a seat at the bar and let her eyes glide over the young man who was tossing the bottles around with a certain agility. She had set the target. When he noticed how she was looking at him, he smiled and made it a more show-worthy event. She didn't take her eyes off him, trying to imagine how his naked body would look like underneath that shirt and those tight jeans.

"Wow, you're really not subtle," the voice sounded.

With a swift turn, she faced the man sitting next to her. She hadn't noticed him before. Dark-brown hair, dark eyes, white shirt, tailored suit, red tie hanging loosely around the neck, and a glass of whiskey in front of him. Not bad to the eye, but older than the bartender she had set her mind to.

"And why should I be?" she said, playfully offended. "Your sex never has a problem with that. Why can't women do the same?"

"My sex... good God," he called out. "If you want to make this a man-woman thing, fine. I just think he's not the right guy for you."

She leaned over, head slightly tilted, and looked at him more closely. Mediterranean. Spanish, Italian maybe. But no accent.

"And who would be the right guy?" she said with a teasing grin on her lips.

He smiled and took a sip of his whiskey.

"Give me a reason why you would be the guy?"

"You need a man, not a boy," he said and threw a quick glance at the barman, who seemed disappointed, having lost the interest of the beautiful woman at the bar.

"That's what you tell me, mister..."

"Nicolas, but people call me Nick."

"And that's your real name?"

"Yes, I am a pretty straightforward guy."

"I can see that," she said and let her finger slide over the rim of the cocktail glass, "but you need a lot more to convince me."

He was up for the challenge as he leaned over and whispered in her ear.

* * *

"I knew I'd still find you here."

Timo turned around. About to go home, he had the jacket in his hand. It was quiet. Most officers had gone home for the day. Behind the counter three policemen were taking the night shift.

"Dr. Olsson, what are you doing here so late?"

"Inspector. I wanted to show you the DNA report."

He took the file she held out in front of her.

"It could have waited."

"And I just wanted to know if everything was fine," she said.

"With what?"

"The funeral and all."

"It was a typical funeral, nothing special," he said calmly.

"You knew her well?"

"Yes, she was almost my mother-in-law, a long time ago," he said with the straightest face. "Pancreatic cancer. She was dead in a year."

He didn't tell her it had been a relief. The mother of his former fiancé had longed for death after her daughter's demise. But she hadn't been strong enough to put an end to it herself. Cancer, as devastating as it was, had been the way out. She had refused every treatment, much to the dismay of her family. At the end of her life, delirious with pain, she had seen her daughter again, and while the morphine had barely taken the edge off the horrendous suffering, her husband had never seen her so happy. Timo regretted not having been there when she had died. They had been fond of each other.

"My condolences with your loss," she said.

The words were hanging like a chimerical curtain between them. Simple words, but the softness and compassion tempered the anxiety and pain. It wasn't just the words; it was her.

She gave him a compassionate smile. That smile reminded him why it wasn't a good idea to be alone with her. But he couldn't stop, and obviously neither could she. Here she was again, standing in front of him unnecessarily, using work as an excuse.

"Maybe you can fill me in on the most important conclusions while I escort you to your car."

"Oh, that's nice, but I really don't need any..."

"I insist," he said, put on his jacket and closed the door, "a lady all alone at night, on an abandoned parking lot."

"Thank you," she said as they strolled down the long hallway.

"So, what did the DNA tell us?"

"Henrik Forsberg isn't the father of Marie's baby."

"What? But he confessed."

"He confessed to protect someone, because the genetic profiling also showed us that the real father is related to Henrik Forsberg."

"Gerard Forsberg?"

"Yes, likely."

He opened the front door and let her step through.

"So he's protecting his father, but why?"

"I think Henrik Forsberg desperately seeks his father's approval," she continued. "He tells the world he doesn't care, but deep down he wants a relationship with his dad, and he clearly is suffering from the absence of his mother."

"Wow, that's a lot of analysis."

"Uh, it's just... that's what I think. Don't take it for granted."

He smiled. "I won't but thank you. This makes sense though."

"He must have known about Gerard and Marie."

"But did they have a relationship or was it sexual assault?"

"You talked to him," she said. "How did he behave?"

"He looked defeated. Sad."

"The pain of losing her," she whispered.

They were now in an almost empty parking lot with only the faint light of the street post casting a shadow over them.

"We need to talk to Gerard," he finally said. "I also think the killer wanted to send a message by dumping her in the water so close to the Forsberg's home. It wasn't coincidence. He knew about Gerard and Marie."

"So, you don't think Gerard is the murderer?"

He sighed. "You're right. I shouldn't make assumptions. I need to be objective. He's a suspect."

For a few moments they were facing each other in silence. So much was going through his mind, and it had nothing to do with Gerard Forsberg or Marie Lång. He remembered that moment in his office when she had turned her head and had glanced through the window. His brain had suddenly gone on hold. Every part of his body had screamed 'Stop!' to absorb the new information. She looked like the woman he couldn't think of without the agonizing pain of loss. He had seen the resemblance before but had ignored that lingering feeling of intrinsic fondness. Now she was standing only a meter away from him and if he reached out, he would be able to touch her. But it wasn't her.

"Oh, I forgot," she said, "we matched one of the fingerprints in

Frank Harket's garage."

"Who?"

"He was in the system. A certain Ilan... something... the last name escapes me. Years ago, he was charged with manslaughter, but acquitted."

"For what?"

"Hit-and-run. The pedestrian died. The old man had neglected a red light while crossing the street."

"Hit-and-run? Does mister Ilan possess a dark-blue car?"

"Yes, but the car was reported stolen in Uppsala the night of Marie's murder."

"Let's talk to the man and see what he has to say," Timo said and took her briefcase as she opened the door of her car. He smelled the familiar sweet scent of her perfume and for a moment let it overwhelm him.

Suddenly she turned, and surprised he jumped back.

"I'm sorry," she stammered as he tried to regain his balance, "I wanted to ask you: have you started looking at houses because I can ask Anton if he has any suggestions. He knows many people in real estate."

"Uh... well, I want to, but I didn't have time yet and I'm not exactly sure what I'm looking for."

He gave her the briefcase and stared at the ground. "My assignment is only until end of the year. I'm not sure what will come afterwards."

"Oh." A shower of disappointment flushed over her face.

"But regardless, I think it's a nice area to invest. So, if your husband has any suggestions, I'm all ears."

She smiled, took place in the driver's seat and before closing the door said, "Good, I'll ask him."

* * *

In the Uppsala forensics lab, Nina was working overtime. Behind the desk in the corner of the empty lab, she was looking at the screen of her laptop. She wasn't working on her daily assignment, but to ease her suspicions about Magnus she had downloaded the last report about the Sandviken case. As an intern, she had access to part of the police files. The disappearance of the footprint scans wasn't the only inconsistency she had discovered. Entries from the records of Alexander Nordin's phone had been deleted. She wasn't expert enough to recover them, but tomorrow she would ask the IT team to look into it.

There was no doubt anymore. Magnus Wieland was involved in the murder of Alex Nordin. Had she been working with a murderer all this time? Sharing personal stories, throwing around jokes, complaining about work and colleagues. All that time, he had kept quiet, had shown no signs. He had fooled everyone. How could a man demean himself to that level of cruelty and evil? Was the love of a woman worth the life of a man? Magnus had deemed so. She would never understand. She would probably never experience the maddening obsession that turns decent family men into killers.

"Nina?"

She jumped up and immediately froze when she saw who it was.

"Magnus!"

He stood in the doorway eyes firmly locked on her.

Think! He's not here to chitchat.

She needed something to defend herself.

Slowly he came closer but stopped when he saw the fear in her eyes.

"What are you doing here?" Nina said. She had tried her best to sound normal, but she couldn't control the tremble in her voice.

"Nina, let me explain," he said and took a few more steps toward the desk where she was sitting.

No gun. No weapon to defend herself. She didn't know what to do. Deny she knew anything or try to reason with him?

"I never wanted to hurt him, I swear," he said.

She was sitting on the edge of her seat, about to run away. She could use the element of surprise and maybe then she would get past him.

"But you did, Magnus. Why? What happened?"

"I don't know," he said.

For a moment, she felt sorry for him as she read the emotion on his face, a kind of remorse.

"You need to make it right. You need to turn yourself in. Tell your story. People will listen."

"Nina, please, don't tell anyone. It was an accident. Please. My daughter, how do I explain it to her?"

"If it was an accident, explain it to the police and they will believe you."

It was a pivotal point in the conversation. She stood up and with her back turned to the wall so she could monitor him, she slowly moved to the other side of the room. She heard her heartbeat in her ears, loud and fast.

Motionless he stared at the floor in front of him, like he was considering all the options.

She took the risk. That moment of inattention was what she had hoped for. She tried to reach the open door, but he was faster.

His hand on her shoulder, a heavy jerk.

She lost balance and fell backward. Her head hit the corner of the wooden cupboard near the door.

He could hardly breathe. What had just happened? He stared at the lifeless body on the floor. Was she dead? Oh, God! He hadn't meant to do this. What kind of man had he become? How could he live with that?

* * *

"Help, help! Please help us!"

The sound of his voice hung between the trees of the forest. Who was he kidding? There was no one.

The cold crept down his legs. The night temperature was still below freezing. And it started to rain again. Icy rain. It hit his bare skin like a thousand needles. His toes and fingers already felt numb. He touched his forehead. Blood. Then he looked behind him. She lay with her back against the tree, her eyes closed.

"No, no, stay with me," he shouted as he ran toward her.

"I can't," she moaned.

"You need to get up," he said and threw her arm over his shoulder. But she was heavier than expected and her body didn't cooperate.

"Leave me. Save yourself! You know what to do."

"No, I won't leave you," he cried, and for the first time his eyes became watery with tears. Until then, he had kept a cool head.

"You have to," she whispered and closed her eyes again.

He felt so drowsy. He had always heard that freezing to death was like falling asleep, like being engulfed by a nice soothing blanket. Painless. How did people actually know that?

He took a deep breath, trying to get more oxygen to his brain. If they didn't move now, they would never survive. With his last strength, he tried to pull her up and get her on her feet. Blood on her hands, face and feet. Where did it come from? Was she hurt? But then he heard the creaking of twigs. Too late.

"Well, well, how disappointing," the voice said. "You didn't get very far."

CHAPTER

16

"**GOOD MORNING, SUNSHINE!**"

Furrowed brows, eyes barely open, she walked into the kitchen to find a naked man handing her a fresh cup of coffee.

"You're still here," Isa said.

After a brief sexual encounter in one of the club toilets, they had gone to her place. It had been fun and exciting; it had been wonderful sex, but now she wanted him to leave. Usually her one-night stands were out of the door before she woke up. He, however, seemed to have no intention of leaving soon.

She took a sip of the coffee, while she got increasingly irritated by the way he kept looking at her. The arrogant twinkle in those dark eyes, the cheeky grin on his face. Instead, she let her glance run over his muscled upper torso. He looked good. As always, she picked the hottest guys, with the right sexual appetite to keep up with her.

"What was your name again?"

"Nick. Nick Petrini."

"Italian?"

"Yep," he laughed.

She never understood why Italians would come to Sweden when they had sun, sea and delicious food.

"And you are...?"

"Why would you want to know?"

"I can't keep calling you sunshine," he said.

He was arrogant and had overstayed his welcome, but, somehow, she liked him.

"Isa Lindström," she said.

"Well, Isa Lindström, nice to meet you." He smiled and held out his hand.

She took it, but instead of shaking hands, he turned it over so the palm would face down, brought it to his lips and kissed it, first the fingers, then the rest of the hand, the inside of her forearm, moving his way up to her shoulder, after gently pulling down the silk robe and exposing her naked body. He went up to her ear and soon she felt his lips touching hers. The skin of his firm upper body muscles caressed her breasts. She took his head in her hands and continued to kiss him, his hands running down her spine. Nick Petrini knew how to seduce a woman. Before she knew it, she felt the cold wall of the kitchen against her back. His hands were now caressing the inside of her thighs, as his tongue made its way to her nipples. She let out a sigh of pure pleasure, completely surrendering to the moment, until the ringtone of her phone interrupted everything.

"Let it ring," he said.

"What time is it?"

"Nine or so," he answered.

She pushed him aside and searched her phone, while yelling, "Shit, shit, shit!"

The phone kept going. She finally found it on the floor near the hallway, hidden under her T-shirt.

"Really shit," she said when she saw who was calling her.

"Who is it?" he asked, barely recovering from the cold shower she had given him after the sensual make-out.

"The boss," she said.

"Why do you care about some gray-haired, almost retired guy?" he said disgruntled and walked up the stairs.

If Timo Paikkala only knew Nick referred to him as an old boring man!

"Yes," she answered the phone.

"Where are you?" the voice said.

"Uh... I overslept," she said, "what's up?"

She shook her head. Not the best way to talk to him.

"Get here as soon as possible! We need to talk to Gerard Forsberg."

"Why Gerard Forsberg?" she said, but he had hung up.

Timo wasn't the most patient man. When he had set his mind to it, things needed to be done, and he needed to see that they were being done.

Nick was looking at her. He had put on his shirt and trousers and stood in the kitchen, jacket in his hands.

"Sorry, I have to go," she said and put the phone on the table.

"Cop, spy, military or you must be one of the few female serial killers on this planet," he said in a serious voice.

"Uh... what?"

"I am trying to guess what you do," he answered, still with an innocent look on his face, "but I'll go for cop."

"How do you...?"

"I don't think it's such a great idea to leave your gun on the kitchen table. I could have been a murderer myself and killed you in your sleep."

She had that annoying habit of being careless with her service weapon.

"And the file next to it...," he continued.

She looked up in terror. The file was about...

"Who's Alex?"

"Nobody."

"His name is on the file, and you talk in your sleep. A lot."

Almost every night, she woke up knowing she had dreamt of him. By the time she got out of bed the details were usually gone, but it wasn't important. Just picturing that he was lying next to her was so pleasant. Last night, she had tried to imagine making love to him, but Nick was so different from Alex, she could hardly reconcile the two men in her head.

"Well, never mind," he said, put on his jacket, took out a small card from the pocket and placed it on the lower wall that formed a barrier between the kitchen and living room.

"I'll be in court for the rest of the day, but I'm free tonight. If you want to continue our special tête-á-tête, let me know."

As he walked out, he kissed her and gave her a flirty smile.

Court? She took the card and looked at it.

"Lawyer. That figures!"

* * *

Magnus opened the door. He hadn't expected to find anyone at home. Anna would be at school and Sophie had a new job, working as an event planner at a small family business in Gävle. When Sophie had told him, he had listened with a certain skepticism, but she seemed happy with the new direction her life had taken. He took the key from the lock. The edges scratched the skin of his hand. Sophie had asked him several times to return the key even though they were still officially man and wife, and the house was as much his as hers. But he had forgotten, and today that forgetfulness served him well. He had to retrieve some items from the house he had left behind when moving out.

He went straight to the laundry room at the back of the house. Baskets of dirty laundry were placed on the floor, and someone had dumped a pile of clothes on the drying rack. Only then he realized the entire house was in chaos. Dust swirled across the floor. In the corners, there were huge cobwebs, and the hallway smelled musty, as if the rooms hadn't been ventilated for weeks. In the kitchen, the dirty dishes were piling up in the sink, and next to the garbage bin there was a plastic bag filled with empty scotch bottles.

He couldn't believe that Sophie, always so meticulous and proud, had turned the house into a ruin. A few months ago, this had been a clean, cozy family home. Was this why she always visited him and avoided him coming to the house? How could he have misjudged her? He thought he was the only one unable to cope with Toby's situation.

And Anna? What kind of home was this for his daughter? A neglectful mother, a father... a murderer. Had he ever thought of the consequences?

There was a soft noise, the squeaks of someone walking across a wooden floor. He looked around, walked through the living room, stopped at the stairs, and listened carefully. It was silent again.

He waited a moment before going back to the laundry room. The washer, placed in the center against the outer wall, was covered with a pile of socks and underwear. He pulled it ten centimeters away from the wall and reached behind it. The wall wasn't plastered, the bricks still visible. For ten years it had been on his list to redecorate the room, paint it, rearrange everything and put nice cupboards in it, but it had remained a line on his list. The procrastinator in him had always found a reason to delay. Lucky for him he had. Behind the washing machine, the bricks at the lower end were loose. He carefully removed them and reached into the hole. It was a perfect hiding place, but he didn't find what he was looking for.

Where was it? How could it be gone?

While Magnus desperately tried to get his arm deeper into the hole, Anna, at home sick, was watching her dad from behind the doorjamb.

That day he had returned from Sandviken. Before picking up Isa from the hospital, he had stopped by his house. Anna had watched how he, all out-of-breath and jumpy, had put a package in the secret hiding place behind the washing machine. He had left the house again in a rush, unaware his daughter had watched the entire scene. It had piqued her curiosity, but when she found the blood-stained gloves and the phone wrapped in a dirty cloth, she knew it hadn't been right. Only gradually the full significance of what she had seen had dawned on her, in the months after the incident.

"Sophie," he said.

No, not mom! What would he do to mom? He wouldn't hurt her, would he?

But he had taken a life once, maybe he wouldn't hesitate to do it again. She had to do something. She couldn't lose her mom too. Toby, her family. All gone.

He got up, and she rushed to the adjoining room to hide.

There was a nagging feeling of being watched and he looked around to see if anyone was there. He walked to the front door, opened and closed it again without going outside. She stayed stock-still, watching from behind the hallway door.

She only left the shelter when she finally heard the engine of the car start and the car drive away, minutes later.

What was she supposed to do now?

*   *   *

Timo found Harald Müller in a cell of the police station. Mr. Müller had been a regular visitor the last years.

"This is how it usually goes: we pick him up twice, maybe three times a month, for disorderly conduct and public intoxication. He stays the night, sobers up, and he'll be gone by lunchtime. He just needs to cool down. Nothing to worry about." That was what the officer behind the counter had told Timo and Berger as he took the keys and escorted them to the cell block.

"And you found him screaming in front of the Forsberg mansion yesterday?"

"Yep. That's where he usually is."

Timo peered through the window at the shabby man, lying on the bed with his eyes closed. He looked like one of those people, old before his age, without a job, without family or friends, lost along the way when he had chosen the path of alcohol.

Probably not a day went by without him being drunk. Those regular visits to the police station were the only moments when the veil of intoxication was lifted, and he could think straight again. But it only took half an hour, maybe an hour at most, for the alcohol cravings to take over. Certainly not a man worth fighting for, but Timo wondered why this man, barely fifty, had wasted his life like that. Choices have reasons, as he always used to say. What was his reason? Linda?

"Tell me about Linda."

Harald opened his eyes and turned, making the metal frame of the bed squeak even more than before. Timo was standing in the corner and Berger was sitting in the only chair in the tiny room, looking at Harald as if he was the worst criminal ever.

"Who're you?" Harald said in his slurred speech, barely able to find the simplest words. The alcohol hadn't worn off yet. And perhaps it wasn't the best time to confront a drunk when he was still dawdling between the haziness of the intoxication and the glimpses of reality and the pain that came with it. The alcohol, the fighting, the screaming. It was a cry for help, a cry from a misunderstood man.

"I'm inspector Timo Paikkala, and this is inspector Berger Karlsson."

"Wadda ya want?"

"Tell us about Linda."

"You're bored or something? Or maybe you think I am some sort of entertainment, like most of your colleagues do? Go away and leave me alone!"

Harald turned his back to the men and closed his eyes.

"Yes, you're probably right. It's going to be a long day, and we clearly have nothing to do. On the other hand, we may be the only people who truly want to hear your story."

Harald got up, leaned against the cold wall and gave Timo a confused look, as if unsure where the conversation was going.

"Do you think something happened to Linda?" Timo said.

"How do you..."

"Why else the drinking? The shouting? The accusations?"

"Linda was wonderful. She was the love of my life. We were together for almost a year. We had plans to move in together until she just disappeared."

"Live together? Are you sure? From what I heard, Linda Forsberg was rather promiscuous. Not the woman to commit to one man."

A confused look on Harald's face appeared and then he suddenly said, "Yes, Gerard and Linda had an open marriage. He had lovers; she had lovers. Plenty."

"Gerard as well?"

"That's what she told me. He killed her. I know he did!"

"If they had an open marriage, why would he kill her?" Berger said.

"Jeez, I knew it. You're just like the lot of 'em!"

He shook his head and lowered his eyes.

Timo said, "I don't understand how a public figure like Forsberg could get away... even would consider killing his wife. The stakes are too high. You're not a stupid man. Tell me why you think something happened to her!"

Harald said with a defeated look on his face, "That day I received a text from her saying that she had made a mistake, that I should go on without her. She needed time and space. She had to disappear for a while. It was the last message I got from her. But she didn't write it. I know she didn't. She would never have signed it with Linda."

"How then?"

"Linlin." He smiled. "That's what I called her."

"And then?"

"I confronted Gerard. He told me she had left the night before. She had sent him a short text message explaining her departure. Fallen in love with yet another man, she wanted to start a new life."

"But she had never left Gerard before?"

"Never."

Harald buried his head in his hands.

"And did her husband say anything else?"

He wiped a tear from his face. "He told me she had sent a few messages to him and the children. He was disappointed, but he didn't think anything was wrong."

"Did you actually see the messages?"

"No. And the police haven't seen them either."

"The police?"

He gave Timo a sarcastic grin. "The police had one conversation with her family after I begged them to look into the case, and that was it."

"So, what do you want us to do?"

Harald leaned back, stared at the wall in front of him and then said, "You could talk to Patrik Mikaelsson."

"We have."

"So, you know," Harald said.

"Why was she upset? Why did she visit Mr. Mikaelsson?"

"Can't you just... leave me alone? I have a headache."

"Why was she upset?"

"How would I know? Patrik said she went to see him, and they had a weird conversation about an accident that happened in the past."

Timo didn't react and walked up to the man.

"Mr. Müller, is there anything else you can remember?"

The man ran his hands through his hair and shook his head.

With a slight nod of the head and a worried expression on his face, Timo left the cell, with Berger walking behind him.

"We're looking at a second murder," Timo said.

CHAPTER

17

GERARD FORSBERG, SITTING in the impressive living room of his lakeside villa, sighed and took a deep breath before answering. That morning he found two inspectors on the doorstep who wanted to talk about Marie, and he knew he could no longer keep it a secret.

"I met Marie in September last year at a party hosted by my son. It's usually not my cup of tea. I've always been skeptical about these things. But Lise insisted. It was love at first sight. I had never seen such a beautiful woman before, but I knew it couldn't be. I'm fifty and she was twenty-two. Strangely enough, we started talking, and it was so liberating, fun. She really understood me. And that same evening we agreed to see each other again."

"And?"

"The week after, we kissed and had sex. She was a very sexual person, but for me it was more than that. I loved her. I even proposed to her. I didn't care how it would look to the outside world. Linda was gone, and I just wanted to take care of her and spend my life with her. But..."

"But?"

"She told me straight she wasn't looking for a man. She didn't want a husband, just someone to have fun with. And she ended the relationship a week before she went missing."

"That must have been painful," Berger said.

"It was. After Linda, being rejected a second time was devastating, but I didn't kill her if that's what you think."

"Marie was an escort girl. That's what your son said. Did you know?"

"Escort girl? That makes no sense!"

He rubbed his hands through his hair. Was everything a lie?

"You think she was hired by someone?" Gerard said.

"What do you think? A thirty-year age difference, a millionaire and a college student with a modest or, let's say, no income. I think you've been played. Any idea who'd do this to you?"

It made no sense. Why would she break off the relationship? If she was after his money, she'd stay with him. It couldn't be true.

"Did you know she was pregnant?"

Gerard shook his head. That was the hardest part. A baby. Their baby.

"Your son confessed he was the father," Timo said calmly. "Why would he do that?"

"He did? I never asked him to do that."

"Did your children know about the relationship?"

"No," Gerard said, confused.

"But Henrik knew, and Marie turned to him. She wanted to end the pregnancy, but according to Henrik, he talked her out of it."

He didn't know what to say. Marie had told Henrik, but he didn't know they were that close. If this was a setup, why hadn't she come to him? Why had she played it through Henrik?

"Not the first time a wife or girlfriend disappears, isn't it?" Timo said. "What really happened to Linda?"

"My wife left me," Gerard said, but the calmness was just an appearance. His fingers penetrated deeper into the fabric of the gray armchair he'd been sitting in since the start of the interview. Deeper and deeper as Timo had talked about Marie and now Linda. This time Mr. Forsberg couldn't contain the anguish and disappointment he had felt over his wife's departure.

"Your wife's way of life: an open marriage, the lovers. You said you approved, but in reality, you didn't. The humiliation, the shame. You couldn't bear it, and her relationship with Müller was the last drop. You killed her."

"I challenge you to prove it," Gerard said. "But I don't think you will. I'll come after you with everything I've got. I'm paying my lawyers a lot. That's why they're so good, and you'll have no chance with this flimsy story."

"Is that a threat?" Timo said.

A sarcastic grin appeared on Gerard's lips.

"You know where the door is," he said and turned his head away from them to look at the lake. Marie. They were wrong about her. She had loved him. It might have started as an assignment, but ultimately, she hadn't gone through with it. She had protected him by ending the relationship.

He would have taken care of her. He remembered her touch, the sound of her voice, the smell of her skin as she lay beside him and ran her hand over his bare chest. He had never felt so alive. This was more than sexual attraction. It was love. How could anyone say he had killed that beautiful creature?

He let his hand run over his face before he broke down and let everything out. The pain, the frustration. He fell to the floor, the wooden floor of the house he had built with the money and success he had gained over the years. But what did it matter if he couldn't share it with the woman he loved?

Outside, Timo and Berger walked to the car. Timo was in doubt. Had this man killed his wife? Gerard had the motive, the opportunity, but it wasn't the entire story. And Marie? It made no sense. Why would he hold her captive for two months to eventually kill her?

The ringtone of Timo's phone disturbed the peace.

"I have to take this."

With the phone to his ear, he picked up the pace, while Berger quietly observed him.

"Okay, keep me posted," Timo said and ended the conversation.

"Something wrong?"

"Yes. Nina Kowalczyk was brought to the hospital in Uppsala. She's in a coma. Brain injury."

"Nina? What happened to her?"

"They think it's an accident. She slipped and hit her head."

"At home?"

"No, in the lab."

He vaguely remembered hearing Berger say, "My God", but his mind was already processing the new information and he quickly came to another conclusion. If his suspicions were true, the situation was escalating, and other people were in danger. Isa.

"Berger, I've planned another visit today, to Ilan Bergman, the guy from the car. Can you handle it? Take Magnus, if you can find him."

"Sure, but...," Berger said, but Timo had already run off to the car.

* * *

"It's time."

The cold metallic voice crackled through the phone. When he heard it, his stomach turned. Was it the stress, the constant pressure of not knowing what could happen? Ilan hadn't slept in days. The voice sounded so other-worldly, as if he were talking to an alien or a ghost.

"You work at Global Law," the voice over the phone said.

"Yes." Ilan could hardly push that word out of his mouth. Breathing was hard. He recognized the panic attack, lurking in the background. Then he looked around. There was no one in the cubicle.

"You can only enter their offices by invitation or if you know the access code that changes every month."

"Uh... yes."

"From now on, you'll provide me the code every month until I say it's no longer needed."

"I can't just..."

"It's not up for debate. Do it! Remember, I know everything about you. I have your car. And I know where to find you... and your wife."

Those last words resonated even more. It wasn't just him anymore. His wife was in danger. What had he done? There was no way out. None.

"When?"

"In a week."

"Okay."

"And if I were you, I'd get myself a lawyer."

"W... what? Why?"

"Mr. Bergman, Mr. Ilan Bergman," the voice said.

With the phone still in his hand, he gave his office chair a twist, so that he was facing the person standing behind him. He didn't recognize the two men.

"Yes," he said.

"Inspector Berger Karlsson, police Gävle," the bearded man said and showed his badge, "we want to ask you some questions about a hit-and-run, and a homicide."

"Good luck," the voice said, then disconnected.

Ilan was rooted to the spot, the phone still tightly squeezed in his hand. How did the voice know? Was his stalker watching him? Where? How?

"Mr. Bergman?"

"Yeah... okay."

"Can we talk somewhere more private?"

"There is a conference room nearby," Ilan said, leading them to a small room across the hall.

The room, without windows, cream-colored walls, was just enough to host a party of five, maybe six people. As he closed the door, Berger immediately asked him, "You own a dark-blue Peugeot 308?"

"Ye... Yes," he said, "but it was..."

"Stolen," Berger said, "yes, we've read the report of the Uppsala police."

Uppsala? This couldn't be right. He had reported the car missing in Sandviken after Frank's murder.

"About three weeks ago, the night before Marie Lång was found dead."

Three weeks ago? What was going on?

"Who is Marie Lång?" Ilan stammered.

"The twenty-two-year-old woman who was found dead in the lake near Stromsbrö. So, it wasn't you driving the car that was seen on the traffic camera a few blocks away from the area where she was found?"

Ilan shook his head. "No, no!"

"What were you doing in Uppsala the day of the car theft?" Berger asked.

"It was a Global Law party to celebrate the new contract."

He still didn't know what story to link to the disappearance of the car.

223

Think!

"And when did you notice the car was gone?"

The palms of his hands started to sweat, and the blood flow pounding in his head sparked the start of a headache.

Breathe!

"What... sorry, can you repeat?" He had to gain time, get his story straight.

"Mr. Bergman, when did you notice the car was gone?"

"Um... when I came back from the party."

"And that was?"

"10:00 p.m. or so."

"Strange, you waited four hours to report it to the police?"

"I... I must have been mistaken. It was probably after midnight. Yes, that was it."

In his desperate attempt to make sense of it, Ilan tried to gain time. Nothing made sense. He had reported the car missing one week later, in the local police office in Sandviken.

The voice. His mysterious blackmailer. Could he have arranged all of that? If that were true, the extent of his influence and power was larger than he had anticipated. This was more than a petty criminal; this went far beyond what he could imagine.

"You are not too sure about that," Berger said.

The arched eyebrow and the ironic smirk on the police officer's face were signs of doubt about Ilan's sincerity.

"No, I am, I am," Ilan said.

This wasn't going well. He needed to get his exploding anxiety under control.

"Do you know Frank Harket?" Lars said.

"Frank who... no, I don't," he said.

Oh, hell, they know. Why don't you just tell them?

"Really? That is strange. We found your fingerprints and DNA in the studio where he was found dead. Murdered. Care to tell us how your fingerprints got there?"

He had been so careful. What else had he overlooked?

"I think I'd like to speak to a lawyer now," he said.

"Then I'll ask you to come with us to the police station."

* * *

Time to bring in the expert. Ilan had called his wife and asked her to contact one of his colleagues. Once over the shock of realizing that her husband was in trouble again, she had asked the first person on her mind to help him. If it were such a great idea, only time would tell.

Ilan had waited more than three hours before his lawyer finally showed up. In the interrogation room, Berger had taken the seat next to Isa. After the false start of the day, she had decided to do something useful, making up for lost time, but the caffeine had not been enough to keep her alert. She struggled to keep her eyes open, much to the dismay of her colleague.

Berger and Isa had never been best friends. When she had been his boss, he had a hard time controlling his endless frustrations with her investigation style. They had conflicted over everything. Whenever Berger said yes, Isa had to say no.

When 'Mr. Lawyer' joined them in the interview room, she was staring into nothingness, not really aware of what was going on around her.

"Okay, let's make this short," the voice said when he opened the door.

Oh, good God!

She recognized him, before he even had set one foot in the room.

"My name is Nicolas Petrini and I...".

He gasped for air when he saw her looking at him, mouth half open, about to say something but not knowing what. It took only one second, before he continued in the same arrogant tone, overtaking most of the people in the room, "... and I'll represent Mr. Bergman."

He took the only seat left at the table, facing the woman he had spent the night with. His overly confident attitude and the smug little smile on his face irritated her beyond measure.

"Has Mr. Bergman been arrested?" he asked and put the briefcase on the floor.

"No, but your client voluntarily accepted going to the police station to answer questions related to Frank Harket's murder," Berger said.

"Is he a suspect?"

"Yes, and we have conveyed this to Mr. Bergman."

"Why?"

"His fingerprints and DNA were found at the crime scene."

"On the murder weapon?" Nick asked.

"No. The murder weapon hasn't been found."

"Exactly. There is no evidence directly linking my client to the murder. His prints were found, as were those of a dozen other people. It only shows that my client and the victim had a business relationship."

"And plenty of other illegal activities," Berger added.

"Do you have proof my client was involved in these activities?"

Berger sighed.

"I didn't think so," Nick turned to Isa and smiled, haughtier than before, with a cruel pleasure that only the two of them knew.

"Your client didn't seem to remember knowing the man," Berger remarked, interrupting the strange moment between Isa and Nick.

"Given his history with the police, he felt pressured. He couldn't think straight. They weren't exactly on a first name basis, but my client admits knowing Mr. Harket."

Nick rolled his tongue and gave them a last smile.

"So, if there's nothing more, I suggest we stop the interview here,"

Nick finally said, looked at Ilan, and signaled him to get up.

"Nice day to both of you, inspectors!"

And with those words he left the room, followed by his client.

She sighed. The back of the chair creaked as she leaned back and gave Berger a look that was supposed to make it clear that he shouldn't interfere. He had felt the tension between them. How was she going to explain this? She could already hear Timo's lecture in her head.

* * *

"Thanks, Nick," Ilan said when they were back in the hallway.

"Don't thank me yet," Nick said, "wait till you see my bill."

He looked at his watch, ignoring the man standing next to him. "I'll take a look at your file. We can discuss it in one of the coming days when I'm back in the office."

"You have to believe me," Ilan stammered, "I have nothing to do with this."

"I believe you," Nick said. "But that doesn't matter. The people in that room must believe you, and you didn't make a very good first impression. How could you not know when your car was stolen? And you're hiding something."

Ilan shook his head a little too vigorously to make it seem believable.

"Don't forget I was there," Nick said. "I was at the party, and I left at the same time you did. It was around 11:00 p.m. and the car was still there."

"I... I..."

Nick grinned. "Oh, God! Where you with a woman when the car got stolen? I won't tell your adorable wife."

"Uh... yeah, that was it."

Nick's smile seemed to widen, and his eyes sparkled. "Maybe it won't get that far, but I'll need her name. Think about it."

"Okay," Ilan said.

Then Nick turned his attention to the woman who had just left the interrogation room. "And now if you'll excuse me, I have a few more questions to ask the nice inspector," he said and left Ilan alone in the hallway.

Dazed and confused, as his lawyer's words raced through his mind, Ilan trudged toward the exit and disappeared.

"So, we meet again, inspector Lindström." Nick couldn't pass up the chance to talk to her.

She pulled Nick aside. "What is this?"

"Well, I was doing my job."

"But..."

"Poor man, though," he mused.

"Why?"

"He doesn't know it yet, but I'm sleeping with his wife."

"Of course," she let out.

He looked at her and smiled, the same grin as when he had entered the interview room.

"What?" she said.

Seeing her become more agitated made him even more determined to continue the game. He came closer, and she pulled back, but she couldn't stop looking at him.

He whispered, "If you want, I'll stop sleeping with her... so you can have me all to yourself."

"Don't let me restrict you in your... activities!"

He smiled and said, "Tonight at eight?"

"That won't happen," she replied, "you're Ilan Bergman's lawyer."

"Sorry to interrupt your interesting conversation, but can I have a word with my inspector?" Timo's voice sounded.

She jumped up.

"What is this?" Timo asked. "He's counseling a suspect."

"I... I didn't know, I swear," she stammered, "I only found out just now."

He sighed and crossed his arms. Out of the corner of his eye, he saw how Nick Petrini was still looking at them, with that overly confident attitude that seemed to be his standard demeanor.

"What am I to do with you?"

"Look, Timo, I know what you're thinking," she said, calmer than she was a few minutes ago, "but I will be professional about this."

"Fine, but don't let me regret it."

He took a deep breath. "Have you seen Magnus today in the few hours you've been here?"

"No, the last time I saw him was yesterday. What's wrong?"

"Nothing, I just need to talk to him," he said. "His wife Sophie, where does she work?"

"She used to work in the city library, but now I think she works as an event planner. They have an office in the center of the city."

"Okay, I'll find it," he answered curtly and ran off direction his office but was stopped by Lars.

She didn't know what to make of it. She still couldn't figure out what he was hiding from her.

"Don't forget, tonight 8:00 p.m.," Nick said and smiled.

"No, Mr. Petrini, we're not going to do that!"

"Well, I see I have competition, but I'm up for the challenge," he laughed and pointed at Timo.

"Uh, what? No! No, no, we just can't."

"Let's see," he said, grabbed his briefcase and waved at her before turning and walking with a steady pace toward the exit.

Timo turned around and said, "Lindström, you're with me!"

"What's wrong?"

"Teresa Ljungman is missing."

CHAPTER

18

THE DOGS WERE BARKING IN THE BACKGROUND. The last sunrays were shining through the foliage, slowly receding as the sun disappeared behind the horizon. Soon darkness would creep over the forest. Timo looked at it with a certain melancholy. Any other moment, he would have taken the time to let it all sink in, but not now. They had a job to do. They had to find Teresa.

He spread the map on the hood of the car that was still warm from the drive to the forest lane where now more than half of the police department was standing. His team of senior inspectors had gathered around him. Only Magnus hadn't turned up.

He ran his finger along one of the straight lines in the center of the detail map.

"The cell towers over here picked up the signal of her mobile phone until an hour ago, when the signal went dead. We don't know if she's still in the forest, but we can't exclude anything. I want two teams, one going east, another west, starting here, where her car was found."

Isa sighed. "It's a huge area to cover."

"Witnesses say the car has been here for a few days," Lars said. "Maybe she's no longer here."

The car on the side of the road, a black BMW, was distracting. A policewoman was marking the area with yellow and black tape and gave them an indifferent glance when she saw the entire team staring at her.

Timo gave Lars his 'so what' face and then said, "We need to be fast; it'll be dark in a few hours."

A young man in a coverall approached them. "There's blood on the driver's seat."

With a slight disappointment, Timo looked at the man. No Dr. Olsson this time.

"And on the passenger seat," the forensic investigator said.

"Two people? She wasn't alone."

"Hard to say. I'll need to test the blood samples, but I believe there was someone else in the car. The seat belt is torn."

"Jussi Vinter," Isa said.

"Why?"

"Come on, Timo. Are you blind? They're a couple."

He should have known. Teresa had been so adamant to make Jussi look bad.

"And have we found Henrik Forsberg yet?" he said and turned to Lars.

Lars shook his head. "No. His phone is switched off. His father doesn't know where he is."

"So he says," Timo said, "Gerard is protecting his son."

"Henrik hasn't been on the grid for days."

"He was the last person Teresa called, and after that his phone was switched off," Isa said.

Lars looked back at the car. "He doesn't want to be found."

"But that's not the case for Teresa. Whoever took her wants us to find her. Otherwise why wouldn't he have switched off the phone?"

Isa sighed. "So she's dead?"

A voice, out of breath, interrupted the briefing. "Sorry I am late."

"Inspector Wieland, how nice of you to join us," Timo said.

Magnus heaved an exasperated sigh.

"And what if she's actually not here?" Berger said. "What if someone took her somewhere else and this is just a decoy?"

"Sivert is checking the traffic cameras," Timo said, "we should know pretty soon."

"Okay, let's move."

The group broke up and while Lars and Berger joined the search for Teresa, Isa needed a moment from Timo.

"Were we so wrong about Henrik Forsberg?" she said. "We should have arrested him then and there."

"On the basis of what? He saw Marie that day, but no evidence that he effectively took or killed her. And why would he target Teresa?"

"Because she knows something," Isa hissed.

What was wrong with him? He wasn't as sharp as usual. For some time now, he was pre-occupied. Was it her? Did she do something wrong? Maybe he was still out to get her fired.

"They're not here," Isa sighed. "He took her somewhere else."

"But he wants us to be here. He knows we'll trace her phone. Why?"

"I don't know. But why aren't you expanding the search to other areas?"

He sighed. "The other teams are swiping his apartment and the Forsberg's home. There's nothing more we can do right now. But you're right. We should have known. Teresa knew something and now she may be dead."

"You can't blame yourself," she whispered, running her hand over his arm as a sign of compassion.

It was refreshing to see a glimpse of his sensitive side. The cracks in his immeasurable confidence suddenly made him a lot more approachable, even though he regretted not being on his guard in that moment of weakness.

* * *

Magnus watched Isa and Timo from afar.

Why were they whispering? Why did she touch his arm? There was something going on between them. He knew it.

Another rival he had to get rid of. Couldn't she just stop being too much Isa? Men were drawn to her like bees to a pot of honey.

"And Magnus, you and I should have a chat."

Magnus jumped up. Lost in thought, he hadn't noticed the boss was suddenly standing next to him.

"About what?"

In his most Timo Paikkala-like manner he gave him a mysterious yet arrogant grin, stared at him for a few seconds too long and then walked away. Could it have been more dramatic? But Timo didn't know he had moved to the top spot on Magnus' blacklist.

He knows too much. Paikkala has to go!

He could get rid of him, like he had done before. But this time, he would plan it a lot better.

* * *

It had been a matter of minutes before the sun had completely disappeared behind the trees. And with the darkness, an icy wind rose. Everywhere, Magnus saw flashlights appearing. In the background he heard the barking of the dogs. He was shivering, but not just from the cold. As always, unnerving sounds were coming from the woods. Like in his scouting years, forests were great during daytime, to hike, to play, to hide, but at night it was a different ball game. It was like there was a madman lurking behind every tree, about to jump in front of him and slash his throat with a knife. Too many horror stories by the campfire.

He stopped, held up the flashlight, and scanned the area. This was pointless. Even if Teresa were still here, they wouldn't find her. It was too dark. A few weeks later and the midnight sun would have given them a lot more time to find her.

"Teresa, Teresa," he shouted.

He recognized the man to his left. Berger.

"She's not here," Magnus said.

"At least, we should try," Berger said.

"We've been looking for hours. If Teresa was still here, we'd have found her by now."

"What do you think has happened to her?" Berger said.

"He took her elsewhere and killed her. We are days too late."

"But Timo thinks...," Berger interrupted.

"Paikkala is wrong. Clearly a lapse in judgement."

"He's keeping all routes open."

Magnus ignored him and continued to spill his slander about Timo. "What do we know about him, anyway? Maybe he was a gigantic failure in Stockholm and that's why they sent him here."

"Perhaps you should concentrate on finding Teresa," Berger said and frowned.

"I heard he came here to clean up the department. Meaning: fire us! Pretty much what he did in Stockholm. Many people complained about him."

"Is that what you heard? Strange. That's not the message I got."

"I see he has wrapped you around his finger," Magnus said.

"It's not like you've been the perfect partner. Where have you been anyway these last days?"

"None of your business!"

Magnus raised the collar of his coat and increased the pace, leaving his companion behind.

"Charming as ever," he heard Berger say.

Ten meters in front of him, he heard Isa walking. The nightly journey turned out to be a bigger challenge than planned. Not only were they unfamiliar with the area, the trail was challenging, covered in rocks and branches.

"Hey, Issie, let me help you," Magnus said and pulled a branch away from her so she could step through.

"Thanks. Jesus, I can't see a thing. This is useless. We won't find anything or anyone."

"My point exactly," Magnus said.

She stopped and turned to him. "Be careful! Don't mess with Timo! He won't hesitate to suspend you. I don't think he likes you."

Magnus let out a whiff of sarcasm and said, "I'm not too worried. The man is bluffing."

"And where have you been? You can't just disappear like that. Is something wrong with Toby?"

"Toby is okay."

"Then what is it? The voices?"

The voices. The hallucinations. They were back. In fact, they had never gone away.

"I'm tired," he said and let his hands run over his face. "Maybe I just need another job. With Toby in the hospital, the apartment in Uppsala and having Anna to take care of every other week. It's just too much."

"Maybe you don't need another job. Maybe you just need some time off."

"Vacation? Yeah, that sounds good. Get away from all of this. And maybe you can come with me?"

She was right. Perhaps they needed some time away from Gävle and his serial killer. Forget about Alex and Toby. Revive the passion.

"Oh, have you heard about Nina?" she said.

"What about her?"

"She had a serious accident. She slipped and hit her head. She's in a coma. I never thought I'd say this, but I feel sorry for her."

She's still alive? But there was no pulse. Idiot!

How could he have made that mistake again? He should have finished her off. He couldn't be that lucky, twice.

"What's the prognosis?"

"It doesn't look good," Isa said, "and even if she wakes up, they think there is massive brain damage. So, she might be a plant."

Perfect.

"Too bad. She was a good person," Magnus said.

And a too good investigator, who shouldn't have poked her nose in things that didn't concern her!

Suddenly they heard fast footsteps behind them. Magnus turned around and pointed the flashlight directly in the eyes of the man who had been so eager to overtake them. The beam of the light blinded him temporarily, and with the hands still covering his eyes, Timo said, "Lindström, Wieland, we need to go. They found something."

* * *

The face was contorted, white, with a blue hue. Leaves and raindrops had stained the body that lay against the tree. The twig pressed between the lips made it look like a farce, something unreal.

Timo had been staring at it for minutes.

"Are you okay?" Isa had quietly inquired when she hadn't seen him move a muscle during the entire time. He was good at playing statue. Motionless, almost carved in stone, just like the corpse. She wondered what was going through his mind.

"Yes," he said.

"It's not your fault, you know," she whispered, opening the jacket the young man had been wearing to expose the wound in the chest.

"I... we should have known they were in danger."

"Timo, you can't carry the pain and trouble of the entire world."

"Lindström, don't make a drama out of this. Let's do our job!"

She looked at the body again. Not what they expected.

"He's been shot. Two entry wounds, as it looks like. And there are bruises and scratches on his forehead."

"Henrik Forsberg," a voice said. "This puts our theory on shaky ground."

Isa turned around and saw Magnus walking toward them.

"Henrik Forsberg is the victim, not the culprit," Magnus said.

"I can see that," Timo said.

"Guys, Teresa Ljungman is still missing," Isa said.

"But she was here."

In the glow of the flashlight, there was trampled ground, as if someone had been dragged several meters over the ground. Timo stopped at the start of the trail and knelt down.

"She was hurt," Timo said and pointed at the bloodstains on the rocks the rain hadn't washed away.

Isa sighed. "Or maybe dead?"

"Perhaps," he said, got up and continued his way, following the path.

"The path ends here." Isa let the light cone run over the tree roots and the sprouting weeds. In the distance, the dogs were still trying to find a trace of the young woman.

"It's too dark," she said. "We should stop and try again tomorrow."

Isa closed her jacket. The rain had stopped, but it was a lot colder than it was a few hours ago when they had been walking around in the other part of the forest. She closed her eyes. Where would a killer take his victim? Why put Henrik Forsberg on display and not Teresa Ljungman? Why those two people?

Magnus was right. They were basically walking blind. In broad daylight this would be a pleasant walk. The path was clean and easy up to the rocks, but beyond that point there was no well-defined trail anymore. She aimed the flashlight at the ground. Tree roots, mud, grass, moss. The rocks were too steep to climb over, forming almost a wall preventing them from moving to the left or straight ahead.

"Teresa," she heard Timo yell.

Magnus was right behind them. He had followed them in silence. And his anxiety and anger had grown by the minute. Why were they always together? They were having sex. Isa had betrayed him with another loser. When would she learn?

On autopilot, with his head not quite on the job, Magnus let the flashlight beam glide over the bushes and rocks. Suddenly he saw an object on the ground, among the leaves and grass, close to the fallen trees, glistening in the light of the torch. Isa and Timo, still unaware of the find, were walking away from him.

Teresa's phone. It had died hours ago. Magnus shifted the beam of the flashlight to the trees next to it.

Timo said, "What's wrong, inspector Wieland?"

Magnus quickly turned around. "I found her phone."

He pointed to the object on the ground, took a plastic bag from his pocket and put the phone in it.

"I think there's something behind the trees," Magnus whispered.

"What?"

"See for yourself," Magnus said and stepped aside.

"This is the only way she could have gone," Timo said, placed his right foot on the bottom trunk, and jumped over.

"Timo, wait," Isa shouted.

The next moment they heard him scream.

And as Timo felt the ground slip from beneath him, he tried to grab every branch and rock on his way to stop the increasing speed at which he rolled down. He didn't know where it would end. The sharp edges of the rocks were scratching and bruising his ribs. The ride down continued until his feet hit something hard.

"Timo, Timo!"

He took a few seconds to catch his breath.

Where was he?

The flashlight was gone. The mud on his hands soiled the painful scratches he'd sustained in his desperate attempt to keep himself from falling. His vision was blurry. He tried to move his foot along what he thought was a rock.

A ledge. Just wide enough to put the tip of his feet. It was good. He was stable, but he knew he had little room to move.

With his chest pressed against the sloped hill, he looked up and saw the faint beam of Isa's flashlight pointing in his direction, with Magnus next to her.

And then he realized it was no longer dark. The sky above him already bathed in the sunrise glow. Shades of red and orange. With each passing moment, he saw the surrounding air grew brighter, until the haze of the night was gone. In the background, he heard the forest come to life.

"Timo, are you alright?"

The sight of the early sun was breathtaking. In that moment he felt so insignificant, as if time stood still, and he forgot why he was there and what dangerous position he was in.

"Timo?"

"I'm fine," he said.

A surge of pain went through his body as he moved his hands along the sharp edges of the rocks. The breathing was painful but manageable, with every gust of air moving the ribcage, bruised by the fall.

"What's that?" he heard Isa say.

"What?"

"Behind you."

He turned his head and glanced down. On one of the lower rocky plateaus, a few meters below him, lay a weird shape.

Everything in his body ached. He looked at his hands. Mud mixed with blood smears. The muscles in his legs were trembling. He couldn't hold on much longer. The only way was down.

He took a deep breath. This should be easy for a mountaineer like him. A hobby he had neglected in recent years.

If he only hadn't been so tired!

He moved his legs and as he slowly descended the cliff, his mind wandered off to Teresa and Henrik. This didn't look good.

When he finally reached the lower plateau, he got a better view of the object. And as he got closer, he could clearly see that it looked like a body.

"What is it?" Isa yelled.

The screeching sound of an owl echoed through the air.

"Timo?"

"It's Teresa," Timo said.

The body lay face down and arms stretched, like she had been thrown down the cliff. He turned and saw the bloodstains on the stones, diluted by the rain and dew. Then he looked over the edge. It was steeply downhill. Through the branches he saw a glimpse of the river below, and he heard the roaring sound of the water cutting its way through the forest landscape. In the background, the lake where Marie was found. What was the killer telling them?

CHAPTER

19

TIMO SLID HIS HAND OVER HIS CHEST. It had been a hell of a night and morning, and he had barely slept. Hours in a hospital room which had been useless. Apart from the bruises and scratches there was nothing wrong with him, but the doctor had insisted on giving him a thorough check-up.

He looked at the picture pinned to the cover of the file.

What a failure! Teresa and Henrik. Dead. The search team was still scanning the area, but so far without results. The killer had hardly left any clues.

Everything was slipping away from him. Maybe he wasn't that great, maybe he just didn't know what he was doing. Such an imposter!

But that morning when he had stumbled into the office, after his unforeseen climbing trip, Berger had joined him with a cup of steamy black coffee and had put it right in front of him with the words, "You deserve it." He had seen Lars passing by, saying, "We'll catch him, boss." At least something positive had come out of this.

He reached for his phone. There was one more thing he had to deal with before he could turn his attention back on the case. As he heard it ringing, he scrolled down and opened the personal file of Magnus Wieland. The nightly trip had opened his eyes. The man was dangerous.

"Finn Heimersson," a deep voice said.

Finn and Timo went back a long way. By chance, their different worlds had collided. He, the son of a wealthy diplomat, Finn, the son of a simple workman who had struggled his whole life to provide for his family. Timo had been fifteen. In his attempt to feel normal and plain, his father had taken them on a bike tour of Uppsala, much to his brother's dismay. And as usual there had been drama when his brother, clumsy and not used to doing any physical exertion, had run his bike into a ditch. With a painful knee—though it looked more like a few superficial scratches—and a twisted bike frame they had rang the doorbell of a neighboring house. And from there it all got started.

He got on well with Finn. Unlike the strained relationship with his brother that was rooted in competition and jealousy, it was an uncomplicated friendship.

Though, the friendship with Finn wasn't that close anymore. They had gone their separate ways, as life demanded. Yet, whenever he was in Uppsala, or whenever Finn came to Stockholm, he had made time to hit the pub and talk about the good old days.

"So, what do you think of Gävle?"

"Not bad," Timo said.

"It seems the commissioner was a little upset about your particular decisions."

"Oh, I see, news travels fast," Timo grinned. Immediately he felt a painful splash shimmer through his body. Laughing and sneezing would be out of the question today.

"Timo, be careful. These vultures are after blood. You know that. You still have some credit with them, but that can change quickly."

"Noted. Thanks for your concern. Now, something else, the reason I wanted to talk to you is Nina Kowalczyk."

"Why?"

"Well, she was part of the team. People are concerned."

"Most of them hated her," Finn said.

Hate was maybe the wrong word, but Timo had also sensed a forced concern from Berger and Lars, a polite inquiry about her situation, detached, but no genuine compassion.

"So, she slipped and hit her head?"

"It looks like it."

"And there was no sign of foul play?" Timo asked.

"As far as we know. The investigation is still ongoing, but it appears it was an unfortunate accident."

"No indication that someone else was with her?"

"Unfortunately, there are no cameras anywhere in that building, so we can't be a hundred percent sure. Why? Do you think it could be something other than an accident?"

Timo sighed and said, "No, not really... how is Ms. Kowalczyk doing?"

"Still in a coma. The pressure on the brain has been reduced, but she's not out of the woods yet. And even if she survives, it's uncertain how much brain damage she sustained."

"Tragic!"

"Yes."

"One last question: what was Ms. Kowalczyk working on?" Timo said.

"No particular case, from what I understood. It was an R&D project, but what was strange, though, is that she accessed the police database about an hour before we believe the accident happened."

"What did she access?" Timo straightened his back and leaned forward, pulling the phone closer to his ear.

"A file related to Mats Norman."

"Interesting. Which file?"

"Phone records of Alex Nordin. Do you think it's important?"

Nina knew something was wrong, and it wasn't just the missing evidence of the footprints. Why the phone records? He opened the drawer and took out the pile of papers lying on top.

"Timo?"

"Uh... no, nothing that I can think of," he said, "thank you anyway for your time and keep me posted on Ms. Kowalczyk's progress."

With those words he said goodbye and started to flip through the pages. The printout of the call listing was inserted at the end of the file. The top line showed the last call was made to Isa's phone. And in the days before his death, Alex had mostly talked to his mother and psychiatrist Dr. Wikholm.

Timo leaned back. Why had Nina been interested in this list? She knew, or at least suspected something. Had someone tampered with the document?

He checked the electronic version in the database, and it matched the hard copy. But the name of the person who had entered it into the system caught his eye.

"Magnus," he whispered.

He had still hoped to be wrong about him, that Magnus hadn't been involved, that Nina's coma was the result of an unfortunate accident, but the coincidences were piling up.

He took the paper and walked to the front desk.

"Constable, I'd like you to contact the mobile carrier and ask them to send me the information regarding Alexander Nordin's phone records. If there is a problem, they can contact me." Timo gave the paper to the female police officer at the counter.

"Yes, sir," she replied.

"Where is inspector Wieland?"

"As far as I know, he hasn't come in," she said.

He looked at his watch. It was almost 3:00 p.m. He had disappeared after they had found Teresa's body. Was Magnus doing a runner?

"Maybe he joined the forensics team," she continued.

"And any news about the search in the forest?"

"No, no news, sir."

He kept staring ahead.

"Sir? Shall I call inspector Wieland?"

He shook his head. Even if they found Magnus, he still didn't know what to do. Other than giving a reprimand, there wasn't much he could do. He had no evidence, just suspicions.

* * *

Isa yawned. Three times in less than a minute.

"Can you stop doing that?" Ingrid said.

The friends were sitting at a table in their favorite pub.

"Give me a break! I've been awake for almost forty-eight hours. If Paikkala hadn't decided to fall off a cliff, at least I would have gotten a few hours of sleep."

"Is he alright?"

Isa leaned backward and gave her an inquiring look.

"You really like him."

Ingrid shrugged.

"Come on, Ingrid, you're behaving like an idiot around him."

It was meant as a kind and playful comment, but Ingrid looked serious. This wasn't just casual time between friends. Ingrid needed to get something off her chest. And as always, Isa had been insensitive to the subtle clues her best friend had sent out.

Ingrid turned the cup of tea on the saucer before she said, "Do you ever wonder if you've made the right choice?"

"About what?"

"Life. Love. At what point did you realize Viktor wasn't the right man for you?"

"Ingrid, seriously! Is it that bad? Are you and Anton having problems?"

"This is just between you and me: I think I'm in trouble."

"How?"

"I think I've..."

Fallen in love with Timo, and I don't know what to do.

She shook her head. Ingrid couldn't say the words out loud. If she admitted it to anyone, it would become real. She could still turn this around. She had to. For Anton, for her boys Kjell and Benno, for herself.

"Never mind," Ingrid mumbled, but the tears were welling in her eyes. Tears of frustration, helplessness, and happiness. The thought of Timo made her happy. That was why it was so confusing.

"Hey, you can tell me," Isa said and took her hand.

"Thanks, but it's nothing. Yes, I like him. I think he's good for the team."

"Hey, you wanted to talk to me," Isa tried to voice her friend's thoughts, "something's bothering you."

Ingrid quickly looked at her watch.

"I need to go," Ingrid said. "I have an autopsy."

The cup of tea was still half full when she got up.

"Thanks for the chat. I'll pay next time."

Only, there had been no conversation. Isa had bombarded her in the past with all her men problems, her doubts about being a mom, her heartache over Magnus and Alex, and now it was her turn, but Ingrid couldn't confide in her. She still had to be the strong one, the rock of decency and everything that was morally good. That image couldn't fall apart.

And why did she need another man anyway? She had a husband, and she should focus on him. Anton was kind and handsome. In all the years she had known Anton, he had been nothing but a loving father, a caring husband who put his wife on a pedestal and adored her.

"Ingrid... wait," Isa said.

But Ingrid had taken a decisive turn toward the exit and had already disappeared from sight.

* * *

The autopsy was in full progress when Timo entered the room. From behind the glass, he could see the two examiners bent over the naked body lying on the metal table. He heard Ingrid Olsson's voice echoing through the loudspeakers, "... the petechiae in the skin further evidence that the victim died of asphyxia... "

From where he was standing, he had a clear view of the body and Ingrid who was standing at the opposite side of the table, face toward him. As the examination moved to the dissection of the neck, the larynx and hyoid bone, his mind lingered away from the case. Dead people and cut-open bodies weren't the problem. He had seen many of those before. Dr. Olsson was the problem.

He was staring at the SCM muscles in her neck, leading down to the protruding collarbones, partially visible under the lab coat. Her neck was so graceful. Her flawless white skin almost reflected the light in the room. Falling in love was usually hard for him. He wasn't the man to get head over heels in love whenever he saw a beautiful woman, but when he did fall in love, it was all or nothing. And these feelings hadn't surfaced in eight years.

This could never happen. He didn't need that in his life. Ingrid was married, and he was kind of her boss, though not officially. He had already been acting like an idiot, putting her in an awkward position and asking stupid questions. It couldn't happen again, but as his eyes moved away from the neck and shoulders, he suddenly noticed her staring at him with an intense gaze, almost looking him straight in the eye, through the observation window. It was like an electricity surge going through his entire body. Her eyes were still locked on him as he looked away.

After the autopsy she seemed very reluctant to talk to him, lingering in the back, pretending to clean up, a task usually for the dieners. Dr. Einarsson, her colleague who had assisted during the autopsy, was the one giving a full report to inspector Paikkala.

"Death by strangulation. It is very clear. He used his hands. As in the case of Mr. Forsberg, we found a superficial head injury, bruises to the temple and minor lacerations to the forehead. Probably she was hit with the barrel of a gun. The other injuries were sustained after death, from the fall down the cliff."

"Anything else found on the scene?" Timo asked and out the corner of his eye he saw how Ingrid continued to label the bags, put them in the box, now and then throwing a glance at the two men.

"No. He was careful not to leave anything behind."

"Estimated time of death?"

"Between forty-eight and twenty-four hours ago. I can't narrow it down any further. The weather conditions make it more difficult to get an accurate estimate."

"They were killed just after the abduction," Timo said. "The killer didn't wait."

"Probably."

"Anything else?"

"Wallet and phone were gone. A twig was stuffed in their mouths."

"A twig." Timo stared at his feet for a while, trying to absorb the information. As he looked up, he sighed and continued, "Did they search the apartments of Henrik and Teresa?"

"Yes, nothing earth-shattering, but the forensics report will be sent to you as soon as it is ready."

Dr. Einarsson, having done his duty to inform the lead investigator, exchanged a few words with Ingrid about another case and then left the room.

She was still busy cleaning up. Not a single glance she gave him, while he stood only a few meters away from her, first still deep in thought then a bit loitering about like a little boy, not knowing what to do. It was embarrassing. He wanted to say something but didn't know how to start the conversation. He was about to leave, when she suddenly said, "Are you okay?"

He nodded and came closer.

"Yeah, why wouldn't I be?"

"Isa said you fell down a cliff."

"Oh, that's nothing."

She lifted her head and looked at him with the same intense gaze she had given him half an hour ago, during the autopsy.

"May I ask you something?" he tried to change the topic, and without waiting for the answer he said, "What do you think about Magnus?"

"Uh... he's fine, I guess," she said.

"He's acting strange. Confused. He's a good detective, but he's been neglecting his job lately."

"That's understandable given the situation."

"Why does everyone keep saying that?"

"His son is dead, braindead," she said. "I'm sorry to say this, inspector, but you have no children. You can't possibly know what it's like to lose a son."

"I'm very well aware of that, Dr. Olsson. So, you don't think there's anything strange with Magnus?"

She hesitated but then shook her head. "If you're so concerned, maybe you should talk to his wife Sophie. She probably knows more."

* * *

Timo went back to his office, grabbed his jacket and left the building.

Emmerson's Glada händelser was five kilometers away from the police station, direction center. His entire body ached, but Timo wanted to walk. He needed to clear his head. Magnus Wieland. This would drop a bomb on the team. The implications would be unforeseeable. A murderer had been among them. And Timo was afraid that by failing to see this he had put people in danger.

After an hour, he arrived at the tall, majestic white building that seemed somehow out of place between the ordinary wooden cabin-like houses. He had been lucky to find the shop open. It was stupid of him not to have checked it before leaving, but the sleep deprivation and the worries had cast a haze over his otherwise sharp mind.

Sophie Wieland was on the phone when inspector Paikkala entered. She was about to order a hundred balloons for the birthday party of a six-year-old.

"Mrs. Wieland," he said as she put the phone down and turned to him.

"Yes, how can I help you?"

"My name is Timo Paikkala. I am a colleague of your husband. I wonder if I might have a word?"

"Now? What is it about?"

"Your husband," he said.

She sighed, crossed her arms, and looked at him with increasing impatience.

"Do you know where he is?"

"No," she blurted, "and I don't care."

"No idea where he could be? With your daughter?"

"Look, we're separated. I'm not his keeper. Is something wrong?"

"Maybe," he said.

Timo wasn't too impressed by her grumpy attitude, and ignoring the increasing hostility and her reluctance to talk, he continued, "Did Magnus ever talk about Alexander Nordin?"

"The guy who was murdered? No, why?"

"I really need your help, Mrs. Wieland," he said calmly.

She took another deep breath, dropped her guard and said, "Look, we hardly talked these last six months. We lived in the same house, but that's about all I can say. You probably know he had a relationship with Isa Lindström while we were still married."

"Yes, I know," he said, "when did that relationship start?"

"More than two years ago, but I only found out ten months ago."

"Did you ever feel he was obsessed with her?"

"Obsessed? You're asking me?"

He narrowed his eyes, tilted his head, and then looked at her calmly for a moment. He wasn't impressed by her sarcastic remarks, and she immediately understood the message.

"No," she finally said, "but..."

"What is it?"

She stared at the window, and for a second, she looked shocked.

"Uh... sorry, I thought I saw... Never mind. I don't know about Isa, but he was very possessive with me. After he had confessed his relationship with Isa and I took him back, he became very controlling. He wanted to know where I went, what I did, who I was with, every moment of the day. Like he could do whatever he wanted, but I was supposed to stay faithful to him. He didn't seem to trust me, while he was the one having the affair."

"What happened then?"

"Nothing really, but it was suffocating and humiliating. Anyway, the situation normalized after a while. We tried to save our marriage, but Toby's accident and... well, it was obvious he was still in love with her. We went our own ways after that."

"Was this the first time he showed this type of behavior?"

"Yes... no, come to think of it, when we first met, I was dating another guy. I broke off the relationship when I met Magnus, but we stayed friends. And I remember that my ex often complained that he felt he was being stalked. It probably had nothing to do with Magnus, but..."

"But your feeling says otherwise."

She nodded.

"Inspector, what is this about?" she pleaded. "Has he done something wrong?"

"I hope not, I really do," Timo said. "When you see him, call me," he leaned over and handed her his card. "And get yourself together. I can smell the alcohol. For your daughter, she needs you."

"What?"

She snatched the card from his hand. He took a deep breath and walked to the exit. The air outside was chilly, and he looked up at the sky. It would soon start raining again.

* * *

From behind the wheel, Magnus watched Timo walk down the street, heading back to the police station. Timo had passed him just as he had intended to confront his wife about the hidden package. He had been standing outside the store for ten minutes and then had walked back to his car.

Why had Paikkala visited Sophie?

Are you going to kill him too?

Alex was right. He didn't trust the man. The arrogance, the way he behaved around Isa. He had to go. But how?

Magnus started the car and slowly passed by Timo who continued his walk, deep in thought, unaware that the man he was looking for was only a few meters away.

He could just run him over. It wouldn't take much to press the gas pedal completely and swing the wheel in the direction of the man. But there were too many witnesses, too many cameras. This had to go more subtly, like the incident in the forest. Plenty of options. He just needed to think it through.

CHAPTER

20

NICK PETRINI WAS A MAN OF HIS WORD. He had rang the doorbell at 8:00 p.m. that day and gotten no reply. The next day he was standing outside her house again. Isa doubted for a moment whether to open the door. Timo's rebuke was still fresh in her mind, but she finally gave in, opened the door a crack and peeked through. He looked so sexy with his white shirt, top part unbuttoned, showing the pecs she had so admired that morning when he had wandered naked through her kitchen.

"What did I tell you?" she said.

"Relax, it's okay. I'm no longer Mr. Bergman's lawyer."

From behind the half-opened door, she directed him an inquiring glance.

"I gave the case to one of my colleagues."

She kept staring at him, pinched eyes, lips firmly pressed together.

He smiled. "At least you should let me in."

"And why would I do that?"

"You owe me," he said with a straight face.

"Why on earth…"

"This is such an important case. Financially I'm losing a lot by giving it away," he whispered as he leaned forward, his head only a few centimeters away from hers. She felt his warm breath on her face. She wanted nothing more than to rip the clothes from his body, throw him on the bed and make mad love to him. And he knew it.

"Are you serious?" she asked, still trying to fight the feelings she couldn't let herself give into.

Without saying a word, he pressed his lips on hers, and her defence completely faltered. She pulled him inside.

*　*　*

"I need your advice," she said, staring at the ceiling. He was still reeling from the sex, taking quick breaths, the sweat running over his naked body as he lay beside her in bed.

"About what?" he turned around. She was still staring at the ceiling, in doubt if she would tell him. He let his hand slide over her arm.

"About adoption and parental rights," she answered and turned her head to look at him.

"Why?"

She got out of bed and disappeared to the living room, but not for long. Holding the letter in front of her, she came back and gave it to him.

There was absolute silence as he studied it. He would judge her, just like they all did. When he finally put the letter down, he said calmly, "What do you want?"

"I don't want... that woman to be the mother of my children," she said.

"Why?"

"What do you mean?"

"He says you haven't seen them in more than five years. I don't do family law but that is abandonment, and it is ground for termination of your parental rights. If you haven't seen or contacted them in so long, why would you object? It seems to me you don't want them in your life."

"How do you know?" she yelled and jumped up.

"Calm down. You asked my advice, and I'm giving it to you."

"Maybe... I might want them back."

"Might want them back? They're not objects. They're children who need a stable and loving environment."

"Can you do something or not?"

He had no right to lecture her. She just needed an objective opinion. And suddenly she realized that was what she had gotten. He was right. She made it all about her. Not a single moment she had thought about what was right for them, her son and daughter.

Six years ago, she had shipped them off to the UK with her ex-husband, thinking they were better off with him, but believing that one day she would be back in their lives. When she would be a better person, a better mother, a better everything, someone to look up to. Now, after so many years, she still didn't feel worthy. In fact, it was even worse: she didn't feel like a mother.

If she gave them up now, there would be no turning back. She would give them up forever. What would she tell them if one day they showed up at her door and asked why? Why had she done it? She couldn't just let go, but she couldn't connect with them either.

"I'll contact a colleague. He can give you better advice than I can but think about what I said!"

"I think you'd better leave," she said.

He sighed, jumped out of bed and dressed.

"Isa," he started, taking the phone from the bedside table, "you'll have to face this at some point: your children and Alex."

"What do you know about Alex?"

"Alexander Nordin. Everyone knows the story, your story, so it wasn't difficult."

She stood before him, fists clenched, trying to find the words.

"I... I..."

"Isa, I can't claim I know you, but I'm concerned."

"Please leave," she said.

He nodded, turned around and left the room.

* * *

The frozen image on the screen had been staring at them for several minutes. Nothing, absolutely nothing. A deserted road. No cars had passed by for hours, except Teresa's black BMW. Her father's car.

"This means he was already there and waiting for them. Do we need to go back in time?" Sivert said.

"No," Timo said and gave his chair a swirl.

His head was blurry, and he was irritated by the slightest sound. Like the annoying, repetitive clicking of Sivert's ballpoint. He had come so close to grabbing it from his hands and throwing it against the wall, when Isa had politely asked the young man to stop whatever he was doing.

"He was already in the car," Timo said.

"You think he picked them up, or they picked him up? They drove to the forest and then it all started? How did he escape?"

"He knows the area well. There was blood on the car seat, although I don't think he shot Henrik there. There were no powder marks or damage from the gunshot. But he controlled them."

"So they didn't escape?"

"I doubt it. He gave them hope and then took it away from them. The killer never intended to let them go."

Timo walked to the other side of the room. Breathing was less painful when he stood upright, as if there was suddenly more room in his chest. "The phone records of Teresa and Henrik. Who else did they talk to that morning? Who called them?"

"Jussi Vinter has no alibi," Lars said.

"And neither does Espen Frisk. Both claim to be home, but no witnesses."

"Espen was in Stockholm. It would have taken him about two hours to get there. He could have done it, but his car wasn't picked up by any traffic camera."

"Gerard Forsberg?"

"He had a meeting with a delegation of politicians until 3:00 p.m. Then he went home, but no witnesses either. His daughter was in Uppsala, taking classes the entire day. She has a solid alibi."

"So, Jussi, Gerard and Espen could have done this."

"What about Linda Forsberg?"

Timo turned to Berger. "What? Why?"

"We've gone through Linda's finances. The last activity dates from the day she disappeared. She withdrew thousands of crowns in the afternoon and since then, no activity. No withdrawals, no deposits. The car was bought a year ago, but the seller didn't remember her. Traffic cameras rarely picked up the car, usually near Hille."

"All of this points to the fact something happened to her," Timo said.

"Or she did a runner? She's hiding."

"What do the phone records tell us?"

Lars said, "The number was used six months ago to send a text message. This was around her children's birthday, as Lise Forsberg told us. For the rest, the number is inactive."

"Do we have an idea which base station picked up the signal?" Timo asked.

"Hille and Stockholm," Sivert said.

"Hille? That's where…"

"The car disappeared," Isa said.

"Near Mrs. Forsberg's house."

"What? Does she have a house there? Now you tell me! How could we have missed that?"

"There are twenty Forsbergs living in Gävle and the surrounding area, but only one in a five-kilometer zone around the base station. A L. Forsberg."

"Great job," Timo said and gave Sivert a pat on the back.

"Okay, let's pay Mrs. Forsberg or whoever lives there a visit," Timo continued.

"Before you go, there's one more thing," Lars said. "Henrik and Teresa knew each other very well. They are featured on many camera images taken in the streets of Gävle. And often with Thore Ovesen."

"Why does that name sound familiar?"

"He used to be Gerard Forsberg's financial director, but he was fired a few years ago following rumors of tax evasion. Gerard decided to clean house and threw out anyone he suspected had anything to do with it."

"So, the dear son was up to something with daddy's money?"

"Maybe, but it's true that Forsberg's companies are under investigation. I'm not exactly sure why. The investigation is classified, but Gerard is trying hard these days to get into the favor of the politicians."

"To stop the investigation?"

"Hard to say."

Isa said. "Or it was his son's move to embarrass his father? That's why he was quick to admit that he was the father of Marie's baby. He didn't want us to dig further and maybe find out what he was up to."

"How does Teresa fit in all this?"

Lars nodded. "Her father. He had a big fight with Gerard a few years ago. He suspected Forsberg of having leaked photos to the press about his affair and illegitimate daughter with a flight attendant."

"Maybe it was Mr. Ljungman who hired Marie to discredit his rival?"

"But the Forsbergs had an open marriage, and this was common knowledge, so it wouldn't be that sensational," Isa said.

"It was Linda who had the lovers, and so far, Gerard had managed to keep it out of the media. But this time, it would be him, and maybe it was more than the open marriage. Maybe it was about Linda's disappearance?"

"Okay, see if there is a connection between Marie and Ljungman," Timo said. "In the meantime, Isa and I are going to visit Linda Forsberg."

"What about EliteGirls?" Lars said.

"What is that?" Isa asked.

"The escort service Marie was working for. There is a meeting later today."

Timo said, "Well, you and Berger will tell us all about that when we get back!"

* * *

The man next to her turned the wheel and drove north.

"I'm tired", Isa blurted.

"Then you should get some sleep," Timo said, keeping his eyes on the road.

"Not that kind of tiredness!"

Although she had to admit, having sex with hot Italian guys didn't exactly help her energy and alertness.

"What then?"

"Tired of worrying about Magnus, my children."

He frowned. "Children?"

"I don't know them. And I don't know if I want to know them."

"Lindström, since when are we bonding? I thought you didn't trust me."

She sighed and looked at the trees. There wasn't a house in sight. Only the long forest road, lined with pine trees. She didn't expect an answer or advice. She just wanted to say the words and thoughts that were haunting her mind.

"Tired of wanting Alex back."

There it was. She was so afraid she'd never be able to get past him or the image of him. That every man she met would never live up to that twisted fantasy.

"May I be honest, Lindström?"

"Yes, although I'm not sure. I feel advice is coming that won't make me happy, but I started it."

Timo smiled and said, "I don't see it. You and Alexander Nordin. You didn't match."

"Oh, God, the same conversation we had weeks ago!"

"No, another conversation. Since you asked, I want to be honest. You don't know what you want, and until then, every man is the wrong man."

"Or every man is the right one," she sneered.

He gave her a quick glance and turned his attention to the road. The long, unpaved driveway to the house, meandering between the trees, was tougher than the concrete street leading to the area.

"Are you sure this is the right spot?" he said as he drove the car deeper into the woods.

"Yes," she whispered and quickly looked at the sky. It was getting dark.

The car passed the gate, and in the distance, they saw the outline of a cottage, almost like a master dominating the area. Behind it, the majestic tall trees they had seen passing by for the last half hour.

The house showed its details as they approached. While it looked like an ordinary Swedish cottage, they could now see it was more ramshackle than initially thought. The walls were gray stone and the paint on the wooden window frames was flaking, but the front door looked new and heavy, recently replaced. Its red color completely clashed with the rest of the house.

Isa peeked through the window but couldn't see anything. Timo had gotten out of the car and had a quick look at the house before taking a walk around the cottage.

"Nobody seems to be home," Isa said.

"That was to be expected."

"What do we do now?"

He walked to the door and knocked, but there was no answer.

"People may be in danger," Isa said.

"There is no one. Lindström, what are you thinking?"

She gave him a faint smile. "Don't tell me you haven't thought of it?"

"We can't."

"I definitely heard a noise. There's someone in there."

"Isa!"

"No, I'm serious. Timo, I heard something."

She stopped and listened again, the rhythmic cadence of her heartbeat pounding in her ears. She was right. There was a noise, something in the background, though, she wasn't sure it was coming from the house. Then she looked at Timo and saw the doubt on his face.

"There's another door," he said.

She followed him as he led her to the back of the house. The wooden door looked less sturdy, and he opened it without any problem. There was no light and as they walked down the hall to the front door, it became quiet again.

They were wrong.

She sighed, but now they were inside, they might as well inspect the place. With her hand on the gun, she followed Timo to the other rooms.

In the hallway were empty cardboard boxes and wooden boards. The rooms were empty. No furniture, but empty plastered walls and the sound of their footsteps echoing across the room.

"Police, is anyone home?"

"There is no one here," Isa whispered. "I was wrong."

"But someone's been here," he said, pointing to the potato chip wrappers in the corner of what should have been the living room.

The windows were covered with thick curtains that reeked of mold and dust when she opened them. Outside, the sun had disappeared behind the trees. It would soon be completely dark.

"When did Linda buy this house?" Timo asked.

"Gerard bought it, but he put it in her name about five years ago."

"Why?"

"Maybe this was Mrs. Forsberg's love nest," Isa said and removed the smile from her face when she saw how serious he was.

"I'll look upstairs," she said.

For a moment, he hesitated.

"Relax, I'm a big girl," she said when she saw the concerned glance.

"There's a cellar. That's where all the stuff usually happens," she laughed, and walked past him to go to the stairs. She heard the cracking of the wooden steps as she went up, gun pointed in front of her.

Upstairs everything was as boring as downstairs. In two of the four rooms she found a closet and a single bed. The other rooms were a bathroom and an empty room she imagined had been used as a study. It seemed as if no one had lived there for a long time.

In the meantime, Timo had gone to the basement. The door led to another staircase. He tried the light switch, but there was no electricity. The stairs were shaky and a few times it felt like the steps weren't strong enough to support his weight.

A feeling of discomfort and anxiety crept over him. Isa might have laughed the danger away, but he wasn't so sure. He really thought he had heard something before. He wrapped his hand tighter around the handguard of the gun. Only his breathing could be heard as he strolled down the stairs. It was so dark. He barely saw where he was walking. He took out the flashlight and let it glide over the walls and the floor.

The room was filled with boxes and open cupboards with shelves containing oil, tools and old rags. He heard the rhythmic trickle of water hitting the floor. It came from behind him. He moved forward, shining the light over the objects on the floor. The room was enormous and covered the entire area under the house.

The sound of water was getting louder. He stopped and let the light cone shine on the wall in front of him. There was a cupboard blocking his way. This didn't look right. His intuition told him there should be no wall. He put the flashlight and gun on the floor and moved the cupboard. It was light and easy to slide aside.

He held his breath. There was a door hidden behind the cupboard. It was a wooden door with several locks. He opened it and let the light shine in the room. He nearly dropped the torch when he saw the red spots on the wall.

Blood. It was blood. And the smell. Urine, mixed with mold and the stench of horror. For a moment, he froze. He saw an electrical heater, standing dangerously close to a pool of water. In the corner a wooden board chained to the wall. It had served as a bed, reflected by the white sheet that still covered it.

He came closer. The light from the torch moved along the walls and then stopped. He held his breath. This couldn't be real. There, scratched in the wall, still clearly legible, was written: "Ollie was here. Tell mom I'm alive."

Those words. A sign of life. Tears came to his eyes.

Then he heard a noise. He had been right. Someone was here, but before he could turn around, there was a blow to the head. The flashlight and gun fell to the floor, and he tried to stay upright, but the pain was too much, and he fell to his knees.

"Isa," he yelled. "Isa!"

Dizziness overtook him, and he lost consciousness.

Upstairs, Isa had heard Timo's screams, and with the gun in front of her, she ran down the stairs. She heard hasty steps running down the hallway to the back of the house. She quickened her pace and ran toward the sound, not knowing if her partner was okay.

The back door was open and, in the distance, in the light of the moon, she saw the silhouette of someone running away from her. She started the pursuit, but the person was faster, and when she reached the forest, she had lost him.

Timo, she heard the voice say in her head, and she turned around and ran back to the house.

"Timo! Where are you?"

She ran down the stairs to the basement. It was darker than upstairs, and her eyes had to adjust to the darkness before she could continue.

"Timo!"

Groans were coming from behind the cardboard boxes. She saw the door and the body on the floor.

As she knelt and touched his face to check if he was still alive, fear came over her. He had rightly been cautious, and she had been stupid not to listen to him. She had put her partner and herself in danger.

"What happened?" he said, tried to get up, but fell down on his chest again.

"Timo, thank God!" she let out.

"Did you get him?"

"Lie still! You may have a concussion. Twice in less than 24 hours, Paikkala. You're well on your way to getting yourself killed!"

"Yeah, I feel your concern," he moaned and put his hands over his head.

* * *

The request for a list of her clientele went down the wrong way with Mrs. Grahn. She was a stylish but no-nonsense woman, in her fifties, who hadn't moved a muscle in her botox-smoothed face since Lars and Berger had joined her in the office on the second floor of the Uppsala business center.

A modern office. The black oak desk she sat at blended nicely with the light gray plaster walls behind her. The large windows on either side gave a view of downtown Uppsala, less spectacular than the skyscrapers of New York where she had lived for several years, but the view of the cathedral towers in the distance gave her always a sense of calm and grandeur. Like she could handle anything.

On the desk, the lamp and a laptop were the only things. Everything was organized and catered to the last detail, minimalistic and sterile. Every item in the room was there because it had a function and was placed almost by the ruler.

"My clients need privacy and discretion. If I gave you that list, I would break my clients' trust. So unless you have a warrant, I won't give it to you."

"That's perfectly within your rights. However, it could harm your defence when we do get that court order and we discover that certain activities of your establishment may be illegal."

"Illegal? Everything we do here is within the boundaries of the law. This is a respectable dating service."

"A dating service for men only?" Lars said.

"We do have female clients," she said.

"Right. And what about your employees? Ninety percent are women. Tall, slim, young. How do you select them? Based on their IT skills?"

"Okay, okay, some men just need a companion for an evening or a few days. We provide that. It's all legal. This is not a brothel!"

"We'd like to see your girls," Lars said, stopped and shook his head realizing the words had come out wrong.

"It's not a catalog where you can just pick and choose!" she said.

"Sorry. We are only interested in Marie Lång."

She took the photograph from his hands.

"Marie. I heard what happened to her. Shocking!"

She had been fond of the girl, although their first meeting hadn't gone well. The girl had been too eager, desperate almost to get the job. One of her friends had given her the connection, and one rainy Monday morning Marie sat in one of the seats now occupied by one of the inspectors.

It wasn't about the money. The excitement, the sex, yes, but Mrs. Grahn had told her it was more subtle than that. It was about tension, attraction, charisma. Marie had potential, but it had taken months to shape the girl with humble upbringing into one of her most successful girls.

"Who were her clients?"

"Inspectors, I can't," Mrs. Grahn said and sighed. As much as she wanted to help them, she couldn't break the trust her clients had put in her. "I can only tell you she was a very popular woman. I was sorry when she left."

"She left when?"

"About six months ago."

"Did she say why?" Berger asked.

Mrs. Grahn shook her head. "Usually there's a man in the picture when that happens, but she didn't tell me."

"Marie had a second cell phone. We didn't find it. Do you know where it could be? She received a phone call just before she went missing. We believe that's important."

"I don't know anything about that. We do recommend our girls to use prepaid phones. That puts our clients more at ease. I can only give

267

you the number I used to reach her."

She scribbled the number on a piece of paper and handed it to Berger.

"There was this one guy though, who was adamant to see her," she suddenly said.

"Who?"

"I don't know his name. I never saw him, but he called me. Several times. At one point, I even thought he was stalking her."

"What else can you tell us about him? Why did he call?"

"It was about six months ago when he first called. He said he had an appointment with Marie, but she never showed up. He wanted to know where she was. I told him Marie no longer worked for us, but he insisted. He called a few times after that."

"Old, young?"

"He sounded old. More mature."

Berger gave his colleague a glance.

"Do you have his number?" Berger asked.

"Don't bother! I got his number traced and it's the phone number of a pub in Gävle."

She wrote the name and number on the paper, still on the desk, in front of Berger.

"Do you think he was one of your clients?"

"I can't say, but he was agitated and angry. He frightened me. He really did. That's why I had my IT guy track him down."

Marie. Should she have warned her? Should she have told the police? It was too late now.

CHAPTER 21

"**OLIVER PILKVIST WAS THERE.** And Marie. But the blood on the wall doesn't belong to Marie or Oliver."

"My God! Then who? Other victims?"

"No, it's animal blood," Ingrid said.

Timo had been silent. Too silent. It wasn't the concussion, nor the contused ribs, but the prospect of failure. Another briefing at the Gävle police station after a phone call from the commissioner giving him an ultimatum. Too many deaths. Not enough progress to get in the good grace of the public. One week and then it would all be over.

"He practiced on animals."

"There have been reports of poachers operating in that area in recent years," Isa said.

"We need to find Oliver," Timo said. "If he's still alive…"

As an uneasy silence filled the room, Timo felt a sad mood settle over him. Everyone was thinking the same. Marie was already dead. The odds of finding Oliver alive were getting slim.

He swallowed a few times before he moved the conversation to another subject. "What did Gerard Forsberg have to say?"

"The man was incoherent and confused," Berger started.

Ingrid gave Berger a quick look. "Gerard Forsberg just lost his son!"

"He may even be responsible for his son's death," Berger said. "The house hasn't been used for years. Gerard bought it as a summer house more than ten years ago. His wife loved it so much he put it in her name as a gift. However, when he learned she was using it as a meeting place for her lovers, he refused to visit it any longer. Harald Müller confirmed he has been there several times."

"And he noticed nothing special?"

"The house was furbished then. He was shocked to learn that all the furniture had been removed, and that it was so dilapidated."

"As if squatters were living in the house," Timo suddenly said.

Isa nodded. "Yes, that's it! Squatters. Like seven years ago."

"When Quinten Hall died."

"We haven't talked to Quinten's parents yet," Timo said, "it's time we did."

"They live nearby. We can be there in ten minutes."

"And someone needs to talk to Espen Frisk," Berger remarked.

"Why?"

"The man called the police station. He says he has information. He asked for you, Timo."

"I'll talk to him later. Quinten Hall's parents have priority. And we should follow up on Ilan Bergman. He knows more about the murder of

Frank Harket. The signal of his phone was picked up in the neighborhood where Harket was murdered that night."

Lars entered the room. "Boss, can I talk to you for a second?"

"About what?"

"The other case you asked me to investigate."

Isa frowned. "What other case?"

Timo ignored her and turned to Lars. "My office. I'll be there in five minutes."

"Timo, what..."

He ignored her a second time and said, "Isa, Berger, you talk to Mr. and Mrs. Hall!"

And before Isa could say anything, Timo had already disappeared.

* * *

"They found Magnus' car," Lars said.

"Where?"

"Near the center of Gävle."

"And Magnus?"

"He hasn't shown up at the police station since we found Teresa and Henrik. His car has been there since yesterday, but no sign of him."

Timo sighed. "Why was he there?"

Lars shrugged. "What's wrong with Magnus? Why..."

Timo looked at the young man. He hesitated for a moment, but now was not the time to bring his suspicions in the open. Accusing a fellow police officer of murder required a certain amount of delicacy, but the gnawing unrest about Magnus' involvement in Alexander Nordin's death was growing. Suddenly Magnus' name had popped up everywhere.

Nina was in a coma. The information from the mobile operator showed that the call to Isa hadn't been the last one, but that Alex had called Magnus after that. But there was still no tangible evidence that

Magnus had shot Alex. However, it was clear Magnus was feeling increasingly cornered, and given his mental state, there was a good chance he might do something reckless and desperate. Timo had to find him. Fast.

"Thanks, Lars. You did a good job."

Timo gave him a distant smile, got up and left the room.

* * *

The car stood in an almost empty parking lot in the center of Gävle. Timo had walked around the vehicle a few times. Candy bar wrappers were lying on the passenger seat and the dust on the dashboard and the dirty windows showed the car hadn't been cleaned in ages. Why did people neglect their cars? Perhaps he was overly concerned about the cleanliness of his own cars, but he loved the look of a well-maintained vehicle shining in the sun. The purity of the leather seats, the spotless windows. Nothing should ever ruin that view. He sometimes spent hours cleaning and vacuuming the interior. Obsessed, his father would say, but he had learned it from him.

Why here? Why now? What was so important here?

Maybe he was overanalyzing it. A moment he thought about issuing an APB, but then he would have a lot to explain. No, he had to track down Magnus himself.

A woman and child were walking across the street. She looked at him for a moment, then turned her attention back to the toddler who tugged impatiently at her arm, but she wasn't at ease. As he watched the distance between her and himself grow, she turned three more times, probably wondering what that strange man was doing by the car.

And as he averted his eyes from the woman, his gaze suddenly fell on Emmerson's Glada händelser. Magnus had been watching his wife. What else had he done? Where was he?

"What a coincidence!"

Timo jumped up. The voice came out of nowhere. Irritated at having interrupted his thinking process, he turned and looked the young man straight in the eye. Espen Frisk was about his size. Tall and slim. He gave a weird, mixed vibe that he'd noticed before. On the one hand a sophisticated, well-groomed man, ambitious, with a hunger to make it in the world, on the other hand insecure and scared. He wasn't sure what to make of it.

"Mr. Frisk, what are you doing here?"

"I live here. Well, close by. Just a few blocks away."

"I thought you were studying in Stockholm?"

"Yes, but I have an apartment in Gävle. Actually, my parents have."

"I see. You want to talk to me. Why?"

"Maybe we can go to my place. I need to show you something. About Quinten."

"I'm, uh... in the middle of an investigation," Timo said.

"It'll take only five minutes. It's important."

* * *

The apartment was modest, less modern and spacious than Teresa and Marie's. Very seventies. Living room and kitchen were one, with a large window facing the street. The couch was old and smelled of dust, but otherwise the rooms were clean and tidy. Too tidy. Timo wondered if Espen really lived there.

"Coffee?"

Exactly what he wanted to hear.

Espen swung the cupboard door open and then sighed. He put the pads in the coffee maker and pressed the button. A rattling sound came from the kitchen.

"What did you want to talk to me about?"

"Quinten and his suicide," Espen said. "Please sit down. I'll bring the coffee."

Timo trudged into the living room and sat down. Once again, he was reminded of how he had pushed every muscle in his body to the extremes in the past days.

"What other information do you have?"

Espen handed him the steamy cup of coffee and walked to the cupboard in the living room.

"I have his diary."

Holding the book in front of him, he returned to the sitting area.

"His diary?" Timo said and took a sip. "How did you get that?"

"I took it with me when we left the house, after Quinten's death."

"You took evidence," Timo said, and leaned backward.

"I thought... I just wanted something of him, and there was nothing special in there, so I thought."

"What do you want to say?"

"After talking to you, it all came back. The drama, the guilt that we couldn't help him, and then I realized I had the diary. I've never read it before, and I didn't think there was anything interesting in it until... well, I'll show you."

He opened the book and flipped through the pages. As Timo watched the young man, the throbbing pain in his head grew louder. Suddenly it was so hard to focus. Espen kept talking, but the words frolicked in the air, like fluffy leaves. He couldn't grasp them.

"I told you he was scared. The days before his suicide, he thought someone was following him. He didn't know who, but in the diary, he talks about meeting with the father of a girl he knew a long time ago. Actually, a girl who was in our class when we were in primary school. He had seen him a few times on the street."

"Do you..."

"Are you okay, inspector?"

His head wasn't getting enough blood. "Yeah, I think so."

"Do you need some water?"

"No. You mean Patrik Mikaelsson?"

"Yes, do you know him?"

The image became increasingly blurred. Why was it so hot?

"I think I'm not okay," Timo said, got up, but immediately felt dizziness take over. He stumbled forward and when he hit the floor, he heard Espen say, "Inspector, inspector, what's wrong?"

* * *

Magnus sat on the linoleum floor in the corner of the motel room. A run-down, second-rate motel he'd moved into after standing in front of Sophie's workplace for the last days, not sure if he should confront her about the disappearance of the package.

The night before, he'd seen her through the window looking at the computer. She was alone and while he was about to go in, he saw how the bluish light from the screen gave her face an almost unearthly glow. The melancholy and sadness of her features shocked him more than he had imagined. She looked so lonely. Only then he realized what he had done. He and he alone had torn his family apart. And they didn't even know how utterly evil he was. He deserved no happiness, no pity.

He had left the car in the parking lot, had stumbled to a nearby store and had bought a bottle of strong alcohol with the idea of drinking himself into a coma, before checking into the motel.

The bottle was still unopened on the bedside table. The moment he had closed the door behind him, the ghosts of his ailing brain had taken control.

Trembling, he was rocking back and forth with his hands over his ears. The voices could not be silenced.

You have to get him out of the way. Timo doesn't deserve Isa. He is competition.

You can do it.

"Stop! Stop!"

And Isa has a lesson to learn. Coward, you can't stop now!

Continuous, no moment of rest. But this had to stop. It was clear. The only way he would ever get peace of mind was to confess.

No, don't!

"I have to," Magnus whispered.

No, you will not do that!

"They'll understand."

You'll rot in prison for the rest of your life. Anna won't understand. Sophie won't understand. Isa won't understand.

He saw Alex sitting in front of him, facing him. He had never seemed so close by. If he stretched out his arm, he would be able to touch him.

Magnus, do you realize this is the end game?

"End game?"

How else would they know we mean it? We have to prepare this carefully.

"I don't know what you mean."

Calm down. It's simple. I will explain. After that, no one will ever doubt you again. Then they'll understand.

CHAPTER

22

QUINTEN'S FATHER LIVED in the suburbs, north of Gävle, with his wife. A simple house with a backyard where the weeds thrived. It hadn't been maintained for years. Seven years, to be exact. After Quinten's death, life had become difficult. Without joy, without passion. Every day was the same. In survival mode, with a certain indifference, because detachment meant nothing could touch him, could hurt him. Quinten had been an only child. Mr. Hall and his wife had poured all their love and hopes into their son. They had feared there wouldn't be enough to divide between different children. Now, all that love had disappeared with Quinten.

"You want to talk about my son," the father stammered when Isa and Berger had introduced themselves and the reason they were standing on his doorstep.

He didn't know whether he could or would talk about his dead son, but his wife had opened the door wider and let them in. She always had strong opinions, and she had one about the suicide. For years.

"Finally, after all those years, you believe us," his wife blurted.

"I'm sorry, what do you mean?" Isa said.

"Quinten's murder. That's why you're here. No?"

"You think Quinten was murdered? It was ruled suicide. We are here because we believe the recent deaths of Marie Lång, Teresa Ljungman, and Henrik Forsberg had something to do with your son's death. I know his friend Espen also mentioned..."

"Wait a minute! Friend?"

Berger nodded. "Yes, Espen Frisk."

The woman waved her hand in the air, as if to get rid of the idea. "Espen Frisk was no friend of my son."

"That's how he portrays himself and that's what we heard from Jussi Vinter and Teresa Ljungman."

"Espen Frisk is a pathological liar. Talk to his family and you'll find out."

"A liar?"

"Quinten was so naïve, impressionable. Yes, they were friends in elementary school. So-called friends. Espen seemed like a decent kid. Helpful, polite. He could tell the most amazing stories about his family, the places he had been, the countries he had visited. It all sounded so plausible at first, but I've always known something wasn't quite right. And then Quinten changed. He became distant, angry, and he spent more and more time with Espen, but, you know, he fed Quinten with lies, poisoned his mind, made him turn against us and our faith."

"Quinten ran away from home," Isa said.

"Yes, they were so vulnerable and Espen took advantage of that."

"It was Espen's idea?"

"Yes, we think so."

"But why?"

The mother sighed. "Quinten called us a few days before his death. He was scared, terrified. He wanted to come home. He realized he had made a mistake."

"Quinten was gay," Isa said.

The father gave his wife a quick glance and then got up. "So what?"

"There are rumors you didn't approve, and that was the reason Quinten ran away from home."

"No, no," the father said.

He still remembered Quinten entering the room and telling them he had an announcement to make. They thought it had been another Espen-esque attempt to get attention. Had they pushed him away? He'd never realized his son had been so confused. He'd never told him he had been proud of him, no matter what. Yes, maybe that was why he left. And there was no way they could make it right.

"He wanted to come home, because he finally realized what Espen had done."

"He said that? What was he referring to?"

"I don't know, but he was disappointed and desperate. He kept saying Espen had lied to him, and he had helped him. He was so sorry for everything he had done."

"Mrs. Hall, I still see no reason to doubt Quinten's suicide."

The father said, "Talk to the man he falsely accused!"

"The teacher?"

"Yes. Then you'll see what kind of devil Espen Frisk really is."

* * *

Timo wanted to keep his eyes closed a little longer before the pain took over. But it didn't take long. The icy water had been dripping on his face, leaving delicate little marks. When he opened his eyes, everything was blurry. He was no longer lying on the soft cushions of the couch. The texture was rough and hard, sticking in his ribs. He ran his hand over it. Maybe wood.

Where was he?

The last thing he remembered was being in Espen's apartment, and then nothing. It was strange. This wasn't a stroke or heart attack. It had been more subtle, paralyzing.

Espen Frisk. Of course! How stupid could he be?

Did it make sense? Maybe. He still didn't see the connection. Espen Frisk had killed Quinten. Why? He had killed Marie. Why? Teresa and Henrik. Why?

He tried to turn around. There was a flash of light, as if he'd been staring at the sun for too long. The image was zooming in and out, focusing, and the next moment not. He closed his eyes again and lay still. And then he heard it. The gentle rhythmic sighs. Breathing. Someone else was in the room. A cough. A sigh. Yes, there was someone.

The anxiety rose. Maybe he was in danger.

A soft cry. Then high-pitched sobbing. It was a child.

He pushed himself up, defying gravity that was trying hard to pull him down again. With blurred vision and muscles depleted from every source of energy, he followed the trail of the sound.

Brown, nothing but brown. Wood. Another drop of cold water hit his face. It was a one-room cabin. There was one window, dirty with dust and barred on the outside, and shelves on the wall that had served as cupboards for pots and utensils, judging by the stains of oil and paint rings that had penetrated deep into the wood.

A bench, he didn't even dare to call it a bench, but a plank supported on either side by two wooden studs on which he had been lying, and in the corner of the room a collapsed figure, folded in a fetal position, hands resting on his knees and his head hidden in his arms. The back rose and fell to the rhythm of the sobs.

"Oliver?"

The boy didn't look up.

Timo knelt and touched his arm. The sobbing stopped, and Oliver looked up at the dark-haired man who was still trying to control the nausea. The boy's face was covered in scratches and dirt.

"Are you okay?"

The boy nodded.

"Do you know where we are?"

He stared at Timo with big green eyes.

"Are you going to hurt me?" The voice sounded so frail.

"I'm here to help you," Timo said and wanted to take his hand, but Oliver pushed it away.

"You can't help me. They'll come for you, and then we'll both die."

* * *

"Janusz Haugen, the teacher, lives in Börlange. It takes an hour to get there."

Isa stared at her cell phone.

"What's wrong?" Berger asked.

"Paikkala doesn't answer his phone," she said.

"Maybe he's busy?"

"Yes, with that secret case of his," she sneered.

Berger smiled. "You're worried."

"About him? No! Why would I be?"

"Really?" Berger said. "You've been distracted ever since Mrs. Hall made these comments about Frisk."

"Espen Frisk wanted to talk to Timo. Why? Maybe... Just leave it!

Let's pay a visit to Janusz Haugen. I'll ask Lars to bring in Mr. Frisk. We have some things to talk about."

The drive to the small, detached house in the middle of the forest near Börlange did indeed take more than an hour.

The paint that was peeling off the walls, the broken and patched window, the missing roof tiles, it looked as if the house had been poorly maintained. Mr. Haugen would claim it was the continuous assault on the house by people who deemed themselves righteous to condemn him as a sexual predator and who therefore thought they had the right to damage everything. It had turned the once clean and rustic villa into a hovel. Mr. Haugen himself was a hermit, though not of his own free will. False accusations had turned his life into a series of problems he no longer controlled. When he opened the door and saw the two inspectors, his first reaction was to slam it and run away as fast as he could, but that would be defeat, and he had refused from day one to give up. It had been tough. He had lost everything. His wife had tried, but he knew she would give in to the constant doubt in her mind that had grown to unprecedented proportions by the time she closed the door and took the children with her.

The area was deserted, far away from the center, but they would know. He didn't know how, but they always knew. The people who were outside his house in the middle of the night, calling him a pedophile, who tried to run him over on the street, who tried to beat him up in an alley. The police on his doorstep would no doubt trigger another episode of pointless assaults. It was so unfair because he had done nothing wrong.

Inspector Lindström told him about the conversation with Quinten Hall's parents and as he listened to her words, he felt his heartbeat increase.

He said, "Mrs. Hall is right. Espen Frisk is a liar."

"So the allegations about sexual assault aren't true?" Isa said.

Janusz sighed. So many times. Repeatedly. But no one listened. Ever.

"Of course not. I am innocent!"

"Then what happened?"

"One moment I'm having a conversation with Espen in my office, the next moment the police are arresting me for assault."

"Be more specific. This happened nine years ago?"

"Yes. I never laid a hand on him. I heard he confided in Quinten Hall that I raped him in my office. Quinten told his parents, and they went to the police. But they didn't have any evidence. They had to let me go."

"So, Quinten's parents had you arrested?"

"Meanwhile, they know they were wrong. They support me."

For years, they didn't realize the damage they had done. They couldn't do anything to make it right, but he had forgiven them. Or so he thought.

"I still don't understand what happened. What was your conversation about?"

"I saw him," Janusz said.

"Where? What do you mean?"

"I saw him the day Jonna died."

"Jonna Mikaelsson?" Isa said. "Why is that important?"

"I saw him in the woods the afternoon when Jonna died. It was a Saturday. I was walking the dog and then I saw them coming out of the woods."

"Them?" Isa said, surprised.

"Espen and Lise Forsberg."

"Lise Forsberg?"

"Yeah. I didn't know they were friends. Anyway, that evening they found Jonna in the lake, close to where I had seen them. I thought it was strange they hadn't come forward. I should have told the police, but I first wanted to talk to them. They were just kids. Who would have thought thirteen-year-olds could do something like that? So, a few days later, I asked him about it. He said he hadn't seen anything, but he was on edge."

"You think he was lying?"

"Yes. He knew more, and he was caught off-guard."

"Do you think they had something to do with her death?"

He bowed his head, stared at his hands neatly folded in his lap. He had gone over this in his head, many times. He shouldn't have meddled.

"I think he... they are responsible for her death. Yes."

"And he knew you knew," Isa said.

Goosebumps ran up his spine again. It had been a deliberate act, devised to discredit someone. Thought through and well executed. Espen and Lise had understood the consequences of their actions: killing Jonna and getting rid of the witness.

"He made sure you wouldn't dive deeper or report them to the police. Because at that moment, no one would listen to you anymore. And Lise Forsberg?"

All those years. Someone finally got it. Someone finally listened to him.

"I saw her once. In a store, a few years ago. I just couldn't control myself. I had to know. I asked her straight what she had done to Jonna. She just laughed and said that whatever comes out of the mouth of a sex offender is a lie, and for someone who lost almost everything there was still one more thing to lose... my life."

"She threatened you?"

He nodded and wiped the tears from his face.

"I've..." Nothing, not a single word, could describe the horror he had endured all those years. He had been walking around with a label someone had stuck to his back. Only this one wasn't easy to remove or erase. Like a skin burn, leaving marks, scars, forever.

"Why? Why Jonna?"

"I've often asked myself that. Jonna was a popular girl. Everyone loved her. She was beautiful, nice, helpful. The perfect child."

"Maybe too perfect?" Isa said.

"Henrik Forsberg was one of her best friends."

"Maybe his sister was jealous?"

Janusz Haugen stared through the window. They could keep guessing, but he didn't care. Espen and Lise had to be held accountable for what they had done. Justice for Jonna, but not for him. There would always be doubt. How could anyone quantify the damage to his life? They had to pay. They had to pay for destroying his life.

"And Marie Lång?"

"What about her?"

"How does this tie in with Marie's death?"

"Maybe she knew. They were all the same age, in the same class, but I don't think they were friends."

"Besides Quinten's parents, have you told anyone else about your suspicions?"

"Yes, Patrik Mikaelsson. A few days ago."

"What?"

"He contacted me. I told him everything."

* * *

The screen showed a man and a woman, supporting a tall dark-haired man. While the timer was running, they pushed him into the back seat of the parked car. Moments later, the car drove away.

"Camera footage of the apartment building where Frisk lives," Sivert said to the police officers who arrived five minutes late at the briefing called by inspector Isa Lindström.

"The camera was installed only a month ago, but it shows Lise Forsberg dropped by regularly when Espen was in Gävle. They know each other very well."

"And the car?"

"Linda Forsberg's car."

"This was six, almost seven hours ago. We need to find the car. We need to find Espen Frisk and Lise Forsberg! They took inspector Paikkala."

"Who says he's still alive?"

"The boss is missing," Isa said. "We have to do everything we can to find him."

With a stern face, she looked at them. Twenty people in the room. Although he had been an outsider, they were all concerned.

And then she said, "He would do the same for each of you."

"The car was last seen in Stromsbrö, and then it disappeared."

"Stromsbrö? Close to the lake?"

"Yes," Sivert said.

They were all staring at her. One wrong decision. So much depended on what she was going to say or do next.

"We need to talk to Gerard Forsberg."

CHAPTER

23

HE HAD BEEN STARING at the window for the past hours. At least it seemed like hours. The light had given way to darkness. He should have figured it out by now. Plans to get out of there. Plan A, B and C, but he had to wait for the fog to clear from his mind, and he didn't have time.

Oliver was sleeping on the wooden bench.

What had the boy been through? He had barely said a word.

Timo closed his eyes. The cyclic breathing was so soothing. The nausea was still there. He wanted to sleep, but that would put him in a vulnerable position. He didn't know what was going to happen, but

Oliver had seen enough to worry about what was going to come. And every time Timo let himself drift off in that state before dreams and blissful paralysis took over, he saw her. Ingrid. The way she looked at him, then walked up to him, took his face in her hands and kissed him.

He couldn't think about her. Not now. He had dealt with danger and death before, but never in such a tangible way. It had never felt personal. This time it was.

He stood up. There had to be a way out. The cabin wasn't that large. Wood everywhere. His hands slid over the veins, and then he dropped to the floor again. For the first time, a wave of panic came over him. What was going to come, would come. He couldn't stop it.

* * *

"Where's your daughter?" Isa said.

Gerard slammed his fist on the table and said, "My son is dead and now you're after my daughter too?"

Isa folded her arms over her chest. "Mr. Forsberg, your daughter has kidnapped a police officer. We need to find her."

"Why would she kidnap anyone? This is ridiculous!"

"What is her relationship with Espen Frisk?" Berger asked.

"Espen Frisk? There is no relationship. They hardly know each other. From school."

"Marie knew him. Did she ever mention him?"

"Yes. She was afraid of him."

"Why?"

"I've seen him at the parties a few times. Henrik knew him better than Lise. Marie avoided him. One time they had an argument, and she ran off. I went after her and found her outside, upset, trembling. She never told me why, but he terrified her. What does this have to do with Lise?"

"Where is your daughter? You have three other properties in the area, but we already searched them, and she isn't there. We're looking for something remote, quiet."

Gerard dropped into his chair.

Was it true? The feeling that there was a monster hiding in the house had been there for years, since the twins were born. And he had been wrong. It wasn't Henrik. It was Lise.

The nights he had woken up, thinking someone had been in the room, breathing, watching, like a predator observing his prey. Days after days. There was a dark presence lingering in his house, lashing out every now and then, hiding most of the time, until the time was right to go for the ultimate kill.

He just didn't know why, but he had always assumed Henrik had sided with Linda after the breakup and Lise had taken his side. She had supported him from the beginning, but now he wasn't sure.

"You won't find it on your list. There is a cabin, close to Hille, in Björkehorns."

"The nature reserve?"

"It's not that legit. The cabin belonged to my parents. It should have been demolished more than twenty years ago, but we've kept it."

"Why the cabin?"

"Lise loves it there. She has always loved it since she was a child. It was her safe haven when Linda and I weren't in a good place."

"Mr. Forsberg, we believe Linda didn't just disappear, but that she was possibly murdered."

"What? Why? Who?"

Isa turned to Berger for a moment as if she wanted his approval before saying, "And we believe your daughter is involved."

* * *

"Get up!"

Every muscle in his body was sore. Timo had fallen asleep, and he wasn't sure what time it was.

It wasn't light yet. He could barely open his eyes when the flashlight shone in his face.

Where was Oliver?

"Get up! I won't tell you again!"

Then he saw the gun pointed at him, and the man holding it. Espen Frisk.

"Take the boy," he heard him say.

There was a second person behind Espen, now moving into the light. Lise Forsberg.

"You look surprised," she said. "You hadn't figured it out yet. You're not the best detective, are you?"

Timo got up and looked her straight in the eye.

"What do you hope to achieve?" Timo said as Espen pushed him to the door. "The police will figure it out and then they will come for you."

"We'll be gone by then. A new life. Somewhere no one can find us. But first, let's have some fun."

"What do you plan to do with us?"

Lise giggled and said, "You'll see."

Outside, the glow of the sunrise filled the air around them. Morning. Probably the last time he would ever see the sun rise and feel the warmth of the first rays on his face. Birds were singing in the background. It went from silence to the reinvigorating sounds that now engulfed the landscape.

Another poke in his ribs. It was excruciatingly painful, but he stepped forward, on autopilot. Oliver looked at him with wide-eyed fear. He knew what was coming. He had seen it before.

"They'll find you," Timo said. "You can't hide."

"Hollow threats," Espen said, motioning them to walk straight into the woods. "The Gävle police is as efficient and smart as an elephant in a lion's cage."

They went on in silence for a few minutes. The path took them deeper into the woods. Lise and Oliver led the way. She had her arm wrapped around the boy's shoulders as if he could run away at any moment. Behind him, Timo heard the cracking of twigs. Focus. He had to focus. Where was plan A? He was scared and he shouldn't be. His training should have kicked in, but he had failed to pick up clues, ways to get out. The fog still hadn't cleared, which was exactly what they wanted. He couldn't be sharp. He had to be weak, weaker than they were.

They stopped in a clearing.

"Björkehorns covers 43 hectares. There's a road to the west. If you can reach it, you'll live. If you don't, you'll die. You have a five-minute head start."

"Are you kidding me?" Timo said.

Espen gave him an ironic grin. "Starting now. If I were you, I'd run."

West. Where was west? Sun in the east. Trees, only trees on the other side. All the same. This was going to be impossible, and they knew it, but he had to try. For him, for Oliver.

"Oliver, come," Timo said and walked over to the boy, but Lise pulled him back.

"No, not Oliver. He stays here."

"What will you do with him?"

"Four minutes to go!"

"Then just shoot me here and now," Timo said, "I know you'll never let me go."

"Okay then," Espen said with an unsettling calm, took the gun in his other hand, and walked over to Lise and Oliver. What followed, Timo hadn't expected. Espen knelt and held the gun in front of Oliver, while Lise took out another gun from the bag she was carrying and pointed it at Oliver's head.

"If you shoot him, you'll live," Espen said to the boy, "if you don't, you'll die."

The boy's eyes jumped from Timo to the gun in the hands of his abductor.

Timo gasped for air. Someone was going to die no matter what. And it'd rather be him than Oliver, a boy who still had his entire life ahead of him. He had to believe that Oliver would survive this, that he would live so his mother would finally get him back.

"Oliver, take the gun," Timo whispered.

Oliver shook his head wildly.

"It's okay," Timo said, "everything will be okay."

"Shut up!" Espen shouted.

Oliver took the gun. It was so heavy that he had to use both hands.

"You know what to do," Espen said.

The boy was still looking at the gun. Then the pupils of his eyes narrowed and widened again. The trembling stopped, and he held up the gun, finger wrapped tightly around the trigger, like he had done it before. The cold metal reflected the light of the early sun. Oliver placed his left hand under the grip, supporting the weight of the gun. Timo could barely breathe as he watched the entire scene unfold. Seconds seemed minutes.

And then, just before the gunshot echoed through the air, his eyes narrowed, and a strange grin appeared on Oliver's lips. In that second, Timo knew he didn't want to die. Not like that.

Pain. Timo staggered and then fell to the ground, his heart pounding out of his chest, dizzy with tension. He lay there for a second and then realized the pain was gone. The bullet had only scratched the skin of his cheek. He waited for more sounds, with all his senses heightened by the adrenaline. He had to get up. The threat was still there. And then he heard the desperate cries of a woman. It was Lise Forsberg.

Moaning.

What had just happened?

Oliver lay on the ground, the gun still in his hand. He hadn't pulled the trigger. Then who fired the shot?

Lise had crawled over to Espen and was holding and rocking him in her arms. The blood was soaking his white shirt. His eyes were closed and there was a cramped grin on his face.

Another gunshot.

Lise ducked. Then Timo knew he wasn't the target, but his abductors were. The sound came from behind him. Someone was lurking in the bushes, in the woods.

Another shot echoed through the air.

He needed a gun. Fast. He and Oliver were in the line of fire. Whoever was shooting at Lise and Espen wouldn't hesitate to shoot them too. They were collateral. He crawled over to the boy, who was still lying between the mud.

Lise yelled after the third shot, "Stop, stop!"

"Stop? You want this to stop, Lise Forsberg?"

The deep voice came from the woods and thundered through the air.

"Who are you?" Lise yelled, swinging the gun in all directions. "Show your face, coward!"

"You're calling me a coward? You, one of the losers who killed my daughter?"

Timo looked up. "Patrik? Patrik Mikaelsson?"

From the darkness of the forest, a figure appeared, black coat and hat, a pistol carefully aimed at the young woman who was desperately trying to get control of the situation. She aimed, but he was faster, shooting the gun straight out of her hand.

She let out a cry, dropped the gun and held her bleeding hand with the other.

"No," Espen's gurgling voice sounded. He reached for the gun that was now lying a few meters away from him, but his failing body, already cycling between consciousness and coma, didn't comply and he gave up.

Timo said, "Patrik, don't do this! Yes, they have to pay, but not like this."

"Stay out of this! This is between me and those pieces of shit!"

"No," Timo said, and tried to get up, but Patrik swayed the gun in his direction.

The man said, "I won't repeat it. I'll shoot you if you come between us."

"Then what are you waiting for?" Lise cried.

Patrik turned his attention to the woman again. "I want to know why. Why did Jonna have to die?"

Lise laughed. A strange, twisted laugh that seemed to get louder and louder. "You want to know why? Jesus, this is so pathetic!"

Patrik's hands were trembling and the finger on the trigger wavered between pulling and releasing. Then he suddenly aimed the gun at Espen and pulled the trigger. The body jumped up as the bullet pierced through the heart with ravaging force, destroying every cell in its path.

"No!" Timo heard the young woman scream.

There was not a moment to lose, and he jumped for the gun lying next to Oliver.

"Police! Put the gun down!" a woman's voice said.

Isa, Berger, and a dozen police officers stood around them.

"No, she's next," Patrik said.

"Go ahead, kill me! I dare you! Then you'll never know."

"Patrik, don't do this," Timo said. "The moment you pull that trigger..."

Patrik looked at him. "What? I'll be a killer? I already am."

Timo said, "You won't win. You'll hit the ground before you can pull that trigger. And then everything is lost. Everyone will hear their story, Lise and Espen's, not yours, not Jonna's. They aren't worth it."

Patrik wavered. Timo felt the coldness of the metal in his hand, as the father almost aimlessly cast his gaze over the surroundings, from

Oliver still on the ground with hands over his ears to the swarm of police officers who surrounded him. It seemed like ages before anything happened.

"Patrik, do it for Jonna," Timo whispered.

Patrik sighed and then lowered his arm. It was over.

CHAPTER

24

"**TELL ME ABOUT MARIE,**" Isa said.

Lise held her wrapped hand in front of her, and without looking up she said, "Don't you want to go back to the beginning?"

"The beginning? Jonna?"

"Beautiful, smart, and popular Jonna. Kids were always hanging around her. They wanted to be her friend; they wanted to be like her. That charisma, even for a thirteen-year-old girl, that confidence. She did it so effortlessly."

"And you were jealous?" Isa said.

Lise shook her head. "No, of course not."

"Then why?"

"Why not?" Lise said and gave them a smile.

"You killed her."

"Of course. I had to."

That Saturday, they found Jonna on the shore of the lake. Lise had been stalking her for months. Jonna wanted to be her friend, but Lise wanted to be Jonna. And there could be only one.

Espen. She had never noticed him until he sat down next to her on a school trip. He said they were soul mates. He'd watched her and claimed he knew what she was thinking and dreaming of. They could be the perfect couple. That same trip, she didn't say a word to him, but she was intrigued, and the weeks after that she observed him. He knew of her growing obsession with Jonna.

"You should do something about it," he told her.

It took months before she trusted him. He was a restless kid. Polite, smart and handsome on the outside, but fighting dreams of torture and death on a daily basis, and it was only a matter of time before things got out of hand.

Jonna was sitting on a rock hanging over the water of the lake. She sat there a lot. The water was eerie and appealing at the same time. She had told her mom she was going to see a friend, but she wanted to be alone. The pressure. They expected so much. Her parents, the teachers, her friends.

When she saw them, she smiled. She had wanted to talk to Lise for a long time. She considered her a kindred spirit. Lise had probably experienced the same high, unattainable expectations as the daughter of a rich, successful man, and Jonna wanted to know how she had managed so far. Henrik Forsberg had told her his sister was weird and not worthy of her attention, but Lise intrigued her.

Jonna stopped smiling when the bullying started. First Lise pushed her. Then Espen tried to get her off balance on that ledge, and when Lise pulled off the necklace her mother had given when she was seven, Jonna could no longer deny it. They were there to hurt her.

Lise picked up a stone and threw it. It hit her on the left side of the forehead. Jonna staggered and a little push was enough to send her over the edge. They looked at the girl below, desperately trying to keep her head above the water, swinging her arms in all directions. She was a terrible swimmer, but she had been in this situation before, and for years, she had planned rescue strategies in her head should it ever happen again.

The panic and the disorientation got in the way. Her legs were so tired, trying to get that vital sip of oxygen every time her head reached the surface and the sunrays warmed her face. With almost superhuman strength, she tried to break the seesaw cycle of going up and down, but it wasn't long before her body gave up, and Lise and Espen watched her disappear into the darkness of the lake.

Isa put the plastic bag with the necklace on the table. The gold necklace with Jonna's name. "You kept it all those years. Why?"

The ultimate souvenir and trophy. She had put it on now and then and had looked in the mirror. At that moment, she hadn't been Lise, but Jonna, the perfect girl she wanted to be, the girl everyone loved.

"Where did you get it?" Lise said, surprised.

"We found it in your room. Your mother knew and she confronted you."

Lise shook her head. "No."

An unfortunate coincidence. That day, Lise had put on the necklace and had forgotten to hide it afterwards. Her mother almost never came in her room, but the night of the reunion, Linda was looking for earrings to replace her broken ones and she found the necklace on the table in her daughter's room.

"That's why she wanted to talk to Patrik Mikaelsson. That's why you killed her."

"I didn't kill my mother," Lise said. "I've thought about it though. She wasn't very subtle. So many questions about Jonna. It annoyed me. And then I realized she had found the necklace and Mikaelsson had told her at the reunion they had never found it on Jonna's body. Nine years too late. But I could handle her. She was weak. She wasn't worthy of my special attention."

"But Marie was," Berger said.

He opened the file and put the picture of Marie in front of her. "Why did she have to die?"

Lise grimaced as she ran her eyes over the young woman's face.

"We had to intervene. She had figured it out, though I hadn't thought she was capable."

"What had she figured out?"

Lise looked at her hands. What was the point of hiding everything? If she wanted to tell their story, she had to tell everything. For Espen. For history. Everyone would remember them, would be in awe of them. What they had done and gotten away with for so many years deserved the proper attention.

"Jonna was the first, and Espen wanted more. He loved to manipulate people."

"Like Quinten Hall? And Janusz Haugen?"

She flashed her eyes at them, and a strange look appeared on her face. Disgust and repulsion.

"Janusz Haugen is a pervert. He deserves to rot in hell!"

"Looks like your boyfriend didn't tell you everything," Isa said with a sarcastic grin on her face. She walked across the room and turned her head to the one-way mirror.

"Espen and I shared everything."

"Why did Quinten have to die?"

"It was a game. Roulette. It could have been someone else. Marie, Teresa, or Jussi."

"But you picked Quinten," Isa said calmly. "Oh, but it wasn't actually you who chose him. It was Espen."

"Both of us!"

"No, Espen manipulated you too. You were no different from the rest."

Isa leaned over and stared at the confused girl.

"Quinten had to die because he knew about Janusz Haugen. Espen had falsely accused him. There was no sexual assault. Espen made it up because Haugen saw you in the forest the day Jonna died. The only way to silence him was to jeopardize his credibility, but your boyfriend made sure it wasn't him who told it. He told Quinten. He knew very well his friend, impressionable as always, wouldn't be able to keep it quiet. Though over the years, Quinten became wary of what Espen whispered in his ear. We assume that a few days before his death he confronted Espen with his suspicions. The big fight wasn't about his feelings for Espen."

She shook her head. "No, it didn't go like that."

"That day Espen made sure they were all stoned, and sensitive Quinten committed suicide. You helped Espen get him into the bathroom while the others were passed out, and there you hanged him. Only, Marie had seen you."

"The bitch! At first she thought it was a dream, but then she saw me with Espen in Gävle. She didn't know we were a couple."

"And then she started to take the same classes, got invited to your brother's parties..."

"And she seduced my father. I watched them, kissing, touching each other, having sex. It was too much."

"Did you know she was pregnant?"

"No, do you think that would have mattered?" Lise said.

"What really happened?" Berger asked.

300

"She was gathering evidence. She got too close, so we had to stop her. That day, I saw Henrik leave her apartment. It was just too perfect. I couldn't help myself. When she left a few minutes after Henrik, I offered her a ride. She had to go to Gävle and had no car. Teresa had already left."

Lise smiled as if it was a pleasant memory. "She wasn't that eager to get in the car with me, but I managed to convince her. I didn't drive her home but to Stromsbrö."

"And she didn't complain?"

"Of course she was scared, but I just wanted to talk to her. About Quinten, about Jonna. It got out of hand. There was a struggle in the car. She hit her head on the dashboard and passed out."

"You didn't just want to talk to her. You wanted to kill her! You already had a plan in your head."

"No, that's not true!" Lise said.

"And Oliver?"

An unfortunate witness. He passed by when Marie's head hit the dashboard. She had pulled the car off the road, in the bushes, hoping no one would see them, but there he was, a nosy, little brat.

"He ran, but he didn't get very far. I dragged him to the car."

"That was risky. Mark Lisberg could have seen you. He must have passed by only minutes later."

"Maybe, but I had no choice. Oliver knows who I am, and he knew Marie too."

"And then?"

"I brought them to the house and called Espen."

"Your mother's house?"

"Yes, mommy's house," Lise grinned.

"And your mommy's car? How did you manage that?"

"Fake ID. I have plenty of them. It wasn't that hard to buy a car pretending to be someone else. Nice touch, don't you think?"

"You must have known Linda was dead?"

"Not really. I could guess something happened to her. She suddenly runs off with a mysterious man. Really? She would never have given up daddy's money. And it wasn't hard to trace her whereabouts that day. But it was in our best interest to play along. No Linda, no one who would ask nasty questions about Jonna's death."

"Going back to Marie and Oliver: why keep them alive?"

"Espen wanted to kill them, but I had a better idea. Marie and Oliver. Interesting subjects to play with. We studied them, starved them, tortured them, to see who would break first, who would kill to save themselves."

The room was filled with a cool draft that sent a wave down Isa's spine. She had never felt such an uneasiness before. Two months. The psychological games, the horror.

"And then Marie escaped," Isa said.

"We let her escape. It was part of the game. Only, she got further than we expected."

"Until someone helped you."

"Yeah! We found her on the road, gasping for air, unable to move."

"And the shoes?"

"Ah, yes. That was my idea. I found it interesting to nourish the fear of the Långs a bit. They deserve it. Especially Bengta. Always so overprotective. And the nonsense she spouted. Unbelievable. No wonder Marie ran away. They also never understood what a conniving little bitch their daughter really was."

"Those people had just lost their daughter," Isa said.

Lise shrugged. Nothing seemed to pull down the wall of indifference.

"And inspector Paikkala? Why him?"

Lise leaned backward, before she said, "The game wasn't finished."

"So he was a random victim?"

The plan was to discredit Patrik Mikaelsson. They had prepared a nice little performance in which Espen would tell Timo about the diary and put the suspicion on Patrik, but Espen had been interested in inspector Paikkala, the strong, confident police officer, ready to save the world. What would it take to break that confidence?

From the beginning, Espen had been stalking him, and it was a last-minute decision to involve the police officer in the game. If Espen had stuck to the plan, they would have been gone by now and he would still be alive.

"Maybe," Lise said and turned to the one-way glass, knowing Timo would be watching.

"What were you planning to do with inspector Paikkala and Oliver Pilkvist?"

The conversation was interrupted by a loud noise from the hall.

"Where is my daughter?" a deep voice said. "I want to see my daughter!"

"Mr. Forsberg, you can't go in there," a police officer said, but the next moment, the door was pushed open, and the devastated father rushed into the room.

"Mr. Forsberg, you shouldn't be here," Berger said, and tried to block the way.

"This is all a misunderstanding," Gerard pleaded. "Lise, I'll get you a lawyer. We'll figure this out!"

Lise shook her head, smiled and looked him straight in the eye. "I killed your precious Marie."

"What?"

"I put my hands around her neck and squeezed. There was this annoying hissing sound she made. So exhilarating! I squeezed harder and harder until it was quiet. And then we dumped her in the lake. It was so poetic, knowing you were there, so close. It was a message. Do you understand, daddy?"

Gerard was frozen to the spot. He opened his mouth, but no words came out.

"Now leave me alone! I don't need your help. I never did. You were only interested in Henrik anyway. Your darling son! Sure, you didn't approve of his life, the choices he made, but ultimately you did whatever he wanted. You helped him, and I... you never saw what I gave up for you! For you! Precious Henrik was about to walk away with all your money and leave you behind with all the financial and legal implications. Henrik and Teresa. That's how much your son loved you! And then you also chose that whore over me! It was humiliating!"

"You killed your brother," Gerard said. "You killed Henrik! How, on earth, could you do that?"

She gave him a sarcastic grin, then turned her head away from him. It was all she had to say.

* * *

"She's a psychopath."

Ingrid sighed and put the file on the table. The entire team was sitting in Timo's office.

"A psychiatrist will have to do a full evaluation, but she's showing the typical signs. Finding pleasure in inflicting pain on others. Dehumanizing them, without empathy, without remorse... it's..."

"Scary," Isa said.

"She confessed to killing Jonna and Marie, but not Teresa and Henrik, and none of the other cases. She said they were just mimicking these murders. And we still don't know what happened to Linda."

Berger felt so exhausted. He couldn't understand how the boss could look so fresh and sharp after all he'd been through. Timo hadn't said a word about the abduction, at least not to them. He had written the story down in his witness statement and that was it. Without drama, without emotions.

"We have to dig deeper," Lars said. "She'll crack at some point."

"We need a different tactic," Isa said, "she shut down after seeing her father."

"What do you think, boss?"

Until then, Timo had kept quiet and had listened to the comments and opinions of his team members like a good captain would. "Why would she tell us about Jonna and Marie, and not about the other murders? No, Lise and Espen didn't kill them."

"But then who did?" Isa asked.

"There was only one person who was looking for revenge," Timo said calmly.

"Patrik Mikaelsson?"

"Yes, it's time to talk to him."

CHAPTER

25

"**SO, THEY KILLED JONNA,**" Patrik said. The police officers on the other side of the table had told him about Lise Forsberg's confession. He could finally grieve; he could finally heal, but his daughter's death had left scars, deep scars. Deeper than anyone could see. He had made sacrifices. He had given up his humanity, his soul.

"I know this must be difficult, Mr. Mikaelsson," Timo said.

"You don't know half of it," the man blurted. "If the police had done their job, this wouldn't have gotten out of hand and people wouldn't..."

"... have lost their lives," Timo said.

Patrik shook his head and let out a sigh.

"Two years ago, you stopped writing letters and emails to the police demanding to revisit your daughter's case. Why? What happened two years ago that suddenly changed your mind?"

"I realized I had to move on with my life," Patrik said. "I finally accepted the official version of her death. I was clearly wrong."

"No. This is what I think happened: you wanted revenge."

Patrik bowed his head. It was better that way. He didn't have to look at those sharp blue eyes that would pierce through his soul, his mind. He wouldn't be able to hide anything.

With eyes fixed on the older man, Timo continued, "Where is Linda?"

"I don't know," Patrik said.

"Sure, you do. You killed her. What have you done with her body?"

"Like I said, I don't know anything about Linda."

"Linda discovered Jonna's necklace in her daughter's room, the necklace Jonna was wearing when she died. She was surprised and didn't know what to think of it. That's why she talked to you about Jonna on the night of the reunion, but that wasn't enough. The fear in her head started to grow. She came to your house a few days later. Did she tell you she suspected one of her children?"

"Where's the evidence?"

"This morning at 9:00 a.m. we found human remains in your backyard, by the cherry tree. The analysis will take a few days, maybe a week, but I'm sure we'll find a match with Linda Forsberg's DNA."

Patrik sighed. "Jonna loved that tree. It hardly bore cherries, but we planted it when she was born. She sometimes sat there for hours, reading, sleeping, dreaming. I can still see her sitting there. It's like... she... they are still there. My daughter, my wife."

The tears came. He hadn't cried for years. Now the drops were falling on his hands and staining the sleeves of his shirt. It was good to feel that pain again. He took a deep breath and then said: "Linda's death was an accident. I never wanted to kill her, but I was so angry. All those years, people treated me like an idiot and then this woman stood before me, with her own messed-up, inadequate words, trying to tell me she knew or at least suspected who'd killed my daughter. And she wanted forgiveness. It was just too much to take."

"It was an accident?"

"I lost my temper. I grabbed her by the arms, shook her. I wanted her to give me a name, but she couldn't, she just couldn't."

"She wanted to protect her daughter," Timo said.

"And then I pushed her, and she fell. She hit her head."

"Why didn't you call an ambulance?" Timo said. "Why didn't you go to the police?"

"I was in a panic. If she had only told me, I wouldn't have... this isn't me!"

"Like it wasn't you when you pulled the trigger and shot Espen Frisk?"

"He deserved it."

"And Teresa Ljungman and Henrik Forsberg?" Timo asked.

"I... they were innocent," Patrik said.

"Yes, they were. You killed them, because you thought Henrik Forsberg murdered Jonna, and you needed him to pay. And Teresa?"

"If only I had spoken to Haugen sooner. I talked to Teresa weeks ago about Marie. I knew this was important. This had something to do with Jonna's death. I shared my suspicions about Henrik with her, but she was so adamant about defending him I thought..."

"She was involved too," Timo said.

"It was a mistake. I'll have to pay for it my entire life. It will never go away!"

Timo jumped up and leaned over to the frightened man. "It's all about you! Not for a moment you thought about the families. How they must feel!"

"Timo?" Isa put her hand on his arm and pulled him back.

Patrik pursed his lips and looked with bated breath at the inspectors. He knew he had done something unforgivable. There was nothing they could say he didn't know already.

"Let's go back to Linda Forsberg," Isa said. "You buried her, but after that you kept texting her family for two years?"

"Henrik Forsberg died thinking his mother left them for another man," Timo said.

Isa gave her boss another concerned look, and then turned her attention to Patrik again.

Patrik said, "She would have left them anyway. That's the way Linda was. A new man every few months. Harald was no different. She didn't care about her family. And they didn't care about her. Why else would none of them have tried to find her? It was so easy to get in the house and make it look like she had packed her bags and had left them. I used her phone to send them the final goodbye note."

"And you also lured Henrik to his death using her phone, using a message from his mother."

"No, I used a disposable phone, telling him I knew something about Linda and Marie. He didn't believe me, but we agreed to meet in Stromsbrö. I told him Teresa should come along as it concerned her too."

"Why wait two years?"

"Because I didn't know for sure," Patrik said. "I had plenty of time to think about it. Linda didn't tell me who, but in my mind, there were only two, maybe three possibilities. Henrik, Lise or Gerard. Lise Forsberg looked so innocent and sincere. I talked to her a lot. But of course, she knew what I was after, and I believed everything she said. So stupid."

"She played you," Timo said.

"Yes. I'm just an old fool. And then you found Marie. Dead. And then I knew... or thought I knew."

"How did you find out you killed the wrong people?"

"Haugen told me."

"Why did you contact Janusz Haugen?"

"The day after they were found dead, I got a call from Bengta Lång. They had found a file among Marie's things that was addressed to me. It was an old newspaper about the case against Haugen. Then I went to see him."

And he had driven around like a zombie when he'd realized he had killed the wrong people and how Lise had been manipulating him all along, poisoning his mind with rumors about Henrik.

"Why would Marie keep a file for you?" Timo said.

Patrik shrugged.

Timo said, "I see. It was you who hired Marie. What was she supposed to do? Seduce Henrik? Get him to talk about Jonna?"

"So what? It didn't quite work. The idiot fell in love with Gerard. She quit and then got herself killed."

"How did you meet?"

Patrik looked at his hands.

"Jesus, you paid her! You slept with her?"

"I didn't sleep with her. How could I? I knew her. She knew Jonna. Yes, I paid an escort girl, but I didn't know it was her. It wasn't until she showed up that I recognized her. We talked about Jonna, Quinten, everyone. I wanted the Forsbergs. Obviously, she wanted them too. We never talked about our reasons. And then, six months ago she suddenly called it off. I tried to contact her, but she avoided me."

"She was in love with Gerard," Isa said.

"And she didn't tell you about her suspicions at that time?" Timo asked. "We believe she already knew about Lise and Espen."

Patrik shook his head.

"Interesting," Timo said, "she didn't trust you."

"Like I said, we never talked about the reasons. I guess her main reason was Quinten's death, not Jonna's."

"Why the show? The twigs?" Isa asked.

"I wanted the world to know what they had done. I wanted them to confess. I needed evidence. But then I had to shoot Henrik. I lost control of the situation."

"How did you get to Stromsbrö? Your car wasn't seen on the CCTV."

"We met at my house. I got in the car, took out the gun and forced them to drive to Stromsbrö, but then Henrik tried to take the gun. I hit him with the grip. Teresa wanted to help him. I really thought I had incapacitated them, but they escaped. Henrik knew the area better than I did. So I was worried I'd lost them, but Teresa was weak, and he didn't want to leave her. I shot him. Teresa still tried to get away, but she didn't get very far. I put my hands around her neck and squeezed."

"And you wanted to make a grand show out of it?"

"She was light. Lise told me Marie was found with a twig in her mouth. Of course, I didn't know she had done it herself. I thought it was a nice touch and it would deflect the investigation. Everyone would think all these murders were committed by the same killer. I wanted to do the same with Henrik, but then he wasn't dead. He tried to escape. He almost reached the road. I shot him a second time and pushed the twig in his mouth. I wanted to put them next to each other, but then I heard voices. People in the area must have heard the gunshot. So I had to leave him as is."

"Four people are dead," Timo said and crossed his arms.

"I'm sorry about Linda, Henrik and Teresa, but I'm not sorry about killing Espen Frisk. I'm sorry about my failure. Lise Forsberg should have died. I was a coward. I could have killed her if I had wanted to give up my own life. I don't care what happens to me now. I've lost everything. There is nothing more to give except my life."

Timo closed the file and got up.

Patrik stared at him. He was tired. The trauma of losing a child, the years of fighting for her right to a fair investigation, but also the realization he was a murderer. He had killed innocent people, and it was too much to carry. When they found his body hanging in his prison cell a week later, the letter on the desk told his story, asking Gerard Forsberg and Teresa Ljungman's parents for forgiveness.

But it was difficult for the families to see beyond the cowardice with which he had taken the easy way out. There was anger because they were not given the grieving process to which they were entitled, where forgiveness could be refused, and revenge could be a lot more tangible than the dreams in which they were lashing out at the person responsible for the death of their loved ones. So many questions and no answers. There was envy that Patrik had gotten his revenge for his daughter's death, and they hadn't. It was all taken away from them. Forever.

CHAPTER

26

"**INSPECTOR LINDSTRÖM?**" said the police officer.

"Yes?"

"Maybe you can help the woman and her daughter sitting there. They have been waiting for a while."

The man pointed to the two crouching figures sitting on the bench in the reception area of the police station. The woman was staring into nothingness, while the girl was preoccupied with her cell phone.

"Sophie?" Isa said.

Isa had spent all morning dealing with the remaining paperwork after Lise's and Patrik's confessions, and she craved for something other than the most creativity-killing task in the world, but a confrontation with the ex-wife of Magnus Wieland wasn't exactly what she was looking for.

"Isa," the woman replied.

Isa turned to the young man. "Can't someone else take care of them?"

"They asked to speak to inspector Paikkala, but I can't reach him. It seems urgent."

"His mobile?"

"He doesn't answer."

"Maybe he already left," Isa said.

"Probably."

Paikkala was on his own crusade, or whatever it was he was doing these days, and didn't want to be disturbed.

"Okay, I'll take care of them. I guess it won't take long."

She took Sophie and Anna into a room that was normally used for short meetings and offered them a seat at the small table in the middle. Anna seemed frightened. Obviously, her mother had taken her to the police station, not quite with her blessing.

"Tell me what's on your mind," Isa said.

Anna looked at her mom as a sign of approval.

"Go ahead," Sophie said and took her hand, "it's okay."

They had never formally met. Isa had seen the girl a few times when she had picked up Magnus at his home, but he had always kept his family and the life he shared with Isa separate. Much later, he had told her the secret about his son's illness, something he had tried so hard to hide from her. She had only met his son in the hospital, lying in an irreversible coma, with the machines that kept him alive roaring in the background. And for the past few months, Anna had avoided being in the same room with her, angry and disappointed about her parents' divorce.

"What do you want to tell me?" Isa said.

Anna's hand went into the pocket of her sweater, her movements going in slow motion, as if she had to think carefully through every step.

The package was wrapped in plastic. She placed it in front of Isa, looked at it, took a deep breath before carefully unfolding it and taking out the phone.

Suddenly, the irritation with which Isa had sat through the entire scene was gone. The blood had drained from her face. Her brain had gone into pause, her eyes and mouth frozen in an expression of horror. The next moment she couldn't stop the flow of thoughts.

She recognized the black cover and the two distinct scratches, one of which ran almost over the entire height of the screen. It had long been the cause of his OCD-induced anxiety. Every time Alex had looked at it, his mind had told him to get rid of it because it hadn't been perfect, but he'd forced himself to deal with the flaw.

Anna pushed the cell phone across the table toward her. Isa still couldn't say a word. So many crazy thoughts were going through her mind, but one stood out. The one she could barely understand.

"Where did you get this?"

"I found it," the young girl said.

And then the tears came. It was a sign. The sign that the most horrific thought was true. Anna hadn't just found it anywhere. She had found it in her home, and she knew who had put it there. She just couldn't say the name.

Sophie took her daughter's hand and then said, "It was Magnus."

Isa could still hear Magnus say 'I love you' that morning in the hospital, at Toby's sickbed. Had she signed Alex's death warrant that very moment by ignoring him?

She had shared the most intimate things with Magnus. They had been together for two years. She had considered him her soulmate. How? How could this man have done this to her?

Her heart was racing. With every thought, it seemed to pick up the pace even more. The burning anger was growing and would finally overwhelm the sadness.

"Where is he?"

Sophie looked at her, afraid of what the woman on the other side, fingers clung to the edge of the table, would do. "Isa, I think you should calm down."

"Where is he?" Isa repeated, the voice trembling, barely able to conceal the anger.

Timo knew. This was what he had tried so desperately to hide from her. How long had this been going on? Who else knew?

She stood up with such a ferocity the chair fell backward, with the sound echoing through the room. She rushed to the door and threw it open with the same fury.

"Where is Paikkala?" Isa yelled.

Police officers and civilians stared at her.

"Where is he?"

Ingrid, standing only a few meters away, walked up to her.

"What's going on?" Ingrid said and took her arm. "You look so agitated."

"I just want to know where your boyfriend is," Isa sneered and pushed her away.

Ingrid took a step back. "My what?"

"Fine!" Isa turned around and with a quickened and determined pace ran toward Timo's office.

The door of his office was closed.

"Timo...," Isa said as she pushed the door open, but then stopped.

This wasn't exactly the scene she'd expected to see: Timo, sitting behind the laptop, looking up at Magnus who pointed a gun at his head. Magnus jumped up, gave her a quick look, and then turned back to Timo.

* * *

An hour earlier, Timo had been so caught up with reading that he hadn't noticed Magnus slipping into the room until he heard the door being closed.

The man he had been so desperately looking for stood before him. The conversation had started civilly. Magnus looked good, not the shabby-looking man who had been walking around the police office for the past few weeks. Calmly he had taken a chair and sat down at the desk of his boss, but Timo didn't trust it from the moment Magnus had entered the room.

"Inspector Paikkala," Magnus said.

"What brings you to my office?"

"I heard you were looking for me."

"How did you hear that?"

Timo changed position so he could move his right hand down, to the holstered gun that was pressing against his hip.

A sarcastic smile appeared on Magnus' face, as he suddenly shook his head and put his hand in the right pocket of his coat. He kept it there for a moment. Timo watched it with increasing concern. There was no doubt. It was a gun.

"Let's come to the point, inspector Paikkala," Magnus said.

"Magnus, be calm!"

"Relax. I just want to talk."

"About?"

Magnus gave him a faint smile. "I think you already know."

"Okay... Alexander Nordin, I suppose," Timo said calmly. "We can talk. I'm willing to listen, but you first need to put the gun on the table."

"In a minute," Magnus said, shook his head again and looked at the corner like he had seen a ghost. He continued, "No, no. I can't do that. Leave me alone. I need to do this."

"Who are you talking to?" Timo said confused, but Magnus didn't answer.

"I need to do the right thing... I."

As fast as Timo had tried to be, Magnus was faster and pulled the gun from his pocket. He got up and moved closer, pointing it directly at Timo.

"Gun and hands on the table," Magnus shouted.

Timo complied. "Magnus, be calm, let's talk about this."

"I tried to tell you, make it right, but you didn't want to listen. And I can see it now: you took her away from me. You're just like the others. He's right. You need to go."

Timo didn't know what to do. Should he go along with the delusion or try to convince Magnus this was a figment of his imagination?

Think!

Where were his negotiation skills, now he badly needed them?

Be calm and reason with him!

He tried to stop the increasing fear coursing through his body. He lifted his head to look him in the eye. If Magnus really wanted to kill him, he would have been dead already.

"Magnus, I don't want to take Isa away from you," he tried.

"You're lying," Magnus said. "I've seen you together."

"No, she loves you, not me."

Magnus shook his head. "No, she doesn't love me, not anymore."

His hand was shaking, when he cocked the gun.

Timo felt the adrenaline rushing through his body. He didn't want to die, not now. There was a time in his life he would have welcomed death, but now he knew there were still things he wanted to live for. He had realized that when Espen Frisk had pointed the gun at him. Now, he needed again a back-up plan, quickly, but there was none. Reasoning alone wouldn't help. He was younger and in a better shape than Magnus. There was a chance he could overtake him. There was a chance, but a chance wasn't enough.

"Alex was a mistake," Timo said, "she knows that now."

"How would you know?"

Wrong, he did it all wrong. Magnus would twist it so that it would always feed the delusion. And the delusion was that he was having an affair with Isa.

The phone rang. He looked at it, but Magnus shook his head.

"Let it ring! Tell me, how do you know?"

"She told me."

"Why would she tell you?" Magnus said.

"You were right. There was something between us, but it's over."

The phone finally stopped ringing.

"I knew it, I knew it," Magnus shouted and then looked at the corner. "You're right."

Timo frowned. Who was he talking to?

"She betrayed you too, with him." He turned to Timo, waving the gun in front of his face.

The phone rang again. In one swift movement, Timo grabbed the phone and put it back. Magnus saw it too late and lashed out. The slap on the cheek was painful but manageable, but more importantly, the test had been successful. He was faster than Magnus. Next time, it wouldn't be the phone, but the gun on the table.

"Don't ever do that again," Magnus said.

"Do you forgive him?" Timo said suddenly.

Magnus stared at him in astonishment. "Forgiveness? Why would I? He isn't real."

"I know," Timo said calmly, "but he owes you. I just want to help you."

Seemingly contemplating what to do, the confusion didn't leave Magnus' face. "You're right. He owes me. He took my Isa."

"Timo,...," Isa yelled as she opened the door, but then stopped.

"Isa," Magnus whispered. Regaining his mental balance, with his lips curled up in a mocking smile, he finally said, "Are you worried about your boyfriend?"

"Uh... no, Magnus, I'm worried about you." She quickly glanced at Timo. "He means nothing to me. Put the gun down and let's talk about it."

Magnus looked like he was about to explode. "Why does everyone want to talk about it? There is nothing to say. Not anymore."

At that moment, also Ingrid jumped into the room. "Magnus? What are you doing?"

"Ingrid, get out," Timo said.

Too many people in the room. The situation could get out of control very quickly, and it did.

"Shut up! Leave me alone! He must die." Magnus pressed the barrel of the gun to Timo's forehead. Timo felt the metal scratch the skin above his eyes. He couldn't think anymore. Was this it? Was he going to die? If Magnus pulled the trigger, no one could save him.

"No," Ingrid cried, "don't hurt him."

From the corners of his eye, Timo saw her almost bursting into tears. He wanted to tell her it would be okay.

"Dad," a frail voice sounded.

In all the commotion, none of them had seen Anna and Sophie enter the room.

"Anna." Her mother tried to pull her back, but Anna signaled Sophie it was okay, and she approached her dad.

"I found the phone and the gloves," Anna said. The tears were running down her face.

"You are my dad, my sweet dad. Remember how you played Lego and Barbie with me when I was young? And it was you who mended my knees when I had fallen again with my bike. You helped me with math,... you... mean so much to me. I can't believe this is you. This is not you."

"You took it?" Magnus said.

"I was there that day. The way you looked. I'd never seen you like that. You took a package out of your pocket and put it on the table, and later you hid it in the laundry room behind the washing machine. Why didn't you throw it away? Why did you have to keep it? Why did you put me in that situation?"

The expression on his face softened. "What situation?"

Police officers took position behind the girl and her mother, guns in hand, ready to fire, but Timo shook his head, signaling them to wait.

"The choice between my father and doing the right thing... telling the police you might have killed someone," Anna cried.

She fell to the floor, while the tears came out in buckets, her body shaking with the flood of emotions.

"Anna," her father's voice broke.

He turned to Timo, stared at him and then put his arm down. Timo took the gun from Magnus' hand, and then the father knelt and took his daughter in his arms.

But the look on Isa's face concerned Timo. It showed nothing, as if she was pondering about something. Her right hand went down along the side of her body, reaching for the gun in the holster hanging at the belt around her waist.

"Isa," Timo said.

Their eyes met. He knew what she was thinking, and he shook his head.

Don't do it!

Her hand tightened and then relaxed. She looked at the father and daughter on the floor, then turned around and walked out of the room.

"I have to go now," Magnus whispered and wiped the tears from his daughter's face. Anna gave him a faint nod and smiled.

The arrest took place in serenity, with only the voice of the police officer, reading his rights, resounding through the room. Cuffed, but head high, he walked with them. Before he entered the hallway he turned. A faint smile appeared on his lips. A sign of relief.

* * *

When the officers left, Timo fell down in the chair and put his head in his hands. What had just happened? He had been careless, stupid, the way he had behaved for so many years. He was disappointed because he thought he had gotten smarter.

"Are you okay?"

Timo jumped up. Ingrid was leaning against the doorpost.

"Yeah. I'm okay."

"No, you're not well."

"I can handle a few more bruises," he said.

"That's not what I meant. You were almost killed. Twice."

He knew she wanted him to talk about the ordeal. He was a policeman, and he was trained for this, but he was still human. And everyone, faced with the possibility of death, falls into a mode of self-reflection.

But there was no time. He had already boxed it and put it in a dark corner of his mind, maybe never to think about it again, like he had put away so many things. Big things, small things. A few years ago he would have kept it there, hidden away, but it had made him think about his existence. Living and wanting to live. And living meant there was a possibility of losing. Not just his life, someone else's, someone he would care for. Was he willing to go through that again?

"Tell me you are okay," she said in the softest voice he had ever heard.

He nodded and said, "I need a moment alone."

"Okay," she said. "If you want to talk to someone, I'm here for you."

"Thank you."

When he was alone again, he sighed. There was so much to fix. He saw the people; he saw their strength and willingness to work together. These were bright men and women, but the events of the last year would leave them in ruins. And there was more to come. Magnus.

He might not be able to save them, but he was willing to try, and in the short time that remained, he would do anything to help them. He belonged here. Not in a building in Stockholm where he could get a promotion, where he could have all the resources he wanted, where he could live an easier life. He wanted to show the Isas, the Bergers and the Ingrids of Gävle that they could achieve so much more.

This was home now, and he had to do everything he could to protect it.

CHAPTER

27

ISA STOPPED BEFORE entering the cemetery. This was harder than she thought. It was a mistake. She didn't need a therapy session in front of his grave. How would it help her? But since Magnus' confession, she had felt the need to talk to him. She didn't know how to deal with the growing anger and guilt.

People looked irritated. She jumped aside. In her indecisiveness she was blocking the entrance. Maybe she needed this stream of people to distract her. She strolled down the wide avenue to the other end of the cemetery, following an old man and his wife, who, flowers in hand, finally stopped at one of the older stones.

The Uppsala cemetery dated back to the seventeenth century and covered almost eighteen hectares. The beautiful avenues, the trees and the sea of green made it an oasis of peace.

However, it didn't help her anxiety. In the distance, she recognized the simple black granite stone that rose above the rest of the neighboring tombstones. She wanted to stop and turn back, but her legs kept going, on automatic pilot. As she approached the grave, her eyes fell on a small item lying on the soil parallel to the tombstone. She didn't recognize it until she was only a few meters away.

A rose, one beautiful red rose. Simple. She hadn't put it there. Neither had Irene. His mother wasn't the woman to do such a thing. Who had? Why would anyone put a rose on his grave? It radiated sorrow and... love. Maybe she read something into it that wasn't there.

She knelt and wiped the dust from the shiny granite. It felt warm and smooth. She ran her fingers along the edges to the ground where the rose was lying. It bought her time. Time to think about what she was going to say. The entire speech she had been practicing in her head was gone, like someone had torn the pages and burned them.

"I don't know why I'm here," she said.

This was so stupid. Who and what was she talking to? Bones? Rotting flesh?

A soft breeze caressed her face, and, in that moment, it felt like someone was standing beside her. His presence so clear, telling her to let go.

"It was my fault."

The tears came. First one, then two, then ten. Her face turned red. Every cell in her body was screaming in unison.

She couldn't make it right. Magnus had pulled the trigger, but she had handed him the gun. After the rage, after that moment when she had wanted to put the gun to his head and pull the trigger in front of his daughter, after the feeling of indignation, the full extent of his betrayal had percolated. That insight had crushed her to the point she could no longer breathe, sleep or think rationally. She had reached the breaking point. It was so easy to blame Magnus, but everyone had played their part in the story. Her lifestyle had been the trigger. Ultimately, she was responsible. How could she cope with that?

Through the tears she saw his picture. Beautiful Alex. So serious, always so serious and sad. She needed to scream out, ask someone for forgiveness, be punished for what she had set in motion so many years ago.

She didn't quite know why, but she needed to lie down next to the slab of granite.

She had been lying there for a while when she saw the gardener, standing on the other side, rake in hand, wheelbarrow beside him, clearing the last dry leaves and early weeds.

She got up, wiped the dirt from her pants and walked over to him.

"Excuse me," she said.

The young man jumped up, removed the earplugs, and pressed the pause button on his smartphone.

"Yes?"

"Do you usually work here? You tend the lawns and take care of the trees and flowers, right?"

"Yeah," he said hesitantly, not used to being addressed by the visitors.

"Do you see that grave over there? Alexander Nordin."

"The guy who was murdered," he said.

"Yes... the guy who was murdered."

He didn't notice how she had repeated his words in a disapproving tone.

"Have you seen anyone visit the grave lately?"

He raised his shoulders.

"Not that I can recall, but I'm not here all the time," he finally answered.

"Okay, thanks," she said and started her walk toward the exit.

"But someone must. There is a new rose every week. The wilted ones are replaced regularly. But I can't say who put them there."

He gazed at the grave for a while and then went on with what he had been doing before Isa had interrupted him.

Who? Who would go through the trouble? And why?

* * *

"Ilan, I have to go," she heard him say.

Nick had been waiting for her at the exit of the cemetery. He put the phone away and turned to her.

"Ilan Bergman? Nick, you can't," she said.

"Are you going to charge him with Harket's murder?"

"We can't be together if you get involved in this case again."

"So you want us to be together?"

He took her hand, and they set off on a tour through the streets of Uppsala. As they walked through the idyllic lanes of the city park, Isa felt like she was in a romcom, where at the end the boy gets the girl, or the girl gets her sexy, handsome man.

Neither Nick nor she had been looking for romance, just sex. Beneath that arrogant exterior, she believed there was a sensitive man who was desperate for love and commitment. Why else would he have called her after hearing about Magnus Wieland? He couldn't say the words out loud; he couldn't ask her how she was doing. His concern was hidden under layers of smoothness, pretending he didn't care, but he did.

He wanted to help her. The only one so far. Ingrid hadn't returned her calls, and she couldn't blame her. The nasty remarks about Timo and her were unfounded and marked by a strange jealousy. Apologies had to be made.

"You annoy me, and you push my buttons, but...," she said.

"But?"

"I like you, Nick," she said.

He stopped and let his fingers run along her face. Then he pulled her closer and kissed her. She closed her eyes. For the first time, Alex wasn't there.

"Thank you," she whispered.

He held her face in his hands as he said: "What do you want me to do?"

"I needed this, to go to his grave."

"It's not your fault. If you are looking for salvation, he won't be able to give it."

"Maybe you should talk to his mother," he continued, wiping the stream of salty water from her face.

A shiver ran down her spine. Irene Nordin? No, she wasn't up for that. Irene would eat her alive. She had been right all along. Isa had been responsible for the death of her son.

"You're right, it's probably too soon," he said and took her in his arms. Her body was shaking violently as she let out all the pain, anger and sorrow at once. Passersby looked at them with concern.

"I'll take care of you," he said.

He had said those words before, but they had meant nothing until now. She hadn't seen it coming and neither had he, but she really cared about him. And she wanted to give this, whatever it was, a chance.

"Nick, you were right. I'm selfish. I should let them go."

"What are you talking about?"

"My children. I should let them go. I won't fight the adoption."

"You're not thinking straight right now. I want you to make the decision with a clear head, not when you're in distress. This is too important."

He was right. She closed her eyes again. It felt good to be in his arms. It felt good to invite him into her home and see him next to her in the morning, waking up after a hard night where worries took over the sleep she so desperately needed.

It would take time.

* * *

Singing birds, babbling water, trees and green grass, just as Timo had imagined it, though the house was in a terrible state. Every room needed renovation, and it wasn't just a lick of paint. Walls had to be torn down, the wooden window frames were crumbling and had to be replaced, and he would have to put in a new floor. It would take months even if he could do it full-time. But there was something charming about the place, and the prospect of doing something practical was appealing. He just needed time. He could spend his weekends on it. Yes, this could be it.

He turned and saw Ingrid staring at him. That look. It had to be in the open. How many times had he tried to tell her about his feelings? This should be the moment. It was just her and him, and a sea of harmony, no one else. What was he afraid of? That she would say yes and that he would lose himself in a flood of lust and emotions that he wouldn't be able to stop.

He felt guilty. Guilty he would choose his own happiness over someone else's. Guilty he would betray the love he had shared once with Caijsa, who had died. Why was she on his mind again? This longing for Ingrid felt so much stronger than what he had shared with his dead girlfriend. It couldn't be, but it was. He just wanted to take her in his arms and kiss her.

Her cell phone rang. She sighed as she pulled it out of the pocket of her jacket.

"Hello... hi, Benno, what's wrong, sweetie," she said and walked to the car so she could have more privacy.

He turned around, feeling defeated. Each time he was confronted with the fact she had a family that needed her. There was no future for them.

As he heard her talking in the background, he looked at the water of the lake. On the other side, he saw the Forsberg mansion. A boat was passing by in the distance, and as the ripple on the water slowly moved toward the shore, his hand went down to the pocket of his trousers and took out the letter he had been carrying for weeks.

"You'll find all the answers in Gävle," he sighed as he read the sentence at the top of the paper. It was as mysterious as the day he'd received the letter in his mailbox, months ago, when he had still been in Stockholm.

Two more letters had followed.

Which answers? What was he supposed to find in Gävle?

He hadn't thought of it anymore until a few months after the first letter when he saw the media coverage of the Norman case. Sandviken, Uppsala and... Gävle. And when they were looking for people to go on a special assignment to Gävle, he hadn't hesitated.

"Sorry, it was my son," she said.

He put the letter in the pocket of his jacket and turned to her.

"No problem," he said, "is everything okay?"

"He is a bit insecure, first time alone at home. I should go back."

"You shouldn't have come," he said without looking at her.

"No, it's fine. It was my pleasure."

Courtesies. There it would stay. Nothing more than that.

"So, will this be the one? You were a lot more enthusiastic about this one than the previous house."

"Yes, I like it here," he answered.

"But I don't think it's really you."

He smiled and said, "Really? Why?"

"I thought you were more the type to go for luxury. Something modern."

"I'm glad I can still surprise you," he said, like they had known each other for years. "Maybe not the old me, but the new me likes it."

"Is there a new you?" she said, surprised.

"There has to be a new me. I need to move on."

And moving on didn't mean leaving things behind but trying to put them into perspective and giving them a place.

"You gave a great speech yesterday," she said.

He smiled. "Thanks."

"People needed that."

"Yeah... with all that's been going on."

"And Isa?"

"She's angry with me," he said.

"She'll come around. And what's going to happen to Magnus?"

"He's charged with murder. His lawyer asked for a psychiatric evaluation to determine if he can be held accountable."

"And the department?"

A deep sigh. "I don't know. This is huge."

People were getting very nervous, from the lowest to the highest ranks. He only knew there was an official vacancy to replace Anders Larsen, and he was asked to stay on for a few more months as superintendent until the new guy or woman would take over. However, this was bigger than the small police department in Gävle. This touched the core of police credibility: a police officer who had murdered someone and had succeeded in falsifying and removing evidence. It couldn't get any worse.

A gust of wind suddenly blew a strand of hair across her face, and with the gentlest touch he removed it and tucked it behind her ear.

"Timo, I can be your friend, but that's all I can be," she said.

"I know."

And that wasn't okay, but he had to settle for that.

He looked up at the sky. In the distance, above the trees, dark clouds were gathering. A storm was coming.

"It's going to rain."

He smiled and then turned to her.

"Come on, I'll take you home," he said and took the keys out of his pocket.

He took one last glance at the water. Yes, he could be happy here. Finally.

CHAPTER

28

"How is he doing?" Oliver's mother looked at Timo.

"As best as it can be given the ordeal he's been through," she said.

She offered him a seat on the couch.

"The psychologist told us it will take some time."

"Anything we can do to help you, just let us know," Timo said and hesitated to take a sip of the hot coffee. It was weird. The last few days he had seen flashes of Espen's face whenever he smelled coffee. Every cup was met with a strange feeling of suspicion, as if everyone wanted to drug him. Maybe they were right, and he should have taken some time to let the abduction and the assault by Magnus sink in. He had mended the physical wounds, but not the psychological ones.

"Thank you. I'm so grateful you saved him. I have my son back!"

She could barely hold the tears that were welling in her eyes. Now they were tears of happiness, two months ago tears of horror and fear.

"I had nothing to do with it. I was captured myself. All credit goes to my team."

"But you kept him safe. That's what they told me."

She looked at him with the kindest smile, but there was something uncomfortable about the way she behaved. There was happiness about finding her child, but also a certain distance, as if she were scared.

"Did Oliver say anything about the kidnapping and the shooting?"

"Yes, he did. He told how Mr. Mikaelsson shot Espen, and how he was almost forced to kill you. About Marie. How frightened she was. How they had told him she was dead."

"He told you that?"

"Yes, why? That's good, isn't it?"

"He's a strong kid. Not many children would be able to talk about the trauma so soon."

"Yes, he's very strong. He wants to go back to school next week."

She got up and took the tray of empty cups into the kitchen, saying, "More coffee?"

"No, thanks."

Timo walked to the window. In the garden, the boy was sitting on the patio, back toward them. A gentle breeze now and then brushed the blond hairs of the child.

"Does Oliver have many friends?"

"A few. Why?"

"Nothing. Have you noticed anything strange in his behavior?"

She stared at him for a while, before answering, "No, he's a normal kid... he's a normal boy."

So much confirmation. Too much confirmation. She was scared.

"Can I talk to him?"

"I'm not sure. The doctor said he needed time."

"But he told you a lot about the kidnapping already."

The mother sighed, and a moment later Timo stood outside, breathing in the fresh air. The mother and son lived in a moderate home close to the forest where Oliver disappeared two months ago. The backyard was small. The grass had seen better days and where there were no bare patches, weeds started to sprout. Oliver was completely focused on his activity that Timo couldn't see from where he was standing.

"Your mom says you're feeling better and that you can go to school next week," Timo said.

"I want to go to school."

"You miss your friends?"

"There's a math competition. There are many great prizes to win."

"So, you like math?"

"I'm pretty good at it."

"I'm sure you are. Is that what you did, in the house and cabin when you were held captive?"

"Math? No. I was thinking about the stories."

"Stories? What stories?" Timo came closer. Oliver's arms and hands were moving back and forth in a rhythmic motion. There was something on the floor in front of him. Little black pieces.

"The stories they show on TV."

"I... don't understand."

"On how to kill people."

"What?"

Oliver turned and said, "There were so many options. I wonder why they chose to strangle Marie."

In his hands, he held the wings of the butterfly he had just torn off. Dozens lay on the floor and with four more live insects left in the glass jar, the killing would continue.

"Do you think you can see it in their eyes?"

Timo just couldn't answer.

"I think you can. The fear, realizing they are about to die."

"Weren't you afraid?" Timo said.

Oliver hesitated. "Yes, I guess I was."

Timo contemplated the answer for a moment and then said, "No, I don't think you were. As a kindred spirit, you played along with Espen and Lise's sick game."

Oliver gave him a radiant smile and then turned to the butterflies. "I guess I'll be seeing you again, inspector. I'm looking forward to it."

* * *

"You did well," the voice said.

"What are you going to do with it?" Ilan's voice was shaking more than he had expected.

"None of your business. By next week, I need the new code, and the card to open the emergency exit."

"I... I can't," he mumbled.

"Sure you can! No one will suspect you. You are taking a few days off."

How did he know? My God, this person knew everything about him.

"When will this be over?"

"No questions. Ever."

There was a silence.

Why would he still help his stalker? He was safe. He should just go to the police. He should tell them everything. He had hit the woman, but he hadn't killed her, and Frank... He hadn't killed Frank either. If he was innocent, it would all come out, eventually.

As if the person on the other end of the line had read his thoughts, the voice said: "Don't ever think you can escape me. I am everywhere.

Your wife leaves for work at 8:00 a.m., sometimes later, depending on whether she wants to stop by the bakery. She takes a lunch break around twelve. On Thursdays she meets her friend from the shop across the street and they go for lunch at a small pizzeria a few blocks away from the office. She usually comes home around 4:00 p.m. Shall I go on? I can get to you and your wife. Anywhere, and at any time. You shall obey me, or people will die!"

He cut the line.

Ilan held the phone in his hand for another minute and placed it on the bedside table.

His life wasn't his anymore.

"Hey, what's going on?" Eve said as she entered the room.

"Nothing."

She ran her hand along his back. Her head on his shoulders, her arm tightly around his waist. This was good. This was what he needed. Why couldn't it always be like that?

"The last few weeks, you seem so down," she whispered. "But everything is fine now. They dropped the charges."

He turned his head to look at her. "Not exactly. They are still looking for the car. And they want to question me again about Frank Harket."

"Why? You have nothing to do with that. Right?"

He sighed and smiled. Her hair was soft and smelled of blossoms. It tickled his neck, but he didn't mind. He should protect her. It wasn't just about him anymore. He had put her in danger. Maybe it was best to go along with what his stalker wanted. How bad could it be?

* * *

The waves rolled in and hit the granite rocks that rose above the water level. The air was saturated with small, salty droplets, leaving a thin water-absorbing film on the skin. The noise was loud but soothing, even mesmerizing. Heavy clouds appeared in the distance. The strong winds would soon carry them to the shore.

He had been awake for ten minutes. Drowsy from the sedation, it had taken him a while to figure out why he couldn't move his arms and legs. Where was he? Water, sea, rocks. He couldn't remember what had happened. He had opened the door, and then nothing. But this wasn't good, wasn't good at all.

His vision was still distorted, and he struggled to focus on the figure in the distance, wearing a red raincoat, blue jeans and black rubber boots. The face was hidden under the hood of the coat, invisible.

The chains were cutting through his flesh. The pain was so overwhelming. He looked sideways at his hands. They were bleeding. The chains were attached to two massive wooden posts. It looked as if he was hanging from a big wooden cross.

The figure came closer. He still couldn't see the face. Was it a man or a woman?

The pain was unbearable, but he couldn't cry, he couldn't shout. The tape over his mouth was so tight. It muffled the cries for help when his attacker finally took the torch and lit it with the lighter. Only then did it sink in what his faith would be. He didn't want to die, not like this. He felt the heat of the fire as the figure approached.

Why? Why? What had he done? He was just a simple man. There couldn't be a more average person than him.

Why? Please!

He couldn't even plead for his life. Even that had been taken away from him.

Desperately he tried to free himself, but the metal cuffs wouldn't budge, and it only caused him more pain. A pain he hardly could feel now the adrenaline was pumping through his body and the fight-flight mode was switched on.

His would-be murderer held the torch in front of his face, so close the heat was already burning his skin. The pain was agonizing. What would it be like if the flames devoured him?

The hooded stranger suddenly moved the torch away and waited a few seconds. The eyes, barely visible under the hood, stared at him with an intensity he had rarely seen. So ominous, terrifying.

Help me! Oh, God, please! Someone, help me!

And then the attacker threw the torch at his feet. Almost immediately the wood caught fire. As the flames moved up, first along the branches and twigs, then the feet and legs, rushing to the torso, arms and head, devouring the flesh, slowly revealing the bones, the body squirming, with the muffled cries getting louder and louder until there was only the sound of burning flames, the killer stood there and watched calmly until the fire had done the job. The stench of burned flesh hung over the sand like a mist. A deep inhale and then the raindrops came. First a few sporadic drops then the heavy rainfall. Too late. What was left were the blackened, smoldering remains of what used to be a man, now being quenched by the cold rain. The hooded figure turned and walked away.

Number one.

AND SO IT BEGAN

BOOKS IN THIS SERIES:

THE FIND
EVIL BENEATH THE SKIN
RETRIBUTION
THE STORM
THE VANISHING
DARKENED HEART

AND... THE STORY CONTINUES

COMING SOON:

BOOK 7 – WHEN SHADOWS RETURN

Printed in Dunstable, United Kingdom